the CastAway Kids

and the Pirates of Zactrala Island

JON STREMEL
CHRIS GRAUE

ISBN: 1492366625
ISBN-13: 978-1492366621

DEDICATION

To moms and dads who allow their kids to take adventures.

ZACTRALA ISLAND

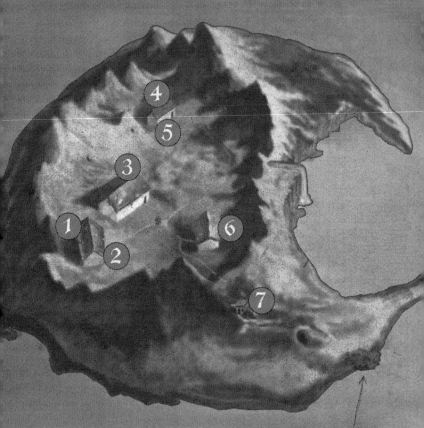

CASTAWAY POINTE

1 - BERTHING
2 - GALLEY
3 - SEED VAULT
4 - CONTROL ROOM
5 - ARMORY
6 - GENERATOR ROOM
7 - GUARD SHACK

CONTENTS

PROLOGUE

Danny hugged the candy bars against his body as he ran out of the liquor store, after being smacked by the shopkeeper with a baseball bat. Sweat dripped down Danny's face as his heart pounded inside his chest. The bat hurt his kidneys and shoulders, but it didn't slow him down. The shopkeeper, Mr. Fong, leaving his daughter to tend the register, chased him onto the sidewalk as his black and orange Giants baseball visor flew off his head. Danny dodged in and out of pedestrians that were walking along the streets of downtown San Francisco. The adrenaline blurred his vision.

"I'm going to kill you, you little brat!" Mr. Fong's pencil-thin legs gained on his thief. Danny scanned ahead. The red-hand light blinked at the crosswalk. Danny didn't have time to push the button to cross the street safely. He didn't even have time to think. Glancing back at Mr. Fong for just a moment, he ran into a display rack in front of a gift shop that was full of cheap sunglasses.

A Snickers bar fell into a small puddle.

It was a relatively foggy morning, so visibility was already low. It had rained the night before and was still overcast. A chill was in the air, and the bustling

Californians and tourists were late for their morning coffee. Danny bolted into the street without looking. A taxi cab nearly hit Danny's left hip as the driver leaned on his horn. Sticking his head out the window, he yelled, "Watch it, kid!"

"Sorry, mister!" But Danny wasn't. He didn't even turn around when he said it. He didn't dare slow down to see how close the liquor store owner was. His head was beginning to pulsate with each step he took. *Dehydrated... Damn.* Right when he was thinking about how much his hip hurt, the shopkeeper threw his bat at Danny's head from across the street.

"Ha ha! Got you!" The shopkeeper also jumped into the street, the same taxi cab from before almost hitting him. "Perfect shot!"

"What's wrong with you, Grandpa?" The cab driver made a crude hand gesture to the shopkeeper. Danny furiously rubbed his head where he had been hit, but he kept running. Mr. Fong smacked the driver's hood and continued the chase, now even more upset, seeing as how throwing the bat failed to stop his culprit.

Licorice ropes slithered through Danny's arms to the ground.

Danny reached the other side of the street, just in time to get smacked in the face by the handle bars of a female biker. He sucked his tongue and tasted blood. "Fat little punk!" The woman yelled back as she wobbled her bike off the slanted sidewalk.

Danny heard the sound of more plastic candy wrappers hitting the ground behind him.

Danny liked the hilly, cracked roads of San Francisco only half of the time. The other half was when he had to trudge uphill. His uncles regularly teased him about needing more exercise, but he usually tried to ignore their bullying remarks. *I shouldn't have had that third bagel this morning,* Danny thought. Danny's chest hurt even more as his faded 49ers jersey was officially drenched with sweat.

His thighs scraped together as he turned to see the shopkeeper taking his apron off and holding it in his hand. Now that he turned and was headed uphill, there was no way Danny was going to outrun him.

Just then, the bells of a trolley rang in the middle of the street to Danny's right. Danny zig-zagged through traffic into the street, onto the track, trailing the trolley up Hyde Street. He outstretched one arm until his shoulder locked. The golden painted pole that riders held onto to was just barely out of reach. With one final stretch his chubby fingers wrapped around the pole and he mustered enough strength to pull himself up.

M&M's and Skittles rolled and bounced down Hyde Street.

The driver of the trolley was an African-American man with a white beard, bald-head, and yellow teeth. He wore a white scarf, which looked more like an extension of his beard, fingerless-gloves, and a black wool petticoat. He always had a short black cigarette hanging out of his mouth that sometimes got so small it singed part of his beard. "Hey Danny, what do you think you're doing? You know it costs five bucks to ride, little man."

Danny swallowed hard between breaths. He clutched his chest and he sat on a very confused passenger's lap. "Hey…Chester…I don't…money…Can I…later?" His panting turned into a loud wheeze. He put two fingers on his neck to check his pulse.

A thirteen year-old girl who looked like she could have been in Danny's grade noticed the blood on his lips. "Are you okay?"

"Never…better." Danny leaned on the pole and glanced behind him. Mr. Fong was becoming smaller in the distance. The stranger whose lap he occupied, a 40-year-old homely southern woman, finally spoke up. "Would you mind kindly gettin' off of me? You're wrinklin' my Sunday dress with your sweat."

"Oh. Yeah. Sorry, ma'am."

Chester pulled hard on the different levers that operated the trolley as smoke blew out his nose. "Come on now, Danny. I can't give you any more free rides. You still owe me from last week when you just *had* to go to that Giants game."

"But I was going to be late! They don't offer refunds. Come on Chester…this is an emergency."

"Unless you're pregnant and ready to pop, bleedin' out your eyes, or the President is with you…it ain't happenin' my man. This is tourist season and I can't be seen giving away no freebies."

Danny checked one more time for Mr. Fong. He was nowhere in sight. Danny let out a heavy sigh. "Thanks anyways, Chester!"

Danny had no choice but to jump off the trolley while it was still moving. *Stupid tourist season*, Danny thought. He landed on the side of the road next to a parked car. Little rocks from the asphalt embedded themselves into Danny's palm when he braced his fall. He quickly wiped it on his jeans, leaving streaks of blood against the pale blue denim.

A pack of gum and three smashed bags of chips were left under the parked car.

Danny could see the green door to his uncle's house up ahead. His legs were numb, his shirt stuck to his skin like duct tape, and he had the mother of all headaches, not to mention a lump forming where he was hit in the head with the baseball bat. *I could go for a nice, cold drink right now.* Danny snapped open the one can of soda he was carrying and gulped down half of it. He poured the rest all over his face to cool off. *Ahhhhh…that's better*, he thought, as he let the can roll down the sidewalk behind him. *My uncles aren't going to be happy I drank that.* They made Danny steal snacks for them about once a week in exchange for rent. They didn't care that their nephew was only thirteen. Danny's gut jerked his skin up and down as he continued to run. Blisters rubbed against the inside heels of his shoes. He was about to cry as he thought about his "weight problem" that his uncles, coaches, and bullies at school reminded him of every day of his life, but he didn't have a chance as he scurried up the steps to his uncle's house.

In one hurried motion, Danny lifted the doormat, grabbed the key, opened the door, stepped inside, closed the door, locked it, and pressed his head against the peephole. The heat from his brow fogged the lens of the peephole. Danny used his pinky to clear it off. The shopkeeper came walking up in front of Danny's house, clasping the empty, abandoned soda can. *Aw crap*, he thought. But Mr. Fong wasn't looking at Danny's door. It looked like he couldn't make up his mind which house Danny ran into. Perhaps he was too far away to tell. For once, all of the look-alike skinny houses in San Francisco came in handy. The shopkeeper crushed the can with his hand in anger, gave up, and trodded back down Hyde Street. Danny looked down into his hands which held the blood dripping from his mouth.

One squished Reese's Peanut Butter cup. That was all that was left from his candy-heist.

Danny leaned his back against the door, sliding down to the wooden floor as he unwrapped his melted chocolatey treasure. He scanned the room for signs of his uncles. All alone. He closed his eyes and smelled it with a long inhale. He took one savory bite and pressed the back of his head against the cold door. He made a happy humming sound as he chewed and caught his breath.

As he sat there, the adrenaline began to wear off. With it, the tile pattern on the floor began to bend and pull in his sight; a dizziness had taken hold. He clutched the rest of the candy in his hand as he sprawled himself out on his back. A static shield filled his vision as he began the process of blacking out.

Right before Danny fell unconscious in the foyer, the last thing he heard was his uncles running down the stairs.

1 UNCLE CESAR & UNCLE JESUS

Danny opened his eyes. *I'm still on the floor.* Not the most intelligent thought, but the only one he could manage through his still splitting headache. His clothes were no longer damp, the blood dried on his lips. His eyes focused on the object directly in front of him: a crinkled, empty Reese's wrapper. Someone had eaten the rest of it, but took the time to place the packaging back on the floor in front of him so that he'd know it was stolen.

An obnoxious laugh roared from the living room. "Head shot!" His uncles were playing video games and blasting rap music.

Danny stared up at a picture of him and his parents hanging in the hallway. When his parents were alive, they kept the house clean. His father's death from diabetes was a great blow to his mother. Already predisposed by her own obesity, the added stress contributed to a heart attack that would leave Danny orphaned at the age of four.

His parents had been successful software engineers, so they managed to leave behind a rather pricey home in an upscale neighborhood for Danny's care. Unfortunately, there was still a rather large amount of debt in the estate that would have to be paid by the inheritor. As his next closest relatives, Danny's uncles took over as his guardians. They sold off what they could and continued to make the absolute minimum payments to continue their brother's plush lifestyle. They only supported themselves with a pizza delivery job of about twenty hours a week split between the two of them.

Uncle Cesar and Uncle Jesus had been entirely unprepared to act as guardians, and not much had changed in the following years. They performed approximately zero maintenance since moving in and had no idea where the vacuum cleaner was even kept. When the downstairs bathroom sink stopped draining, they simply surrounded it with buckets that were emptied only when the stink of mildew became too overwhelming for Danny to tolerate.

In fact, this was the only way that any chores got done nowadays. Danny acted as his uncles' personal maid. He was the only one who ever cleaned, did laundry, the dishes, or any other chore. For his deeds, he received no allowance or reward of any kind. There wasn't even any good food to cook, just a freezer full of frostbitten pizzas and junk. They forced Danny to "hook them up" by making him steal groceries about once a month. If he didn't, they threatened to kick him out of the house or just generally make his life more miserable.

Uncle Cesar called out, "Hey, tubs! Finally getting up?"

He pushed himself up off the hardwood floor, leaving behind a Danny-shaped sweat print in the layer of dust below. Danny stumbled into the living room, trying to ignore the lightheaded feeling he got from standing to his feet. "Which one of you took my Reese's?"

Neither Cesar nor Jesus turned their gaze from the television screen; even a single second's distraction could make the difference between virtual life and death. "*Your* Reese's? You mean *our* Reese's."

Only eighteen months separated their birthdays, but the years had weathered them so similarly that they were difficult to tell apart. Their receding hairlines were neck and neck; their postures identically slumped. It did not help that both men had a penchant for goatees and bandanas which they felt made them look like they might belong to a gang. The reality was that neither of them had enough friends to start one nor had they ever been in a fight. The easiest way to tell them apart was that Cesar typically wore a flat brimmed baseball cap with a flannel shirt buttoned only at the top. Jesus wore tank tops and used his bandana as a do-rag.

Jesus chimed in, "If you're gonna rob the liquor store, couldn't you at least do yourself a favor and grab yourself a Slim-Fast?"

"Where's he going to hide a Slim-Fast? He's bursting at the seams," Cesar piled on. "You can't wear skinny jeans when you're shoplifting!"

"Skinny jeans? Any pair of jeans that kid wears are skinny jeans. They don't make 'em any bigger!" Jesus and Cesar exchanged a high five without looking away from the screen, then took simultaneous chomps into their greasy Hot Pockets. This was pretty much the nicest food ever served in the Herrera household.

Danny's pride was wounded, but no more than any other typical day. "I'm just bulking up before football tryouts. I'm gonna make the team this year."

"You've got plenty of bulk already, *ese*," Cesar offered. "You can stop now."

Jesus added, "Yeah, I'd say your lifelong effort has really paid off."

Danny fumed, "You're just jealous I'll be playing football all summer while you guys sit around doing nothing."

Finally, they paused their game. "Oh yeah? How are you going to play for the team while you're at fat camp?"

Cesar's words stopped Danny cold. "What did you say?"

He continued, "Oh, we didn't tell you? Yeah, you're going to fat camp all summer."

A rage welled up inside Danny, "What? Why?"

Cesar squinted, "Are you serious?"

Jesus elaborated, "We're sailing the *Thug Life* out to Catalina and we can't have your chubby buns weighing us down." The "*Thug Life*" was Danny's father's old sailboat. It was one of the few possessions his uncles held onto. It used to be called the *Odyssey II* but Cesar and Jesus thought that *Thug Life* had a better ring to it. Danny disagreed.

"It turns out it was way cheaper than getting you a babysitter," Cesar chuckled.

"Plus, this is the third time in a row we sent you on a run and you came back empty-handed," Jesus added. "We have no use for a *tortuga gorda*." Jesus has been calling Danny "fat turtle" since he was in diapers.

"I'm thirteen years old, I can take care of myself."

"Oh yeah, we're gonna leave the blubbery bandit unsupervised for two months," Cesar sarcastically replied. "We'll get thrown in jail the minute your chubby cheeks gets caught by the cops."

Furious, Danny exploded, "That's not fair!"

"Fair?" Cesar asked. "You think it's fair we got stuck taking care of you? Would it be fair if we just dropped all our fun plans so you could do whatever you wanted? How selfish can you be, *homes*?"

Anger wasn't going to get Danny anywhere. His entire summer was at stake and he had to find a way out of this. "What if I make the team?"

Cesar and Jesus laughed. Jesus was the first to be able to speak, "That's a good one."

"No, really," Danny pleaded, "what if I make it? There's mandatory workouts all summer. If I miss, I can't play in the fall!"

Cesar was unmoved, "Why do I care if you get to play in the fall?"

"Well," Danny improvised, "if I'm on the team, that means I'll have practice after school. And games. I won't be around as much because they'll keep me busy." By the expressions his uncles were making, he could see this strategy was beginning to work. "Summer workouts are like all day. By the time I get home, I'll be faster and able to go on more food runs for us, and it's way cheaper than fat camp. It'll be free!"

Jesus appeared to be running the numbers in his head with great difficulty. "His math checks out."

"Okay, mijo," Cesar relented, "if you make the team then you can stay home."

"Yes!" Danny pumped his fist in victory.

"Don't get too excited, chubs. You've never made the team before. When you fail, you still have to go to fat camp."

"This year's going to be different," Danny said, "I can taste it."

Jesus turned their game back on. "Maybe you should stop tasting everything, Danny. That's probably where all the fat comes from."

As loudly as he could, Danny stomped up the stairs to his bedroom, slamming the door shut behind him. His entire summer hinged on tomorrow's football tryouts.

March 15th

BLACK SEA

Captain Morell called me into his stateroom at 1630 this evening with dire news. A message had come in stating that my father had been killed in action. I asked the skipper if I were to be given any leave time to make funeral arrangements seeing as how I am his last living relative and next of kin. He denied my request.

When pressed further as to why he would deny me what every sailor (and especially a Lieutenant of my caliber) is promised when a family member dies, he told me that the Navy doesn't want to acknowledge the death of my father. "The 'Powers That Be' want to keep his mission and work top secret. By acknowledging his death," he continued, "they acknowledge his life, and what he did with it." He said that because he was an admiral, and my mother was not alive to receive any kind of life insurance, that I would be receiving a hefty sum of money.

Captain Morell further ordered that I not mention anything to the crew or even the other officers, and that I carry on as if nothing had happened. He then said that "if there is no further mentioning of this matter, a Navy and Marine-Corps Serve Medal would look good on your chest." My father told me so little about his mission, I didn't even know what to keep silent about.

My father dies. Hush Money. Medal for my silence.

I'm not sure which to be most upset about. I am certain, however, that tonight marks the night that I am officially fed-up with the Navy, with America, and with all of their damn secrets.

Ever since I lost my left eye in a training accident, and the Navy's version of treatment was simply an eye-patch, I have been questioning my government's competency. (By the way, I am still checking the mail daily for my glass-eye that was ordered months ago.) Like my eye, they see every problem as something to cover-up, rather than to come up with a solution to fix it and put into place actions that can prevent future problems.

It is getting late. The seas are rough. Dinner was terrible. My roommate is seasick. The Boatswain's mate of the Watch just announced 'Tattoo, Tattoo' across the ship, which means I have 5 more minutes to write before it's lights out.

I'm not sure what, I'm not sure when, and I'm not sure how...but I will seek justice from the US government and avenge my father's death. I am the last remaining male in my family, and when we pull into port in Somalia in 18 days, I must begin my separation paperwork.

Rest in Peace Father,
Lt. Kerry Vasser (SWO)
USS Montibello CG-16

P.S.

Can't sleep. Perhaps a bit more writing will help clear my mind.

As I juggle between reflections of my father and thoughts of swelling hatred towards the Navy, I cannot help but remember the last day I saw my father. It was a cold December morning when I hid in the back of his station wagon on his way to work when I was a child. He picked up a suited man in front of a government building.

Believing they were alone, they spoke of a secret island in the Pacific and something called a "Super Nova."

They drove across town discussing various travel arrangements for my father. The suited man opened his briefcase and began shuffling through some papers. At one point, my father drove over a bump in the road, knocking some papers to the floor of the car and beneath the seat. Curious, I grabbed one of the papers. I had time to read a latitude and a longitude when suddenly my father's passenger put a gun to my face. Thinking me a spy, he began yelling at me. Luckily my father turned and made the man put the gun away, explaining that I was just his son.

My father was furious with me. He asked me what I saw and heard. I lied and told him nothing. I pleaded that I was only there to follow him to work. He pulled over to the nearest bus stop, gave me fare home, and said, "I'm going away for a very long time. You're the man of the house, Kerry. I can't tell you where I'm going, but never forget that you're my son."

 Then he drove away, never to return to me or my mother again. I don't think I'll ever forget how lonely I felt. Abandoned. I cried the entire bus ride home, thinking it was my fault he was leaving. I'll never forget that feeling.

Just like I'll never forget those coordinates...

2 TRYOUTS

"I think I'm gonna throw up." Danny keeled over a water fountain. He was sweating so much that little pools of water formed under his armpits and around his neck. "Maybe if I eat something, I'll feel better." He reached under his football helmet where he had stashed a chocolate bar.

"Candy will only make things worse." Eugene Applebaum, a scrawny boy who had lived down the street from Danny his whole life, rubbed Danny's back in a reassuring way. Most of Eugene's clothes were too big for his pint-sized body, including his cowboy boots and thick-rimmed glasses that his grandmother gave him. His distinctive red cape, which he wore as part of a Superman costume five years ago, flapped in the breeze. He was wearing it on the first Halloween that he and Danny managed to dodge their long time bully, Erik Berman, before he could beat them up and steal their candy. Ever since, he'd worn the cape daily for good luck, which it had not always managed to bring him. Regardless, as Danny's best friend and living shadow, he was always there for support.

"I just need a little energy." Danny unwrapped the

chocolate bar furiously and shoved the entire thing in his mouth. His cheeks filled up so much he could barely see over them. His nose whistled a little as he tried to breathe through it and chew at the same time.

Danny continued to lean on the water fountain that stood at the entrance to the fenced-in field area where football games and track races were held. It was the end of the school day and the sounds of cheerleaders practicing echoed in the distance. The sun was blaring, but the grass was still wet from last night's fog.

"Why do you care so much about making the team this year? You hate exercising."

"My uncles told me that if I don't make the team they're gonna send me to fat camp."

"Now why would they do something like that?"

"That's what I said."

Danny shoved another candy bar into his mouth. "I almost got caught stealing from the store again." He threw the wrapper towards the trash, missing it by two feet.

"At least you're not trying out for the basketball team," Eugene excused Danny's poor aim. Danny splashed a little water on his face before putting his helmet back on, and he and Eugene made their way towards the bleachers near the football field.

"Fat camp doesn't sound too bad," Eugene continued. "My parents want to send me to Wilderness Camp. They think I need to toughen up. I would much rather go to Computer Camp, but they said that building a cyborg bodyguard is unrealistic. And you wanna know the worst part? I'm not even allowed to bring my cape."

"Sounds like suicide if you ask me."

Danny and Eugene reached the football field. Tryouts were in full swing, with half the school watching from the aluminum bleachers. Coaches were standing on the sidelines taking notes on their clipboards. Danny sat down on the first bench, bending down to tie his cleats.

"Eww Danny, cover your butt-crack." The disgusted

voice behind Danny came from Miko Tanaka who was sitting just one row up. She had a textbook resting on her lap, her thick black glasses and bangs covering her dark brown eyes. Miko spent most of her time trying not to be noticed. She was arguably the smartest girl in school, and would have skipped a grade too, but she spent a lot of her after-school time in detention with Danny. When she wasn't studying or playing the violin, she was usually hanging out with Danny playing video games or Dungeons and Dragons.

"Sorry Miko, this uniform doesn't fit me like it used to." Danny had tried out for football all three years of junior high, wearing the same jersey each time. If today went well, he could finally live his dream to play as a Fighting Prospector at Bay Harbor High School next year.

"Well I came out here to support you before I go to band practice, so at least have the courtesy to not flash me your back-canyon."

"Don't worry, Danny, I'll cover your shame!" Eugene stretched out his cape to conceal Danny's crack. "Hi, Miko! What are you doing homework for? This Friday's the last day of school."

"Oh, I didn't tell you? My parents are sending me to conservatory for the summer at UC Berkeley to get better at violin. I think their goal to make me the most stereotypical Asian in San Fran is almost complete. So my dad got me this-" Miko held up the textbook called *Mozart's Mind.* "Apparently he said that any kid can play classical music, but I'll be the only one who knows *why* I'm playing it...Blek!" She closed the book in disgust and put her head in her hands.

Danny watched a kid getting slammed into the field. "I have a feeling this is gonna be the worst summer ever."

"Why? How are your uncles torturing you now?" Miko asked.

"Fat camp," Eugene chimed in.

"Eesh... Bummer."

"Bummer summer! Hey that rhymes!" Declared Eugene. He put his hand up for a high five from Miko, but she simply rolled her eyes. Danny's palms sweat as he observed the coaches yelling the names of the kids on the tryout sheet.

"Cooper!"

"Davis!"

"Ferguson!"

One by one, boys and girls would run onto the field, throw a ball to a receiver, catch a pass, then dart in between defenders, trying not to get tackled. Some did well, and others did really well. This intimidated Danny a great deal.

He walked over to the bench to grab a towel for his palms. He nodded to the towel boy who had just folded his last towel onto the stack.

"Hey kid, your towels are all dirty," mocked Erik Berman from behind, not noticing Danny. Erik was taller than Danny by almost a head and entirely built out of muscle. When not concealed by a helmet, his flaming orange hair stood as a beacon of terror on a daily basis to Danny and his friends. Starting last year, every opposing coach asked for his birth certificate at games to prove he wasn't some ringer from a local junior college. But no, sadly for Danny, Erik was just some sort of genetic freak of nature who seemed created to make his life miserable.

"No, they're not," the towel boy retorted, "I just washed them."

"Then why are they all covered in dirt?" Erik flipped the bench, sending every one of the meticulously folded towels flying into a giant pile of mud.

Erik chortled to himself deeply as he trotted onto the field. The towel boy looked over the wreckage and sighed. "Don't worry," Danny kneeled down, "I'll help you out."

"It took three whole loads to get all these done," the towel boy lamented.

Danny scooped a handful of dirty towels and tossed

them into the nearby hamper. "I don't know why he feels like he can be a jerk to everyone."

Right at that moment, Shayla Nichols approached Danny with her arms stretched out holding what appeared to be a necklace made of dandelions she picked herself.

"Hi, Danny! I made this for you!" Shayla proclaimed with a huge smile on her face. Shayla always had an immense amount of energy and a happy aura about her. She smiled more than anyone Danny knew, even in the worst situations. Her dirty blonde hair reached her waist, and was almost always down. A devout vegetarian, she was really into nature. Not satisfied in merely taking care of her own garden at home, she could usually be found watering plants or pulling weeds anywhere in the city she thought was necessary. She usually smelled like potting soil and wore blue coveralls. "You should wear this necklace under your uniform for good luck!"

"Thanks, Shayla. I'm gonna need it." Danny smiled as she placed it around his neck and tucked it into the front of his uniform. Danny felt better having all three of his friends by his side.

"Be careful out there, those guys are barbarians," Shayla warned. "I mean, can you believe one of them threw this chocolate wrapper right next to the trash can and didn't even think to pick it up?"

Danny eyed the familiar packaging guiltily. "Er, yeah. Who would do that?"

The crowd of students watching the tryouts burst into a loud cheer. Miko, Eugene, Shayla, and Danny all turned at the same moment to see what the excitement was about. Apparently, Cody Nichols, Shayla's cousin, who had been the school's quarterback since 6th grade, threw a spectacular 40 yard pass that was caught by another kid trying out for the team. Girls loved Cody, which was only one of the reasons Danny couldn't stand him. The other was that he was the best friend and co-conspirator of Danny's own personal bully, Erik Berman.

"Herrera!" The head coach screamed.

Danny threw his last few towels into the bin. He pulled out a shot of espresso in a can from his back pocket. He had a hard time pouring it through the helmet, but he managed. While a waterfall of cold coffee cascaded into his mouth, Shayla suggested, "I don't think that's a very healthy choice right before playing a sport. Remember what I always say? 'If there's a commercial for it on TV, it's probably not healthy.'"

Danny burped loudly and crushed the can. He was about to toss it aside when he caught Shayla's eye. He slowly set the can down on the bleacher and said, "I'll come back for it later."

Shayla smiled, "Thanks, Danny."

"Go, Danny!" Eugene squeaked.

"You're a rockstar!" Miko screamed.

"Go easy on him Cody, he's my friend!" Shayla cupped her hands to her mouth to shout to her cousin who was stretching on the field, getting ready to throw the ball to Danny.

Okay, Danny, show time. Focus. I don't wanna go to fat camp...I don't wanna go to fat camp... I really don't wanna go to fat camp...

Danny took his position on the field at the line of scrimmage. Some girls in the bleachers giggled at him and mocked him loud enough for Danny to hear. "He's already sweating and he hasn't even done anything yet..."

"Totally. He looks like six pounds of crap in a five pound bag."

"He's going to bring back the term 'pigskin' if he makes the team."

The players on the sidelines joined in, "Are you serious? This fatty is gonna have a heart attack before he even takes two steps!"

"How's anyone supposed to fit in a huddle with this guy?"

"He's like a Mexican Shrek! Viva El-Shrek-o!"

"Oink oink piggy piggy!" Came a familiar voice. It was Erik Berman. He was in uniform on the field, leaning on Cody's shoulder. *Great. He's here…*

Danny pretended he couldn't hear them. The players continued to make oinking sounds until half the bleachers had joined in. Danny was surrounded by the sounds of pig noises and could barely hear Cody when he finally yelled "Hike!"

Danny sprang forward as fast as he could and bolted down the field. His pants began to fall around his waist as he sprinted forward, throwing off his balance. A quick tug fixed the problem temporarily, but soon they were riding even lower than before. He turned to see the football spiraling towards him. He reached out to grab it, but the ball went faster than him, and he missed it by about six whole feet. He was so off kilter at this point he stumbled to the ground and landed in a puddle of mud.

The students roared with laughter. Danny pried his face mask out of the dent it had pressed into the ground. He spit out some grass before standing up to examine the damage. He was covered from head to toe in mud, and discovered a huge rip in his pants along the backside.

"He just tackled himself!"

"Nice underwear, Donkey Kong!"

Danny looked to the sidelines where his friends sat. They were the only three not joining the crowd in heckling.

"It's okay, Danny! Try again!" Shayla yelled from her tippy toes.

The head coach stepped over to Danny. "All right, Herrera, dust yourself off and let's try some tackling. A big fella like you might make a good defensive lineman."

Danny hobbled back to the line of scrimmage, chest pounding and out of breath. He bent down and got into position, his underwear flashing everyone behind him. The crowd recoiled in a simultaneous "Eww!"

Danny closed his eyes and took a deep breath, trying to

silence out any outside distractions. When he opened them, he was face to face with his own private nightmare: Erik Berman.

"Fancy meeting you here, Jiggle Jugs," Erik cackled.

"Come on, Erik," Danny pleaded, "I swear you can beat me up in the usual place after school, just please, please, please let me make the team."

"That doesn't sound very fair to the rest of the guys."

"Just this once," Danny whispered. "Please at least don't kill me."

"Now where's the fun in that?" Erik sneered, crinkling the freckles across his face.

"Hike!" came the call from Cody.

Erik started forward like a cannon. Danny's eyes grew wide as he braced himself for impact. Flinching in the face of the mass hurtling towards him, he stepped back, attempting to cushion the hit he was about to take. In a split second, Erik had reached him with a devastating shoulder under Danny's ribcage. The wind had already been knocked out of him before he found the turf.

Wheezing for air, Danny laid flat as Erik stood up and off of him. Looking down at his helpless body, he called to the others, "Hey, let's pile on top of him and flatten him like a pancake!"

A moment later, half of the players jumped into a huge pile on top of Danny, each kid putting more and more pressure on his chest. Still scrambling for air between gasps, Danny screamed in pain. "Stop it guys! Get off me!"

The coaches ran over to them blowing their whistles and pulling kids off the pile.

"All right, all right, break it up! Break it up!"

The kids turned their backs to Danny and proceeded to the other side of the field. Erik lingered behind for just a moment to spit on Danny. "That's for trying to ruin our good team, Porkus! Get it? It's pig-latin."

"More like pig-latino!" another player added.

Cody slapped Erik on the back. "Nice hit." He looked

down at Danny, shaking his head, then they walked off together.

The coach outstretched his hand to Danny to help him up. "Come on, son."

"Did I make the team?"

"No. Not even close."

"But, coach, you have to give me another shot. Maybe I'm no lineman, but Cody over-threw the pass!"

"Looked a little more like you couldn't keep up with it. You've got a lot of heart, Herrera, I'll give you that. The problem is that your big heart is surrounded by bacon grease and cheesecake. Try again next year, and maybe don't wear the flower necklace."

Danny was crushed. He didn't accept the coach's hand, but instead waved him away and remained lying on the grass with his eyes closed. He fought back tears as the rest of the kids continued on the other end of the field.

At that moment, he couldn't help but think about how both of his parents died from weight-related issues. He had promised himself he wouldn't allow the same thing to happen to him, but here he was, feeling like he could die.

I can't believe I didn't make it…What am I going to do? I can't go to fat camp…I can't face my uncles….They're going to tease me so much when I tell them this…I don't wanna be here anymore…

"Are you all right?"

Danny opened his eyes. Shayla was trying to determine if Danny was still alive while Miko and Eugene huddled around.

"My life is over," Danny responded.

Eugene panicked. "You're dying? Do you want to go to the hospital? We should take him to the hospital. I love the hospital."

"He's not dying," said Miko. "Here, let's get you up."

"Just let me rest here for a minute. I have nowhere special I want to be." The tryouts had ended, leaving Danny and his best friends alone on the field as the bleachers cleared. Miko shrugged and sat down on the

27

grass to join him. Shayla and Eugene followed suit.

"Your life isn't over," Shayla consoled him.

"Yeah, just your summer," Miko offered.

Danny sighed, "It just isn't fair."

"I know," Shayla picked a clover out of the grass. "I'm getting sent off to my Aunt's pig slaughterhouse in Wyoming for six weeks. It's going to be *so* gross!"

Eugene pondered, "You ever think maybe adults get jealous that they don't have summer vacations so they dream up horrible ways to torment us in our spare time? Like maybe they have some sort of secret club where they build a giant robot that can determine what we'd least like to do with our own summers."

"Summer vacation is supposed to be a break from boring reality," Miko rested her chin on her violin case.

"I need a break from my parents," Eugene picked grass off his boots.

"And my uncles," Danny added. "I can't believe those bums are sailing down to Catalina while we're-" Danny sat up with a shot, interrupting himself. "I have an idea."

"On how to make a bigger robot to fight the evil robot?" Eugene was still on his own train of thought.

"No. Better. Meet me at the lighthouse tonight." Danny sprang up with his mind racing. "I think I have an idea that can save everyone's summer."

CG-19

IAW OPNAVINST 5100.23
USS MONTIBELLO CG-19
APRIL 8TH
USNAVY CLASSIFIED
DOD FILE SERIAL #: 310TICOc-73.99_FOXTROT
INCIDENT SEVERITY CLASSIFICATION: ALPHA
COMMANDING OFFICER: CAPTAIN JAMES T. MORELL
SHIP MAA: CHIEF PETTY OFFICER ROGER WADLOW (SW)

SUBJECT: BLUE-ON-BLUE/UNACCOUNTED ABSENCE (UA)
PERSONNEL FILING REPORT: ENSIGN SHAWN WEST

I, _Shawn West_ , DECLARE THAT ALL EVENTS DESCRIBED IN
THIS REPORT BE TRUE TO THE BEST OF MY KNOWLEDGE.
ON FRIDAY, APRIL 4TH, LT. KERRY VASSER (SWO) AND MYSELF
SIGNED OFF THE SHIP AS LIBERTY BUDDIES, IAW (IN
ACCORDANCE WITH) CAPTAIN'S OCONUS (OUTSIDE
CONTINENTAL UNITED STATES) POLICY. LT. VASSER AND I
LEFT THE SHIP AT 1734, IN THE PORT OF MOGADISHU IN THE
COUNTRY OF SOMALIA. WE TOOK A CAB TO A NIGHT CLUB
CALLED "THE WHISPER ROOM," SIX MILES FROM THE PIER.
THERE, WE CONSUMED ALCOHOLIC BEVERAGES, AND DANCED
WITH LOCAL WOMEN. LT. VASSER HAD AT LEAST FOUR
PITCHERS OF BEER AND SEVERAL MIXED DRINKS. A GROUP OF
MARINE OFFICERS WHO WORE CIVILIAN ATTIRE BEGAN
TEASING LT. VASSER ABOUT HIS EYE PATCH AROUND 2230.
LT. VASSER BEGAN YELLING ANTI-AMERCIAN AND
ANTI-MILITARY COMMENTS AT THE MARINES. THE FIRST
PUNCH WAS THROWN BY LT. VASSER. THE MARINES THEN
TACKLED HIM. I ATTEMPTED TO HELP MY SHIPMATE STAND UP,
HOWEVER HE PUSHED ME AWAY. HE CONTINUED TO ATTACK
THE MARINES UNTIL ONE OF THEM PULLED OUT A KNIFE AND
STABBED LT. VASSER IN HIS RIGHT SHOULDER.
AT THIS TIME, 2313, I CALLED THE SHIP'S MASTER-AT-ARMS
(MAA), AS WELL AS SHORE PATROL FROM A LOCAL PAY PHONE
WITH A CALLING CARD. DURING THE CONFUSION, LT. VASSER
RAN OUT THE BACK DOOR HOLDING HIS SHOULDER. THERE WAS
BLOOD RUNNING DOWN HIS ARM. HE DID NOT SAY TO ME
WHERE HE WAS GOING OR HIS MEDICAL CONDITION. I HAVE NOT
SEEN NOR HEARD FROM LT. VASSER EVER SINCE.
I HAVE TRIED CALLING HIS CELL PHONE, BUT IT HAS BEEN
TURNED OFF BY HIS PROVIDER. LT. VASSER HAS MISSED SHIP'S
MOVEMENT AND IS NOW UNACCOUNTED FOR.

NAME: _Shawn West_

DATE: _XX-4-8_

3 MIDNIGHT MEETING

Danny rolled up to the lighthouse in his trusty old go kart. Looking something like a bumper car that had come loose from the ride, it was black with a tan stripe down the middle. Danny thought the stripe made it look like it went faster. In reality, it couldn't get up the hills very quickly, even with a lighter driver at the wheel, but it sure beat the extra effort of bicycling around town.

The gang had been using the lighthouse as a place to hang out since two summers ago when Eugene accidentally started a fight with some seventh graders and they needed a place to make a getaway. They discovered that although the keyhole turned, the door could not actually be locked or unlocked from the outside. It was their own secret hideaway whenever the four of them needed to escape from the world, which happened about once or twice a week.

The building, itself, was in a shabby state of disrepair. The bulb had long since been removed as the lighthouse had been decommissioned years ago, the once white paint was now chipped and weathered, and the black roof tiles, or what remained of them, were cracked and off kilter.

Danny knocked on the door. From inside came

Eugene's muffled voice, "What's the password?"

"Eugene, open the door."

"Correct you are!" Eugene swung the door open gleefully. "You can never be too careful."

Up the dingy, spiraling staircase they climbed into the former lantern room where Miko sat waiting, and asked, "Who's there? Is that you Shayla?"

"Nope, it's just Danny," Eugene proclaimed as he sat gingerly next to Miko while being careful not to sit on his cape.

"Ugh," Miko slumped back to the floor where she was playing with a lighter, "I was really hoping for that healthy trail mix she always makes."

"I've got it!" A gleeful Shayla bounded up the stairs.

Eugene was startled, "Shayla! You didn't say the password!"

"Oh, sorry, Eugene, open the door." She handed off her plastic bag of trail mix to the starving Miko. "I used organic unsalted peanuts, raisins from my cousin's best friend's winery up north, mangos from my backyard that I dried myself, free trade almonds from the farmer's market, and a new kind of gluten free whole grain cracker sticks I found online."

Miko heard none of this as she rooted around the bag touching everything. "Okay, but these are just regular M&Ms, right?"

Shayla sighed, "Yes, but don't just pick them all out."

"Here, look, I took a peanut too." Miko revealed a single peanut on top of a handful of chocolate. She tossed it behind her as she ate the rest, hoping Shayla wouldn't notice.

Shayla went over to the window to water the herb garden she'd planted a few months back. She mostly used plants from her garden at home in her cooking, but she felt it added a homey touch to the lighthouse. Eugene inserted a playing card from an anime show he watched into the slot on a laser gun toy. It lit up, indicating some sort of bonus point score in a game that none of the others understood.

Danny stood before the rest of his friends, cleared his throat, and began his speech, "So, I bet you're all wondering why I gathered you here today."

"Oh, yeah! The big idea!" Shayla recollected. She, Miko, and Eugene sat cross-legged on the rug that Miko had found next to a dumpster. They watched Danny intently.

"What," Danny continued, "is the problem that we all share this summer?"

Eugene shot his hand up.

"This isn't class, Eugene, you can just answer."

"Mosquitoes."

"What?"

"Yeah," Eugene pressed on, "Every summer I end up bitten head to toe. Don't you guys hate it?"

The girls nodded in agreement. Miko tried to toss some of her customized trail mix into her mouth, but she missed the mid-air catch. Danny rubbed his forehead, "No, guys, the summer camps. The violin classes. The slaughterhouse. We're all getting sent away to places we don't want to go."

The room filled with a mixture of "Oh" and "That's right."

"Up until now, everyone's been telling us what to do and bullying us around," Danny made his case. "During summer vacation, someone has always had to look after us, and when the adults didn't feel like doing their job, they abandoned us into someone else's care for a few months. But next year is going to be different. We'll be in high school. We're practically adults. And soon, we won't have any summers left because of college prep courses or summer jobs or internships or a million other reasons that can take away our vacation. But this is it; our one chance to use this freedom for something amazing. We should be the masters of our own destiny. And the way I see it, our summer belongs to us. Not your parents, not my uncles, not anybody else, and we should be able to spend it the way we want."

Miko objected, "But Danny, I *have to* go to conservatory. My parents signed me up already. I can't just tell them I don't want to go. Believe me, I've tried." Another M&M bounced off her lip.

"And that's why we don't tell them." A hush fell over the room. "We're all expected to be gone for almost an entire summer. If we play our cards right, we can use that time for the coolest adventure of our lives without anyone having a clue."

Miko was the first to be able to respond, "Okay, so what do you propose we do?"

Danny reached into his pockets and pulled out some folded sheets of paper. He smoothed out the creases and showed his drawing, "We, my friends, will be sailing to Hawaii."

Crude though it may be, Danny's drawing sold the total package. It featured, front and center, a sailboat with stick figures representing each of the four of them. The sun smiled with sunglasses on, and an arrow reached from a rough map of San Francisco to the Hawaiian island chain. "All we have to do is get out of our commitments, steal my uncles' boat from the harbor, and set a course for an island paradise."

Eugene thought aloud, "How are we going to fool our parents into thinking we're at camp?"

"Well, that's going to take some clever planning. As

long as I leave the house on the right day, my uncles won't think twice about where I might be. They'll be so focused on their Catalina Island trip and happy that I'm out of their hair. They won't even notice."

Shayla bounced gleefully in her place, "My aunt's slaughterhouse is completely off the grid! She doesn't even own a phone, so I'll just send her a snail mail saying not to expect me. Then I'll send letters to my mom periodically with my aunt's return address about what a wonderful time I'm having."

"See guys? That's the kind of thinking we're going to need."

Miko spoke up, "Well, I'll have my cell phone where I'm going. What am I supposed to do if my parents call me while I'm in the middle of the ocean with no service?"

Danny excitedly responded with, "Call whoever's in charge of the conservatory and tell them that you are no longer attending due to a flu or something. Then record a voicemail saying that cell phones are banned at conservatory so as not to disturb the creative process, in case your parents call. Then we'll set up a charging station. Here. In the lighthouse so you'll have full power and reception. And just leave your phone here."

"What about me?" asked Eugene.

"You're going to Wilderness Camp Eugene. Cell phones aren't allowed anyways. Just call them and cancel."

"Can I cancel because of too many mosquitoes?" Eugene asked excitedly.

"Yeah. Sure. Whatever."

Miko excitedly popped up with an idea. "Oh! We can have a taxi pick us up from our houses so that our parents don't see where we're actually going!" She turned to Shayla and exchanged their elaborate, secret handshake to celebrate her idea.

"But wait," Eugene paused. "What about when my parents drop me off at the bus to Wilderness Camp? They're super over-protective and won't let me take a cab.

They say only New Yorkers and drunks use taxis."

"Hmmm…" Danny hadn't planned on that. "It's okay. We'll think of something by then."

Miko asked, "Won't your uncles notice if their boat has been stolen?"

"Yes, but they'll think I'm away at fat camp. So as long as they don't suspect *me*, we're in the clear. And when we return from Hawaii I'll just leave it alongside a pier. They'll think that teenagers stole it, used it to party, and then abandoned it."

Shayla, Eugene, and Miko sat for a moment pondering the possibility of Danny's plan actually working. Occasionally the silence would be broken up with questions, each of which Danny had an answer to.

"Where will we stay in Hawaii?"

"On the boat or camped out on the beach."

"What about gas?"

"We'll buy enough with the combined allowances your parents are giving you for camp. I can fill my gas cans from my go-cart."

"How will we know how to get there?"

"The boat has a GPS and a radar. We simply enter an address from Hawaii and it will take us there."

"Well, if we're going to steal a boat and sail the open seas, I think we're going to need a name," Shayla declared.

"Call me Gene the Mean. Yarrr!" Eugene curled his fingers and began hook-attacking Miko. Miko calmly lit her lighter and said, "Stop or I'll burn your cape."

Eugene stopped immediately. "Ah! Okay! Fire bad! Fire bad!"

"No, not like that. Like for *us*," Shayla continued. "As a crew."

Suggestions flew wildly about the room. Many of them had something to do with skulls, Miko's were just deemed too violent. All of Eugene's ideas were in some way related to super heroes or robots. Finally, Danny settled the argument. "The Castaway Kids." Everyone sat back and let the name bounce around in their minds.

Shayla nodded her head. "I like it."

"Me three," threw in Eugene.

"Sounds good to me," Miko shrugged.

"Do you even know how to sail, bro?" The kids turned to the top of the ladder to see where the voice had come from. It was Cody, Shayla's cousin. He was out of his football uniform now and leaning against the railing of the stairs. One hand rested in the pocket of the school's football jacket and his skinny jeans were high enough to expose his red kicks. He swept his shaggy blond hair out of his eyes.

Shayla sprang to her feet, "Cody! What are you doing here?"

"I ate dinner at your house. Your mom told me to bring you a plate here," he handed her a plastic grocery bag that held a plate of mixed spinach salad and a vegan casserole.

Danny swallowed hard, "How long have you been standing there?"

"Long enough to know you guys are going on a suicide mission."

Danny glared at Cody. He felt as though his sacred space had been violated. *He's going to ruin everything...*

"I'll ask you again, do you know the first thing about sailing a boat?" Cody's calm resilience stood in contrast to Danny's rising fury.

"Of course I do. I've been out like a hundred times."

"Oh really," Cody stepped into the room further. "By yourself? Or with someone else telling you what to do?"

Danny's face was turning red. His anger and embarrassment at being called out interfered with his ability to quickly shout out answers as he'd been able to do when only his friends were asking them. He shook his head no.

"What was that? No you haven't? Or am I wrong?" Cody was unmoved.

"Not alone," Danny grunted.

Cody pressed him further, "So you don't know how, then."

"Yeah, I do!" Danny insisted.

"Okay, then tell me this; at what wind speed do you need to reef the sails or risk capsizing?" Danny started to sweat under the pressure of Cody's question. He'd always been in charge of tying lines and preparing for the boom to swing, but he only ever did what one of his uncles told him to do so. He folded his arms and looked at the ground, unable to answer. Cody continued sarcastically, "Yup, sounds like you're ready to sail across the Pacific."

"Well I guess that plan's out the window then." Miko put her headphones on and leaned back. This time, she tossed a small handful of M&Ms, ensuring one or two would make it in her mouth.

Shayla picked at her casserole with the plastic fork she'd found in the bag, "Gee, I hadn't realized how much I was dreading the meat packing plant until I almost didn't have to go."

"Yeah, I bet there's not even any mosquitoes out in the middle of the ocean," Eugene lamented.

"I was hoping to meet a cute musician in Hawaii." Miko closed her eyes and smiled.

"Sorry to burst your bubble, guys," Cody said, "but Shayla's my cousin and I'm supposed to take care of her. Sometimes that means dealing with reality."

Eugene tried to cheer up Danny. "Well, maybe it was a little too ambitious. What if you just sail us over to Oakland instead?"

"How are we going to hide in Oakland all summer?" Miko fired back. "My mom works in Oakland. It's like twenty minutes away."

"Besides," Cody went on, "it's not the distance that matters. Any water can be unsafe if you don't know how to sail. That's pretty much the first rule."

"All right, Cody, we got it." Danny stared out at the

ocean. "The dream is ruined. Give it a rest."

"Can you sail, Cody?" Eugene asked.

"I worked the last couple of summers taking tourists out sightseeing in the bay," Cody answered. "They made us get certifications."

"Well, why don't you come with us?" Shayla perked up suddenly. "You can be our Captain!"

This was too much. Danny had been trying to fume silently, but this made him boil over. "Are you kidding me? Cody can't come!"

"But he's the only one who knows how to sail the boat," Miko stated flatly. She was trying to present logic to Danny without further provoking him, but it wasn't working.

"Oh, yeah, sure. Let's spend a whole summer getting away from all the jerks that treat us like outcasts in close quarters with the worst offender! Eugene, remember that time Cody and his friends stuffed your locker full of dreidels?"

"It wasn't as bad as the time they tied me up with my cape and called me 'Super Jew,'" Eugene recollected.

"And, Miko," Danny flailed wildly as he spoke, "how many times have they thrown pencils at you in class and told you to stop sleeping?"

"Racist jerks," Miko huffed. "I've never slept in class before!"

"If this trip is about anything, it's about having one summer getting away from guys like Cody. And you're all telling me you'd feel better if he came with us?" The room went quiet. No one had an answer for Danny's question.

"Look, this isn't personal," Cody put up his hands in indifference. "It's just the truth. If you try and do this alone, you're not going to make it. I can't go to Shayla's funeral knowing I could have prevented it, so I'm going to have to tell somebody."

Cody started to leave when Shayla stopped him, "No, Cody, don't tell on us! Just come with us. You can be the captain so we get there safe, and we'll all put the past behind us and start fresh. We'll be nice to each other and we'll have a good time." She looked at Danny. "Right?"

Danny pursed his lips for a moment, thinking. Eventually he asked, "People are going to expect you at football practice."

"There's a private training camp that's always trying to recruit me. As long as I stay in shape, I can tell everyone I'm there all summer."

Pacing the room, Danny realized he didn't have much choice. He was either spending the summer with Cody or at fat camp. At least with Cody he'd have the rest of his friends too. He walked right up to Cody and looked him in the eyes. "You might be sailing the boat, but I'm still the captain. Got it? And Erik Berman isn't invited."

"Fine. Whatever," Cody submitted. "I'm just coming along to make sure Shayla's safe."

"Does this mean we're back on?" Eugene asked.

"It means we've got a lot of work to do," Danny turned to face him. "Now tell me about this bus drop off for Wilderness Camp. We're going to need a plan."

ARTICLES OF AGREEMENT

This contract applies to all persons on board The Mogadishu (formerly the USS Montana). Allegiance to these provisions is sworn by the undersigned. Any disagreements or circumstances not provided for here are to be decided solely by Captain Vasser and by no other man.

I   All weapons are to be kept clean and fit for service at every moment.

II   Treasures and items of value are to be distributed in equal shares amongst the crew with one share to each man upon completion of the voyage. Quartermaster shall receive two shares, the master and gunner shall each receive one and a half. The Captain forgoes a share of all such items save for the weapon codenamed "Super Nova."

III   The Captain and only the Captain shall be entitled to the Super Nova.

IV   No man is permitted to game at cards or dice for money.

VI   Lights to be out at nine o clock for the night. Any crew wishing to engage in after hours drinking shall do so only on the weather decks.

VII   Desertion of ship or quarters in battle is punishable by death or marooning.

VIII   If any man shall lose a joint in time of engagement, a stipend of 6,500,000 Somali Shillings shall be issued. A limb shall warrant 13,000,000 SOS.

IX   Drunkenness in times of engagement shall suffer a punishment deemed by the Quartermaster and voted by the majority of the company.

X   This agreement null and void only upon safe return to home port with Super Nova and all acquired bounty.

K Vasser   Captain
Mu'Mmar   Quartermaster

4 EUGENE'S ESCAPE

The following week the kids were so busy they hardly had time to sleep. Immediately after school, they'd set about taking care of all the little things they'd need to set off on their journey. Shayla sent the letter to her aunt, Miko loaded up on supplies, Danny stole the key to his uncles' boat and had a copy made. They'd even hit every gas station around town, asking the attendants for gas for the go kart which was secretly how they'd been filling up the boat. While the rest of the kids were celebrating their graduation from middle school, Eugene was trying not to let on that he had strapped the cafeteria's entire condiment supply under his cap and gown. The last major uncertainty revolved around the plan to spring Eugene from Wilderness Camp.

Eugene did a surprisingly good impression of his father on the phone, so he was able to get himself off of the roster, but there was still the little matter of his parents expecting to bring him to the bus. Danny ran through his plan in his head while sizing up their supplies at the light house. Eugene and Shayla were sorting and packing while Miko set up her voicemail. "Hi, you've reached Miko Tanaka. You're probably my mom or dad. Cell phones

43

aren't allowed here, so I won't get this message till I see you…so probably don't bother. Uh, bye." She turned to the others, "Was that good?"

"It was a little awkward," Eugene responded.

Miko pursed her lips, "Hmm, like 'teenager-who-thinks-cell-phone-rules-are-dumb' awkward or 'teenager-stealing-a-boat-for-the-summer' awkward?"

"Mostly the first," Danny said. "I think you'll be okay."

Cody clanged his way up the metal staircase. "Oh, look who decided to show up," Danny called out. "Somebody's finally ready to put in a little work to get this show on the road."

"Uh, yeah, about that," Cody hesitated. "Change of plans. I got your text about tomorrow…it's not really a good day for me."

The room stopped. Everyone looked from Cody to Danny. Danny threw his hands in the air, "What do you mean? We have to make sure Eugene doesn't get shipped off to camp."

"Can't you do it without me?"

Danny tried to restrain his frustration, "Not really. I made the plan using five of us. Why won't you help?"

"Look, Danny," Cody wasn't his usually collected self. Danny was getting hot under the collar, but Cody seemed absent and distracted, "I'll sail your boat, but I'm not going to be able to be there tomorrow. Besides, I don't want to do a bunch of illegal stuff and get in trouble."

"We're already stealing a boat!" Danny burst. "And we need to save Eugene. If everyone doesn't do their part, we might blow this."

Cody sighed, "No, *you're* stealing the boat. I'm just keeping my cousin from dying because of your stupid plan."

Eugene spoke up, "Cody, don't you want to go?"

"Frankly," Cody looked him in the eye, "it's probably smarter if none of us go."

That was when Danny lost it. He'd had enough second-guessing and nay-saying to last a lifetime. "You don't get it, do you? Maybe it doesn't matter for you whether you stay or go, but it matters to us. You don't know what it's like to be different or outcast from everyone else, but we have to put up with it all the time. We have to try and hide in the middle of the crowd at school every day, and then our one chance to be ourselves, we get sent off to some stupid place we don't want to go." He pushed Cody back towards the stairs, "You don't have problems like we do, so just leave us alone. We'll figure it out without you."

"I'll see myself out," Cody said. "Good luck, guys."

A hush filled the room. Danny's face was still red from the confrontation. Shayla asked him, "Can we really do this without him?"

"Maybe," Danny stared out the window. "But it's going to take a lot of luck."

A gentle breeze rustled through the leaves of the bush behind which Danny was crouching. He tried to put the previous night's argument out of his head as he held up his binoculars. Focusing the lenses, he pointed them toward the bright yellow school bus, patiently loading the students as they arrived one by one. A man in military camouflage checked the name of each one off of a clipboard as they waved good-bye to their parents.

"I still think we should have brought more road flares," came Miko's voice over the walkie talkie.

Danny knew this had more to do with Miko's penchant for things that set on fire and less to do with the actual details of the plan, so he ignored her statement. Besides, if all went well, they wouldn't need to use a single one of them. He spotted Eugene's parents driving up to the bus stop. "Ok, everyone look sharp. The bird is in the air."

Shayla's voice crackled over the radio, "That means Eugene's here, right?"

Danny took a moment to collect himself. They'd been over these codes a thousand times. He tapped the walkie talkie to his forehead, "Yeah, that's right. Remember, don't let Eugene's parents see you."

"Ten Four," Miko answered.

"Seven Eleven!" Shayla, of course, meant "ten four," but Danny knew this was as close as she was going to get. He put the binoculars back up and watched Eugene and his parents get out of the car. Eugene looked nervously over his shoulders, visibly trembling. *Hold it together, Eugene, don't give us away.*

The army-print man found the name of the next kid on his roster as Eugene crept up. He had been instructed to be sneaky, but it was coming across a bit more suspicious than Danny would have liked to see. He picked up his radio, "Now!"

Shayla sprung from an alleyway and made a beeline for the camouflaged man. She smacked right into him, causing him to drop his clipboard. "Oh, I'm sorry, mister, I didn't see you there!"

The man bent over to pick up his papers, "That's all right, it just means the uniform is working."

"Say, you look like the outdoors type. Maybe you can help me with my toad." She produced an oversized Pacman frog from her pocket, "I want to give it a name, but how am I supposed to know if it should be a boy's name or a girl's name?"

While the man tried to deal with Shayla's intrusion, Eugene, his eyes fixed wide in fright, floated behind him and up the steps into the bus. He found a seat and waved out the window to his parents. Danny got on the radio, "The sparrow is in the nest."

Shayla grabbed the radio in her pocket. The

46

camouflaged man hadn't noticed as he was rotating the frog in his hands and examining it closely. Her mission complete, she didn't let him finish his thought before snatching back the frog, "You know, maybe I'll just call it 'Sam' to be safe. Thanks anyway!"

She made her escape, back the way she came. Danny smiled at the success of the plan so far. Eugene shot him a thumbs up out the window of the bus, but then Danny looked back towards the curb. Eugene's parents were still standing there. Danny shook his head and waved his hands wildly back to Eugene. He got on the radio, "We've got lingerers. Plan B, everyone, Plan B!"

"Ha! Yes! Firing up the flares," Miko could hardly contain her excitement. The last couple of kids got checked off the list and on the bus. The door closed and the bus started to move. *Great, now we definitely need Cody*, Danny thought.

Danny hoped for the best, fired up his go kart, and exploded from the bushes. He bounced along the uneven sidewalk, but the little two-stroke engine struggled to keep up.

The sidewalk was crowded. He hadn't counted on it being trash day, and the added obstacles made Danny's drive something of a slalom course. He darted past a rather confused looking dog tied to a light post when Miko came in over the walkie, "Everything's set up here. Give me a buzz when you turn up 10th street."

Danny looked up and checked the street signs. The intersection he was currently crossing was 10th, and the bus showed no signs of slowing to turn. "Mayday! Mayday!" He screeched into the radio, "The driver is not, I repeat *not* using 10th street!"

This was exactly the moment he had been dreading. There were two routes to the freeway that the bus driver could have taken. Danny had planned to have both covered, but Cody's refusal had left him a man down.

Horns honked all around Miko from the backed up

traffic, "What do you want me to do? I've got like a dozen of these flares going off in the middle of the street."

They had to stop the bus before it got on the freeway. Once that happened, Eugene would be long gone, headed off into a wilderness that wouldn't be expecting him. Danny knew that if Eugene was caught, he wouldn't last long before confessing the entire plan. Their entire summer hinged on getting Eugene off that bus. "You have to try and cover for Cody. Book it to 8th street! Move the flares!"

Miko froze at the order. She looked at her line of glowing red road flares. "Awesome."

As Danny fumbled with the radio, an old woman in a tattered pink robe and mismatched curlers in what remained of her thinning, grey hair wheeled her recycling bin out to the curb. Danny swerved hard right to keep from plowing straight through her, managing only to clip the corner of the container with his bumper.

"Watch where you're going!" she wailed after him, but Danny had bigger fish to fry now. Sparks shot up where the undercarriage scraped the curb and Danny was flying down the road on the wrong side of the street.

A convertible slammed on its brakes to stop short of plowing into Danny. He tried to weave back onto the sidewalk, but his tires were too small to climb back up the curb. The bus was pulling ahead, and Danny couldn't afford to lose it. He swung back out into the street, splitting the gap between two passing minivans.

Her hands straining to contain a dozen roaring road flares, Miko sprinted past a row of shops. She held them up over her head, the flames shooting backwards, giving the impression that she was some sort of Wile E. Coyote experiment gone awry. Danny's voice crackled over the radio, "The bus is turning, are you in position yet?"

Miko was not in position, and she wasn't sure if she'd make it in time. She had no free hand with which to communicate this back to Danny, but she kicked her pace into a higher gear.

Out of the corner of her eye, she spotted a shortcut. She could chop off an entire corner by passing through two sets of glass double doors in the plaza to her right. She broke towards them as fast as her legs could carry her, through the confused crowd.

Danny had made his turn, still in hot pursuit of the bus. He had no idea of Miko's status, so he dare not lose sight. Eugene's face pressed up against the window. He mouthed something, but Danny could not take his eyes off the road long enough to read his lips. His white knuckles gripped the steering wheel tightly, the ball of his foot aching from the unnecessary extra force with which he pressed down on the gas pedal.

And finally, at long last, brake lights. The bus came to a sudden stop and so did Danny. "Great job, Miko!" Danny barked over the radio. "We got it!"

"Got what?" Miko managed to fumble her radio on. "I'm almost there, I promise!"

Confused, Danny pulled over towards the curb. He caught a glimpse around the bus where, rather than a pile of road flares, he saw a line of traffic cones blocking off the lane. On the sidewalk, overseeing the disarray he had created was a grinning Cody.

Miko finally arrived, her flares still burning. She chucked them into the street before she had a chance to notice the cones. "What?" She asked no one in particular. She tried to act casual while catching her breath. Looking over, she saw Cody watching her. "Oh. Hey. Glad you came through."

He shrugged. "I had some things to take care of, but I guess I'm happy I had time to help out."

Miko smiled back at him. "Cool man, but I think we should run. I'm pretty sure I just ran through a whole bunch of public places screaming with flaming sticks above my head."

"Oh. Yeah. Good idea." Cody and Miko disappeared

behind a nearby dumpster.

Eugene gave another thumbs up out the back window. Breathing a sigh of relief, Danny returned it. Inside the bus, Eugene opened up a small canister from his backpack. From his vantage point, Danny could not see the swarm of mosquitoes, but he could see the sudden flailing of the other kids attempting to swat them all away. The counselor in camouflage let out a high-pitched squeal as he threw his safari hat at the army of bugs. A moment later, amidst the chaos, the emergency exit door on the back of the bus swung open and Eugene rolled out, latching it behind him. He crawled back to Danny's go kart and squeezed into the second seat, "For a minute there, I thought we weren't going to make it."

Danny smiled, "The Castaway Kids never leave a man behind. Now let's steal ourselves a boat."

CLASSIFIED D.O.D. FILE #5300.1138-CV/SPS

SATOC PIER WATCH 0200 - 0800 MAY 21ST

132 NAUTICAL MILES EAST OFF THE COAST OF MANILA, PHILIPPINES

SATOC (SATCOM Operations Center) - CHIEF PETTY OFFICER ELECTRONICS TECHNICIAN AMANDA VESKI (SW)

CALLER: (STATIC) HELP! HELP ME! PLEASE SEND HELP!

SATOC: THIS IS SATOC NINER ONE. PLEASE IDENTIFY YOURSELF.

CALLER: OH THANK GOODNESS!…(STATIC)…IS CARGO SHIP SAVANNAH USNS-106. WE'VE BEEN ATTACKED BY TERRORISTS. THE SHIP IS SINKING! REPEAT, THE SHIP IS SINKING! I NEED HELP!

SATOC: SAVANNAH, SATOC. WHAT ARE YOUR COORDINATES?

CALLER: UM, I'M NOT SURE…LET ME CHECK THE RADAR. WAIT ONE. …(INAUDIBLE)… OKAY, I THINK WE'RE AT 14.64 DEGREES NORTH, 117.75 DEGREES EAST. PLEASE HURRY!

SATOC: AM I SPEAKING WITH THE CAPTAIN?

CALLER: NO! THE CAPTAIN'S DEAD! THEY SHOT HIM! I'M THE ONLY ONE LEFT! MY NAME IS…(STAT-IC)…AS THE CHIEF ENGINEER! THERE IS A HUGE HOLE IN THE PORTSIDE HULL! MAJOR FLOODING! MASS PERSONNEL CASUALTIES! THERE WAS AN EXPLOSION! THEY TOOK EVERYTHING!

SATOC: WHO TOOK EVERYTHING?

DRAFTER NAME		TYPIST:	
MARK TRAN, SATOC COMMANDING OFFICER		IAN LARSEN	
PRINTED NAME AMANDA VESKI			
SIGNATURE *Amanda Veski*		CLASSIFICATION CLASSIFIED	

CALLER: TERRORISTS! OR PIRATES! I DON'T KNOW…THEY SPOKE ENGLISH AND ARABIC, I THINK. WE DIDN'T SEE THEM ON THE RADAR! THE SHIP IS PAINTED ALL BLACK WITH NO LIGHTS ON! THEY'RE INVISI-BLE…(STATIC)…TOOK MONEY, JEWELRY, AND HELICOPTER PARTS! THEIR CAPTAIN CAME ABOARD WITH 30 OTHER MEN. MOST OF US WERE SLEEPING. THEY KILLED EVERYONE!

SATOC: ARE THEY STILL ONBOARD?

CALLER: NEGATIVE, THEIR SHIP IS PULLING AWAY NOW. I THINK IT'S A CRUISER. MAYBE AMERICAN. THEY SHOT AT OUR REFUELING STATION AND BLEW IT UP. SOME OF THEIR MEN WERE KILLED IN THE BLAST. THEIR CAPTAIN LOST BOTH HIS LEGS! I SAW THEM CARRYING HIM BACK TO THEIR SHIP. HE LOOKED AMERICAN. PLEASE HURRY! THAT HELICOPTER WAS DESIGNED TO LIFT A TANK! IT'S EXTREMELY DANGEROUS IN THE WRONG HANDS!

SATOC: SAVANNAH. I'M SENDING A REQUEST TO THE NEAREST US NAVY SHIP TO COME HELP YOU. I'M PICK-ING YOU UP ON MY RADAR NOW… THE NEAREST DESTROYER IS THE USS CARTER HALL. I'M SENDING A MESSAGE TO THEM NOW. IT MAY BE UP TO TWO HOURS BEFORE THEY CAN ARRIVE.

CALLER: THAT'S NOT FAST ENOUGH! I CAN BARELY HOLD ON IN THE PILOT HOUSE. I'M STANDING ON THE PORT BULKHEAD. THERE'S WATER UP TO MY KNEES. I HAVE TO ABANDON SHIP.

SATOC: SAVANNAH. STAY WITH THE BOAT. STAY NEAR THE COORDINATES YOU GAVE ME. WE WON'T BE ABLE TO FIND YOU.

(RADIO SILENCE)

DRAFTER NAME	TYPIST:
MARK TRAN, SATOC COMMANDING OFFICER	IAN LARSEN
PRINTED NAME AMANDA VESKI	
SIGNATURE *Amanda Veski*	CLASSIFICATION CLASSIFIED

5 UNDERWAY

Night fell and the whole gang regrouped behind the dumpsters on the far end of the parking lot at the harbor. Miko was the last to arrive, lugging two empty shopping carts with her. Shayla and Cody began shoveling their supplies into the carts. Eugene protested, "Are you sure we won't get in trouble for taking the shopping carts?"

Danny rolled his eyes, "I guess at least we'll have a more interesting rap sheet."

Shayla stacked the last box of food, "Is that everything? Do you have the key?"

"Of course," Danny produced the silver key he'd copied earlier that week. He had it on a rubber keychain that read "Aloha" that he bought from the hardware store in honor of the trip.

They began their inconspicuous creep along the edge of the parking lot, ducking by the fence, all the way to the entrance to the harbor.

Raising a fist to signal a halt, Danny peeked around the corner. The night was crisp, the orange glow of the city lights illuminated the layer of clouds an ominous shade of grey. Down the rickety, wooden docks, the beam of a flashlight bobbed up and down. Danny quickly retreated for cover. He counted to ten slowly in his head before peeking back around. The night watchman passed by, turning down another walkway along the pier.

"Move out."

Miko and Cody pushed their carts behind Danny, following his lead to his uncles' boat. It had been some time since they'd taken him out, but he remembered vaguely where their dock was located.

He guided them down the second pier from the entrance, keeping one eye on the security guard. The flashlight was safely pointed away from them, but he watched like a hawk in case that changed. They moved slowly in order to keep the shopping carts from banging on the ridges between the planks.

Danny scanned the rows of boats, looking for the right one, and then he saw it. Eight docks down on the right, the distinctive bright hull of *Odyssey II*, now painted over shoddily by his uncles with *Thug Life*. Out of the corner of his eye, he saw the watchman's flashlight swing around. He'd reached the end of the pier and was coming back towards them. "This way," Danny whispered, "Hurry!"

They quickened their pace and pulled up alongside the boat. It was twenty-four feet long, a brilliant white with a blue streak along the side. Rolled up at the bottom of the mast was the great, white sail. Being the only thing his uncles truly loved besides themselves, the boat was kept in perfect condition at all times.

Cody hopped aboard, receiving loads of supplies from the others on the dock. The beam of light grew closer with each passing moment. Anything soft they simply chucked aboard. The more delicate, heavier items were taken by Cody and silently set down with as much speed as they could manage. With the carts emptied, Shayla, Eugene, and Miko all jumped aboard.

Not wanting to arouse suspicion, Danny decided to shove the shopping carts over the edge of the dock. He pushed one over when Cody called out to him, "Toss me the key!" Danny reached in his pocket and flung it to Cody. The second it left his hand, he knew he'd thrown it short.

He watched in horror as the key plunked off the hull of the boat, dropping into the murky water. Like some sort of slow motion train wreck, he couldn't avert his eyes. *This is it. Our entire summer, everything we've planned and worked for, down into the harbor on one bad toss.* He was frozen in terror, horrified at what he'd done but unable to move.

In the split second it took for his brain to start pondering what juvenile hall would look like, Cody made his move. In a single leap, he was over the side and down into the water, shoes and all. Miko scampered to the railing, watching as the ripples dispersed into the natural wake of the sea. All eyes were fixed on the spot until finally a hand shot out of the water, grasping tightly to the key. Cody gasped for air, "I got it!"

Miko pulled Cody up and Danny shook off his haze. He ditched the second cart, untied the last rope, and leapt into the boat. The engine purred to life and they eased away from the pier. By the time the night watchman's flashlight fell upon the boat, it was too far away for him to notice it was being captained by an unruly gang of thirteen year olds.

Once clear of the breakwater, squeals of excitement were released all around. Danny howled into the cool night sky, Eugene swung around the mast, his cape flapping in the breeze. Miko and Shayla had their own private dance party. Even Cody, wet and wrapped in a towel, couldn't help but smirk in approval.

They raised the mainsail and entered the coordinates for their destination in Hawaii into the GPS. Sailing off into the unknown, the city lights slowly faded over the horizon until they disappeared completely.

The celebration continued well into the night, Cody manning the helm. One by one, the rest of the kids fell asleep, lulled gently by the rolling of the waves.

"Hey, Danny," Cody called out. Danny's eyes snapped open. He hadn't even managed to make it down the stairwell to the beds down below, he'd passed out right there on one of the padded seats. "I'm fading fast, can you take the wheel?"

Danny sat up, rubbing his eyes. The sun was bright on this beautiful, cloudless morning. The *Thug Life* stood as a stark contrast to the blanket of blue sky and ocean surrounding them. "Yeah sure," Danny stumbled over to the controls.

"Keep it pointed straight, be aware of fuel levels, check the GPS now and again, and try to take any waves head on."

Through a yawn, Danny waved Cody off, "Yeah, yeah, I got it. I'll call you if anything comes up." Cody gave a mock salute before disappearing below deck.

The view was simply breathtaking. Danny liked the way he could see the curvature of the Earth, uninterrupted by hills and buildings. While he was glad to have his friends here with him, these few, quiet moments sailing the boat alone gave Danny the sense of absolute freedom he'd been craving.

Over the next several days, everyone found their niche and something of a routine began to form. Shayla found herself as the de facto chef, whipping up some of the most creative meal options the crew had ever had. For example, one particularly sunny afternoon, Shayla made what she called "Salad Pockets." It was a Romaine lettuce leaf cupped like a taco, stuffed with carrots, tomatoes, purple cabbage, broccoli, and croutons, and eaten by hand. It saved creating more dirty dishes too, since they only brought one steel wool brush for cleaning.

Miko ended up as the DJ for two reasons: the first was that she had been the one with the foresight to bring an mp3 player and stereo dock, the second was that she was the only one capable of navigating through her collection of obscure bands to find fitting, mood appropriate music. She soon found out, however, it was impossible to find anything that everyone could agree on, so most of the time they listened to Eugene make up his own parody songs, usually about whatever it was he was doing at the time.

For his own part, Eugene did what he could to contribute around the boat. He was always happy to help tie some lines or refill the fuel tank, but he spent most of his time either seasick or trying not to be seasick. Being unable to swim, he insisted on wearing a life jacket at all times under his cape.

Cody and Danny split steering the boat between the two of them. When there was a prevailing wind, Cody put up the sail and cut the engines. When none was to be found, Danny would give Cody a break and run the boat on gas. He took it upon himself to try and learn tricks for sailing the boat from watching Cody, but never by directly asking a question. Danny refused to clue Cody in that he was jealous of yet another of his talents.

From the steps down to the kitchen, he spied on Cody's technique, which right now consisted of doing very little but watching the seas ahead. Danny felt around in the paper towel he used as a plate for another bite of his snack. Using several of the desserts on board, he'd concocted an old favorite of his: the Snack Cake Jambalaya. This comprised of a Twinkie, Ding Dong, and a Ho Ho, finely chopped, then tossed in an ice cream cone to provide a random sampling in every bite. The sugar took the edge off his bitterness towards Cody.

Shayla came from the front of the ship where she'd been sunning herself, "Look! I found some seaweed! We can make nori tonight!"

"Cool, have fun with that," Danny munched into another bite of his creation. "I'll stick to real food though."

Shayla pouted, "Danny, maybe you should save some room for dinner."

"Nah, it's okay," Danny talked between chews. "Don't worry about me, I've got plenty here."

"Yeah, but I mean, I'm going to put together something for everybody. It's really the same amount of work no matter how many of us eat it. Maybe if you try it you'll like it?" Shayla hinted strongly.

Danny missed it entirely, "I don't know; is that stuff even clean? Sounds kind of gross to me." He let out a resounding belch.

Shayla was hurt, but tried not to let it show. She squeezed past Danny to drop off her find in the kitchen. "I was just hoping I could find something healthy for you, that's all."

Danny muttered loudly, "Oh great, as if I don't get enough fat talk at home, now I have to hear it out here too."

"I didn't mean anything like that, I-"

"Yeah, sure. You want me to stop being so fat. So does everyone else. There's nothing I can do about it." Danny wiped his fingers on his shirt.

Shayla retreated quickly, attempting to repair the damage she'd done, "No, really, I wasn't trying to make fun of you! I was just trying to-"

"You can help me by leaving me alone." Danny stomped towards a relatively unoccupied part of the boat where he could get a little peace. Shayla was left alone in the kitchen to decide whether she was crying more out of guilt or for the insult of her cooking.

The next morning, Danny was the last to rise. Shayla and Miko were playing a magnetic travel checkers game on the deck while Eugene tried to figure out what other parts of the boat he could stick the pieces to.

"Look what I found," Danny shouted, reaching on his

tippy toes into a cupboard above the bed. He pulled out two sturdy fishing poles and a tackle kit.

Shayla gasped, "Oh no! You're not going to hurt the fishies, are you?"

"Well, I mean, I guess we're going to try," Danny responded apologetically.

"Strong pass," Shayla huffed, going back to her game.

"I thought we were all about eating things we dragged out of the ocean," he said under his breath. Danny held a pole out to Eugene, "Want to give it a shot?"

Eugene grinned and snatched the pole. "Yes, I do!"

They rooted around the pantry to find a bit of bait. Danny settled on gummy worms while Eugene managed to scrounge up some leftover eggplant chili Shayla had made two nights ago, which he wrapped in a piece of tin foil. *Hopefully the fish like the eggplant chili more than we did*, thought Danny.

"Fun fact: fish like shiny things," Eugene stated to nobody in particular.

Danny hooked a gummy worm to his line and fed another to himself. "One for the fish, one for me," he sang. He caught Shayla watching him out of the corner of his eye, so he spitefully tossed back a couple more.

"Hey, just so you guys know," Miko said without looking up from the chess board, "I brought some homemade puppy chow as a dessert for the day we pull into Hawaii. I was going to bring it out sooner, but I want it to be for a special occasion. Oh, and Shayla? Checkmate."

"Rats." Shayla turned her attention back to Danny and Eugene.

They cast their lines out from the back of the ship, dangling their toes into the water below. Each time they reeled in their empty lines, Eugene would tweak his bait. He added a tail made of foil, opened a small hole, added some more chili, each time having some sort of logic for the change. Danny didn't care much about such adjustments; he had no idea if there were even any fish around here and his gummy worm was just the right weight for him to put out a good long cast.

Cody explained that when fishing in the ocean, the motion of the boat in the waves tugs at the line regularly. It bends and dips slightly, leaving amateur fisherman to wonder whether or not they may have a nibble. Danny and Eugene pulled in their lines hopefully, finding nothing but their bait several times. When a fish finally did latch on, however, there was no doubt. Eugene's line began to quiver just a bit more than it had been. Suddenly, it seized and whirred, "I got something!"

Danny reeled in his line and chucked his pole on the deck, "Reel it in! Have you got it?"

Eugene grunted as he angled the tip of the pole. "I think so." He put a foot up on the railing for leverage.

The fish led him on two full laps around the boat. He was stepping over lines, ducking the sail, all the while Danny shadowing him ready to lend his support. A rainbow glimmer reflected just beneath the surface. "Get a net!"

Danny bolted below deck. There was no net in the cupboard, he'd have to improvise. He grabbed Shayla's duffel bag, dumping the clothes onto the floor. She cried after him, but Danny was already gone.

By now, the fish's head was peeking up, just barely out of the water. Eugene was wincing hard, his arms beginning to give beneath him. "Scoop it up!" Danny leaned over, reaching out with the bag. He hooked his foot around the railing and stretched as far as he could. Positioning the bag under the fish, he folded it shut and zipped it up.

"Got it!" Eugene helped pull Danny back onto the boat, the bag flopping mightily in his hands.

Miko and Shayla came up to look. "You turned my bag into a prison!" Eugene apologized and brought the bag over to show them his conquest. What he managed to come up with was a 35 pound yellow fin tuna.

Miko was more impressed than Shayla was disgusted, "How'd you know how to do that?"

"Simple," Eugene smirked, "I played a lot of *Ultimate Fishing 5000*. It taught me everything I know. Besides, it's the one sport that being unnoticeable and quiet gives you an advantage."

Eugene offered to clean and gut the fish so that Shayla wouldn't have to. Before they could throw it on the grill, Shayla stopped them, "Thank the fish."

Danny looked at Eugene. "Uh…the fish is already dead."

"Maybe it is, but that doesn't mean our manners are."

Eugene shrugged and offered a quick word of thanks. "Food is great, food is good, thank you fishy, let's eat fish."

Shayla chimed in, "I prepared something while you were fishing in case the inevitable happened." She unfolded a page from her notebook and cleared her throat. Cody rolled his eyes. Danny guessed that Cody had seen several of these ceremonies at family Thanksgivings. "It is a great and noble thing you have done for us, Mister Fish. You served the earth with honor and dignity, and now your life has come to an end. We thank you deeply, from the cores of our being, that you have offered this great sacrifice to enrich our lives and our bodies." She made a gesture towards the sky before giving her blessing to continue the cooking process.

They took down the sail so Cody could take a break and join them. Sitting around the grill out on top of the deck, they sliced off bits of it at a time. They all agreed it was the best fish they'd ever tasted.

Cody finished first, darting off down the stairs. When he returned, he had a football with him. "Anybody want to play?"

"I'm not sure there's enough room for that," Danny said between bites of the tuna.

"Aw, you're just worried about a repeat of tryouts,"

Cody flipped the ball as he spoke.

Danny's cheeks started to turn red, "You're the one who overthrew the pass!"

"I'm pretty sure you were the only one out there who couldn't catch up to the ball," Cody took his shirt off as he spoke.

Miko blushed. Eugene raised his eyebrows, "Whoa, Cody's like, comic book ripped." Danny shot him a look. "What? It's true! He looks like Green Lantern!"

Cody tossed the ball to Eugene. "Come on, put a little lead on me." Cody started jogging towards the front of the ship. Eugene let go something of a lame, wobbling lob out over the edge of the boat into the water. Cody leapt and front-flipped in the air, coming up with a catch before splashing spectacularly into the water. "Woo hoo! Come on in, the water's fine!"

Shayla and Miko had both worn their bathing suits under their clothes, so they quickly threw off their outer layers and dove in. Eugene didn't want to risk learning how to swim in the middle of the ocean, so he stayed up top as the designated quarterback. A few cannonballs and 360s later, Danny had to admit it looked like fun. He changed his pants for a pair of swim trunks and lined up for a throw. "Hit me, Eugene!"

Cody kicked in the water and turned to watch, "Uh, Danny? You might want to take your shirt off first."

Danny looked down. He hadn't forgotten to take his shirt off, he was simply hoping they wouldn't notice. Wearing shorts was a big enough challenge for him. Going publicly shirtless was a battle he was not yet ready to fight, especially with someone as athletic as Cody in the audience. "No thanks, I'll keep it on."

"Whatever…" Cody muttered. Danny heard him, but he pretended like he didn't. *Luckily he's not trolling me,* Danny thought. Eugene put up his throw and Danny set off. He tried to catch the ball and do a flip, but succeeded at neither. The ball bounced off his head and he belly-flopped hard onto the ocean surface.

Cody laughed, but Eugene genuinely complimented him on the size of his splash. Danny was proud to have done something impressive and decided to ignore Cody.

After about an hour, they grew tired of swimming and climbed back into the boat. Danny clapped his hands, "Let's hoist the sail and get a move on!"

"I'm not so sure that's a good idea," Cody objected. "See those clouds to the west? Those are cumulonimbus clouds. They usually mean a storm is coming."

Danny examined the clouds. The sky was clear above them, and the clouds in the distance didn't appear any different from the ones that blanketed San Francisco on any given day.

Cody continued, "We should probably hang out here and let them blow by. Or maybe even run a bit south and east."

"That's in the total opposite direction," Danny dismissed him. "Let's just keep following the GPS. We've lost enough time here already. "

Cody seemed as if he was going to further the argument, but instead he shrugged and helped hoist the sail. "You're the captain," he said, staring at Danny with discontent.

He's just trying to sound smart to make me look stupid, Danny thought. *Cumu-whatever clouds. He's just jealous that this awesome trip wasn't his idea.*

Back underway, night fell and the sky grew dark around them. It was so nice and warm, they brought their blankets up above to camp out underneath the stars. Eugene called out excitedly, "You guys! Look! A shooting star!" Miko and Shayla oohed and aahed at the splendor.

Danny came up from below with some life jackets for pillows in one hand and a violin in the other, "Miko, you didn't tell us you brought your violin."

"I had to," she responded. "I couldn't leave it at home. What if my parents found it?"

Shayla clapped her hands giddily, "Play us something!"

"Eh, you don't want to hear it. Violin music is boring."

Danny handed the instrument to her, "Who cares? Play us something. It'll be fun."

Reluctantly, Miko took it. Danny laid back on his lifejacket and looked up towards the stars. Miko began to play. Danny didn't recognize the tune, but it sounded classical. He thought it was beautiful and mysterious, a perfect symphony for a majestic night at sea.

As she played, Danny watched Shayla slowly nod off to a peaceful, deep sleep. *She's beautiful,* Danny thought. *There's no way she'd go for a guy like me. She probably thinks I'm a fat jerk. It's all Cody's fault. He brings out the worst in me. Then again, she did agree to follow me on this crazy adventure...*

Danny's eyelids became too heavy to lift.

THUD!

Danny jolted awake. The ship rocked violently. *What was that noise?*

MEDICAL LOG – DR. RASHEED DARZI

05/21 - Captain Vasser triaged at 0515. Patient presents with
bilateral disfigurement of feet and lower legs. 36% 3rd degree
burns on lower extremities upon admit. Morphine administered
at 0520, 2.5 mg IV q4h PRN for pain. Sodium Chloride 0.9%
continuous infusion 30mL/hr. Burns immersed in cold water for
30 minutes. Gauze bandages applied. Tourniquet applied below
knee bilaterally due to excessive bleeding at laceration sites.
Patient monitored for neurogenic shock.

05/22 - Thorough assessment of Captain Vasser reveals
significant ligament damage to lower extremities, decreased
muscle tissue, multiple bilateral compound comminuted fractures
to fibula and tibia. Patient was educated on the necessity for
amputation including risk for widespread, systemic infection
under the present conditions. Evaluation: the patient
understands the risks and consents to bilateral below the knee
amputation (BKA).

Skin grafts prepared for upper leg burns. Remaining burns
monitored for healing.

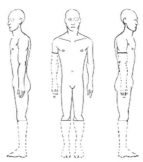

05/23 - 1400 - Education for experimental prosthetics completed.
Consent for procedure obtained. Mechanical leverage in new legs
expected to provide the ability to walk with minimal physical
therapy, and the ability to perform extraordinary feats outside
the normal range.

Request has also been made to proceed at this time with patient's long awaited eye surgery. An untested camera lens-enabled visual prosthesis will be fitted in place of the currently empty left eye socket (model HVX-242L).

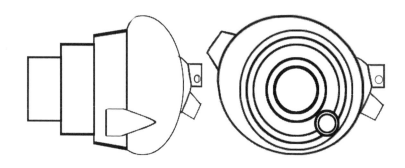

model HVX-242L

5/25 - 0600 - Lengthy surgery has been completed. Both carbon legs are set in and camera receiver installed successfully. Upon waking, Captain will be presented with camera attachment to gauge accuracy and response time.

6/12 – All reports satisfactory from prosthetic. Captain reports, "They work better than I expected." Scheduled installation of new hydraulic assisted robotic arm for depleted shoulder muscle and cartilage in right arm for 1000 tomorrow morning.

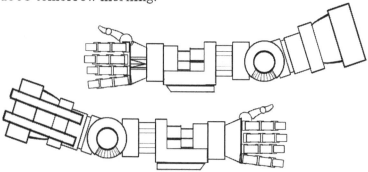

6 CODY'S STORM

Danny threw off his blanket and stood alert, scanning all around him. Cody was the only one awake. "What'd you do?"

"Try to stay calm," Cody responded, "but very slowly, look into the water just over port side." Danny turned left and looked into the deep blue waters, squinting against the early morning sunrise. The placid waters were cut only by the shimmering reflection of the sun on the surface of the water, and then he saw it.

A gray, looming fin.

Danny panicked, *I've led my friends out into the middle of the ocean to be eaten by sharks.*

Shayla stretched, poking her head out of the sleeping quarters, "What's going on? Are we there yet?"

"Go below deck," Cody warned. "We've got a little bit of a situation here and the last thing we want is anybody falling in the water."

"Oh no! Is it the kraken? It's the kraken, isn't it?" Eugene's voice lamented, muffled through his sleeping bag.

WHAM!

Another shark slammed into the side of the boat.

Danny steadied himself on a rope, "No guys, it's just a couple of sharks."

"Sharks?!" Danny couldn't see Miko, but the succeeding clangs and bumps he heard coming from down below painted a pretty clear picture in his head of all the things she must have knocked over in her panic.

Cody was visibly nervous, but he focused that energy on keeping the boat steady. "We probably attracted a bunch of fish with the trash we've let go overboard. They want nothing to do with us."

"Except eat us alive!" Eugene zipped himself shut in his sleeping bag.

"Cody's right," Danny said, "there's no reason to freak out. We'll stay below deck as much as possible."

Shayla reached out to Cody, "Cody, come down here now! You're supposed to be protecting me! You can't do that if you get eaten!"

Cody didn't move, "Sorry, Shayla, but someone's got to run the boat. Don't worry, we'll be through this soon enough."

Miko suggested that they take down the sail and ride it out until the sharks were gone. An argument broke out about how long that would take and whether or not they were safer moving or sitting still until Danny broke through, "You guys, we're on a schedule. We have to keep heading towards Hawaii or we're not going to make it."

"Actually, I've got us headed South-East right now." Danny turned around and glared at Cody. He checked the instrument panel and sure enough, they were headed well in the opposite direction of the route.

"What are you doing? There's an arrow right there!" Danny tapped the GPS a bit too hard.

Cody pointed off into the horizon. "That thick blanket of cloud cover is probably a tropical storm. The storms usually head North-West, so if we're going to try to avoid it, we've got to backtrack a little."

Danny stared blankly at Cody. He looked back to the

clouds. *They're just clouds*. The sky was clear, after all, the waves were calm. WHAM! Another shark crashed into the boat. "How would you even know that?"

Cody kept his eyes in the sky, "I told you, I used to take tourists around the bay on boat trips. They make us study weather patterns and take a class in order to get a license."

Danny grabbed the controls and shooed Cody away, "Well, I'm the captain of this boat, and the weather forecast before we left didn't say anything about any sort of tropical storms. I say we keep heading towards Hawaii."

"But Danny, the weather changes." Danny turned the boat back towards the GPS' course. "And apparently when we go the wrong way, we head into shark-infested waters. Let's go the right way, like we're supposed to, and everything will be fine."

"It's not that simple, Danny! You have to trust me. Just let me navigate!" Cody and Danny were shoulder to shoulder, struggling over the controls.

SLAM!

A huge hit from a shark suddenly sent Cody flailing backwards and off-balance. He hit the back of his knees against the side of the boat and fell overboard.

"Cody!" Shayla ran above deck and peered over the side. Cody came up for air with six sharks circling the boat. She screamed, "Help him!"

Danny, Eugene, and Miko ran over to the edge of the boat. Cody was trying not to panic and tread water slowly. Shayla smacked Danny in the shoulder, "You pushed him in!"

"No, I didn't! I swear! The shark must have tipped the boat," Danny tried to defend himself.

"I could really use some help here, guys!" Cody's voice trembled.

"There's a ladder on the starboard side," suggested Miko.

"There's no time! You need to lower something down

to me."

Danny turned to Eugene and tugged his cape off. "Sorry, Eugene." Danny wrapped one end of the cape around his fist and lowered the other end into the water. Cody grabbed it and pulled up on it. The cape ripped a little.

"My cape!" Eugene exclaimed.

Cody continued to pull himself in. Miko and Shayla pulled up on the cape as well. Just then, a shark snapped at Cody. Luckily, he jolted to the side in time to smack against the wall. The shark was only able to bite off a piece of his shirt.

"We need to distract them with something." Danny looked around the boat. He reached into the nearest bag and pulled out a plastic container that held Miko's puppy chow. He popped the lid off and tossed it in the water.

"My puppy chow!" Miko cried out. "Sharks don't like snacks, Danny. They like blood!"

"We almost got him!" Danny's face turned red as all four of them grunted and flung Cody aboard with a final pull. They all sat and caught their breath.

"Everyone okay?" Danny asked.

Cody, Shayla, Miko, and Eugene all stared at Danny with extreme frustration. The sharks continued hammering away at the boat. Cody shook his head. "You're unbelievable, bro." He got up and went down below.

BAM!

"It was an accident! I didn't mean to-"

"Just stop, Danny. I don't want to hear it." Shayla followed Cody.

BOOM!

"Next time you decide to throw food overboard," Miko stood, brushing herself off and adjusting her glasses, "throw your own damn food." She left downstairs.

SLAM!

"Miko, I'm – I'm sorry. I'll make some more when we get back." Danny called after her, but she was already below deck, ignoring him. Danny turned to Eugene who was examining his now torn cape. "Oh no…I can fix that, Eugene, I promise," pleaded Danny.

"I don't think this is something you can fix." Eugene raised his chin and tied his cape around his neck. He sighed a heavy sigh. "I guess I'll help the others with breakfast." Eugene looked at the boat's controls. "Well, you got what you wanted, Danny. The ship's all yours." Eugene disappeared below deck.

WHAM!

Wow, Danny thought, *I really messed up big time.* He could hear clanging coming from the kitchen below, low chatter, and the smell of eggs. He knew he couldn't go down there just yet. *Will they ever forgive me?*

BOOM!

Another hit from the sharks shook Danny out of his pity party. *I need to make up for this. I need to get us back on course and safely to Hawaii. Then they'll forget all about this.*

With a new sense of determination, Danny stood and took the controls, riding the throttle forward.

Frustrated that they'd lost progress, Danny gripped the tiller tightly. He fought back tears and put his worries behind him as he focused on his sailing. Now he'd finally have a chance to practice the things he'd watched Cody do by himself. He seemed to have found a knack for it, and before long he noticed there hadn't been any bumps from the sharks in quite some time.

As the day went on, the bright, clear sky overhead grew dingy, gray, and overcast. The wind began to pick up, allowing Danny to really catch a good speed. The rest of the Castaway Kids stayed below deck playing board games and generally ignoring Danny. A light rain began to pour on Danny's face. *Ha, this isn't so bad. My uncles and I have been out in the bay in a little rain like this plenty of times, and we always made it through okay.*

It was no sooner that Danny had this thought that he found himself facing down a nearly vertical wall of water.

"Uh…guys? Guys! Help!"

The rest of the kids came bursting out from the decks. Cody seized command immediately and barked orders all around. "Lower the sail!" then "Tie down the jib!" The crew scrambled about, securing all the lines and doing their best to keep up. The ship tossed like a leaf in the wind, slamming in all directions. Danny sat on a bench, bewildered. *I can't believe I screwed up again.*

Each wave they encountered sent a rush of water sweeping over the deck. It took quick minds and quicker hands to grasp onto something solid before their feet were pulled out from under them. More than once, Danny knocked his face into the hard, plastic hull as he held on for dear life. Waves came in like rollercoasters, pulling the ship up to the towering crest of the wave. Once peaked, the bow tipped forward, lingering just a moment as the kids looked straight down the edge. Then off it raced down the watery cliff.

Over and over again they took these beatings, each one higher and stronger than the one before. Screams were lost completely now to the wind, and tears were masked by rain.

It was hard to imagine that the storm had begun in daylight, but with the sun now completely set, true darkness shrouded their view. Hours went by as they fought to keep the boat afloat. Cody grasped the controls tightly as he shouted and pointed to one side of the boat. The rest scrambled quickly in the direction of his point, using their weight to tip the boat back from the brink of turning over.

Exhausted and fueled only by adrenaline and fear, Danny gripped tightly with his arms and legs wrapped around the center mast. That was when he felt it. A sudden wave from the side rocked the ship with such force that Danny couldn't even remember feeling the impact, only the sensation of flying through the air that followed. Into the water he went as the boat tore into pieces.

He bobbed in the water, kicking to keep his head above the surface. A rather large piece of the wreckage floated by and he climbed on top of it. "Danny!" A cry came from behind him. He could barely hear over the howl of the wind and the crash of the waves, but just at the faintest level he heard her voice.

It was all Danny could do to keep himself on top of the debris; he could be of no assistance to her. He shouted back into the wind, attempting to guide the voice towards him. A hand emerged from the water. Shayla pulled herself up, spitting water and choking for air. The two of them clung to their makeshift raft, adrift in the raging sea.

They laid flat, gripping the edges, sliding down the slopes of the still monstrous waves, unable to see any of the others.

What have I done…?

SON OF ADMIRAL LIAM VASSER, KERRY VASSER HAD ALWAYS WANTED TO JOIN THE NAVY LIKE HIS FATHER. CAPTAIN OF THE VARSITY ROW TEAM, THE FENCING TEAM, AND THE CHESS CLUB, VASSER HAS ALWAYS HAD A COMPETITIVE SPIRIT. GRADUATING TOP OF HIS CLASS WITH A MAJOR IN MECHANICAL ENGINEERING AND MINOR IN MIDDLE EASTERN STUDIES, VASSER CAN SPEAK ARABIC FLUENTLY AND IS KNOWN AROUND CAMPUS FOR MAKING "THE BEST CHAI TEA ON THE EAST COAST." HE HOPES TO SOMEDAY CAPTAIN HIS OWN SHIP.

7 SHIPWRECKED

GASP!

Danny shot up out of the water and drew a deep breath. Another wave had toppled him from his makeshift raft, sending him under water yet again. The salt water stung his eyes and he could barely see. He opened them just long enough to catch a glimpse of another wave cresting over his head, so he ducked under to avoid being pounded again.

He resurfaced and struggled to find his bearings. The wreckage he'd used to float on, which he could now see was the rear portion of the ship's hull, was drifting off to his right. It had flipped over, but was still floating. Without Shayla. *I have to find her.*

Danny spun around, peering through the storm for where Shayla might have been flung to. He didn't know what he could do to help if he found her, but she was helpless alone. The horrendously cold, miserable water overwhelmed Danny's senses as he tried to keep a clear head. The wreckage floated further and further away, leaving Danny to struggle to stay above the waves on his own.

In the distance were two flailing arms. With all his

might, Danny paddled towards them. He struggled mightily against the current, making very slow progress for the amount of energy it took to move. As he got closer, he could see that the arms belonged to Miko. He called out to her, but she didn't hear him. Danny pressed on until she saw him and swam towards him.

Exhausted from the effort, Danny nearly went limp by the time they grabbed each other. What had started out in Danny's mind as a rescue operation of Miko became reversed as she ended up supporting most of his weight.

"Where is everyone?" she shouted at him.

"I don't know! I lost Shayla, I haven't seen anyone else." Danny yelled back in reply. His temporary relief in finding someone and relaxing his fight with the tide distracted Danny from the ever present battle against the raging waves. By the time he'd noticed that one was towering over him and Miko, it was pouring down on top of him, sending Danny back into the deep.

Defensively, he covered his face with his hands. It was lucky that he did, because on his descent he came crashing into a sandy bottom.

What? Where am I? Why am I hitting sand in the middle of the ocean?

Positioning his feet beneath him, Danny managed to push himself back up towards the surface. Miko had made the same discovery, shooting Danny a confused look. He shouted at her to follow him, heading with the current. Each time they ducked a wave, he felt the bottom coming closer until at last he could stand.

They waded onto the shore. A few feet of sand, pounded by the surf, was enclosed by tall, cragged rocks. Gasping, they flopped to the sand, just beyond the reach of the water. "Where's everyone else?!" Miko shouted her question. Danny shot up, unable to rest his weary bones.

Eugene was bobbing with the tide on his way in. His bright orange life preserver had kept him above the water for the most terrifying ride of his life. Shaken but okay, he had found the shore beneath his feet as well and was walking the last few steps out of the water. Danny ran to him, helping him onto the sand. Eugene felt around his neck in a panic, "I lost my cape!"

Danny wasn't listening. He scanned the shoreline. Some of the debris had made it near the shore. A couple of water bottles, some boards, and what might have been an empty cooler were briefly mistaken by Danny as being people. But then he saw something else. A body lay on a jagged rock about fifty yards to his left. "Come on, Eugene!" Danny pulled Eugene with him, Miko chasing after.

Cody lay on his back, water racing over him. He gripped his right shoulder and grimaced. Danny, Miko, and Eugene scooped him up, walking him ashore. They set him down on the sand, breathing heavily and attempting to recover. Danny laid down on something jagged. It was Miko's old stereo dock that had washed up beneath him. He cleared it out of his way and melted into the sand.

Another wave rolled in, splashing its way up to their feet. "We can't stay out here, the tide is coming in," Miko was scrambling backwards, butted up against the rocks as the sand slowly retreated into the sea.

Lightning flashed across the sky, illuminating the intimidating cliffs above. Up the cove in which they'd landed, there lay a break in the rocks. "Follow me!" The Castaway Kids scrambled up the rocks after Danny. Looming ahead was a menacing cave. "We'll take shelter in there!"

"What? No way! What if there's a bear in there?" Eugene froze on the rocks.

Cody was strangely calm through his pain, "There aren't any bears in the South Pacific, Eugene."

Eugene wasn't totally satisfied that Cody was right, but a loud clap of thunder encouraged him into getting out of the rain.

The inside of the cave was dark and damp, but it was

high enough off the water that they had no fear of the rising tide. Clambering inside, they huddled together for warmth. Not two seconds passed before Danny bolted away yelling, "I'm going back for Shayla!"

Emerging from the front of the cave, he perched himself on a rock for a better view. Lightning above lit up the water where, just for a moment, he thought he spotted Shayla's head poking out of the water amidst the wreckage.

"Wait for me, Danny!" Shouting from the cave, Cody tried to push himself up, but he collapsed under the pain of his elbow.

"No, Cody," Miko pleaded, "you need to rest."

Outside in the rain, Danny's eyes narrowed. With hardly any strength, he knew it was up to him to find her.

Flying down the rocks he went, splashing into the tide. He ducked a wave, fighting against the current as he went. Out past the break point, he bobbed and scanned. He saw bits of debris everywhere, but there was no sign of Shayla. He needed a better vantage point.

The next rising wall of water came surging towards him. Danny let himself float up to the top of it, paddling with all his might. Stretching his neck up and peeking out, he looked down across the waves. There was Shayla, wrestling with a large ice chest. Unable to grasp a hold or get on top of it, she kept rolling off and dipping into the water.

Danny slid down the back side of the towering wave, locking on to Shayla's position. Danny kicked and paddled as hard as he could until his shoulders and thighs were numb. It was a matter of seconds before he swiftly grabbed her, wrapped her arms around his neck, and angled back towards the shore. "I got you. I got you. It's okay. It's okay," Danny reassured her.

Paddling in was easier since he had the tide with him, but Shayla's added weight and the crashing of the waves added significantly to the task. It was made harder still by Shayla's death grip on his throat.

He warned her when he planned to duck a wave, but she was so out of breath from her extended time in the water that she came up gasping for air each time. When they finally reached land, the sand was mostly covered by the rising of the tide. Shayla coughed up several mouthfuls of water. Danny grabbed the back of her coveralls and helped her to her feet. They hugged the rocks and dragged themselves up into the cave where the others were waiting.

No one had the energy to speak. They simply laid there, panting and puffing with their eyes fixed upon the raging storm outside.

It was Cody who first raised his voice after some time, "Come on, guys, let's climb in a little further in and see if we can find someplace dry." No one responded, not even with a nod, but they all obeyed this command as they couldn't think of anything better to do.

The deeper they went, the darker and smellier it became, but it certainly did seem to get a bit dryer. The rocks grew in size until they found a relatively flat surface upon which they could rest. The sounds of the raging storm outside were now a distant, muffled white noise.

Shivering mightily, Eugene lagged behind. He cried suddenly, "Ow!"

"Are you okay?" Miko quickly got back on edge.

"I'm fine, I just rolled my ankle a little on this piece of driftwood." Eugene stomped on it, teaching it a lesson for how it wronged him. "That's a hazard."

Hoisting himself up, Eugene collapsed onto a large, flat rock with the others. Wet and cold, they curled up to attempt to stay warm while the frigid surface below sucked the heat out of them. The growl of Danny's stomach broke the silence.

"Did anyone manage to bring anything from the boat?" Miko asked.

In the panic of the storm, they had only focused on saving themselves, not any supplies they might have needed. Cody instructed the others, "Check your pockets."

Most were empty, whether or not they had been this way before they fell into the water. "I've got my rosin block for my violin," Miko said. "That's useless…"

"All I have is some of the steel wool from scrubbing the dishes," Shayla tossed it into the circle.

"Any matches?" Cody asked hopelessly. "We're going to catch hypothermia if we don't start a fire." They all shook their heads.

Danny's eyes lit up. "I have an idea. I'll be right back." He scampered out of the cave. Having now rested, he found that muscles he did not know existed were now remarkably sore. Carefully, he navigated his way back to the edge of the water and snagged the stereo dock he'd spotted earlier.

Danny clambered his way back into the cave. "Grab that log you found, Eugene!" Eugene retraced his steps and found the log. It was weathered and rough, two large branches sticking out the side of it, just big enough to give him a bit of trouble carrying it.

"Is it dry?" Danny asked.

Miko felt the edges of the wood. "Seems like it."

Danny tore the back off the stereo and removed the nine volt battery. He peeled away chunks of bark from the log, combining them with several small sticks he'd found on his way back in. Placing the steel wool next to the edge of the log, he stuck the head of the battery into it. The wool began to ignite immediately, a glowing ember travelling across it. Danny placed the log into it and fanned it with his hands. Slowly but steadily, a flame began to form, giving some much needed heat to the weary travelers. They crowded in, warming their hands by the fire as it continued to grow. Danny searched the floor, now with the slight illumination, and brought over a few more bits of wood to toss on top.

"Guys…" Shayla was looking up towards the ceiling of the cave. Following her cue, the others slowly turned their eyes upward when they saw what had her attention.

Bats. Everywhere. Hundreds of them.

"Dude, that's so gross!" Miko's eyes were fixed on the bats, terrified that if she looked away, they'd come for her.

"Great," Eugene let out his frustration. "We survive the storm of the century just to be devoured by vampires!"

"Nobody panic," Cody whispered, "they're easily disturbed. But if we stay cool, we should be fine." They stared at the bats in silence. Just then, the fire popped loudly, sending sparks into the air.

Like a rushing wind, every single bat dropped down from its resting place and took flight. Screaming and ducking, the Castaway Kids turned their backs to the onslaught of flying creatures.

"Get it out! *Get it out!*" Miko smacked her own head ferociously, attempting to free a bat that had become tangled in her hair. Eugene, from his own crouched position, delivered the finishing swat that sent it on its way.

Shayla's instinct for the duck and cover earthquake drill position fared well for her. Several bats flapped around her, but none became entangled with her hair. Danny popped his shirt over his head while Cody simply sheltered his face with his good forearm.

Finally, a quiet fell over the cave. The bats had fled and the kids had the space to themselves. The crackling fire, the crashing waves, and the booming thunder were all they could hear.

"What do we do now?" Eugene wondered aloud.

"We have to wait out the storm before we can do anything," Cody answered.

"Where are we?" Eugene asked.

Danny and Cody exchanged glances, hoping the other would have an answer. "I don't know," Cody admitted.

"I'm scared," Shayla hugged her knees up to her face, staring into the fire.

Miko scooted over to her. "Me too." She looked to Cody. "After the storm, what do we do?"

"Well, since we left our cell phones back in the

lighthouse," Cody rubbed his arms lightly, recoiling when he found the spot with the most pain, "I guess we just hope to get rescued."

Danny rubbed his hands in front of the fire. He was still regaining the feeling in them. "Someone will find us. They have to, right?"

"I don't know," Cody responded bleakly. "I have no idea where we are and no one knows we're out here. I wouldn't keep my hopes up."

Miko stared wide-eyed into the fire. "We're all going to die."

Shayla tried to keep their spirits up, "Maybe we can find someone here that can help us!"

The news sank in for each of them in silence. The most they could do was huddle together and gaze into the fire. Shayla coddled Cody's injured arm while Miko leaned against her. Eugene rested his head on Cody's shoulder like a lonely puppy. Danny sat by himself on the opposite side of the fire, suddenly feeling very cold and alone. "I...I'm sorry, guys." No one said anything back to him. No one even looked at him. As exhaustion took hold, one by one they all nodded off.

Just before he fell asleep, one final coherent thought repeatedly crept across Danny's mind: *We're going to die and it's all my fault.*

Missing boat,
reward if found, $20

415-981-7625 415-981-7625 415-981-7625 415-981-7625

8 ZACTRALA ISLAND

Danny, Shayla, Eugene, Miko, and Cody emerged from the cave, squinting as the morning sunlight swept across the beach. The soft sand was still cold from the previous night's storm, but the thick air was warm and humid. The Castaway Kids gazed into the clear blue ocean. The horizon was unobstructed. No sign of the *Thug Life*. *I wonder what my uncles are going to think....How are we supposed to get back to San Francisco? Where are we?* These and several other thoughts of worry raced through Danny's head.

They all smelled of salt water and looked a mess. Miko's black eyeliner had slithered down her usually pale cheeks. Eugene dumped sand from his shoe and dug his pinky finger into his ear, trying to clean the grains of sand from the chaos of last night. He had the worst time sleeping out of the whole group, often waking up shaking and screaming, which in turn woke Danny up several times in the night. Cody squeezed his shoulder while he rotated it, checking to see if it had gotten any better after a night's rest. Apparently it had recovered to the point that he could stretch it with some hesitation, but the wince he made at the extreme points of motion demonstrated it was not fully healed. Shayla's hair looked exactly the same, long and everywhere. She wrung it and twisted it like a towel, right before shaking it around violently like a dog. Danny's stomach growled, but he was otherwise unscathed from the night before.

"We could've died last night. We got really lucky," Miko stated morbidly.

Danny felt guilty and embarrassed. The five of them just stood there gazing out to sea. Perhaps Danny was searching the horizon for answers, but none appeared. The gentle waves rocked back and forth as the sun continued to beat down on them. Not a cloud in the sky. Almost as if the storm didn't happen.

Eugene broke the silence. "Is this Hawaii? I imagined a lot more luaus."

Danny turned and focused on the island itself. Besides the small amount of beach they were standing on, there wasn't anywhere for them to go. To his right was a large cove that opened to the sea. It was blocked by giant rocks, trees, and cement pillars. It seemed man-made, as though it was once a harbor or passage through the cliff.

To his left were more rocks. Giant reddish-brown boulders with vines, shrubs, exotic flowers and dangerous looking trees growing all around it. Neither direction could be accessed by foot.

Directly behind them was their cave. Danny made a mental note: *"Castaway Pointe" is what I'll call it. The spot where I almost got us all killed...a good way to remember it.* Above Castaway Pointe Cave was a small, twisting path. It looked awfully treacherous and led to the top of the mountain that dominated over the rest of his view of the island. The trail disappeared over a ledge and through some trees, so it was hard for Danny to decide if it was safe or not.

"I don't think this is Hawaii," Danny finally answered. "The last glimpse I got of the GPS said we were still several days away."

Miko stared blankly at the sea. "Our boat is gone, there's no sign of any other boats...there's no sign of anyone. Anywhere. We're lost. We have nothing. No money, no cell phones, no way to get back home. We're stranded on a deserted island, and we're all gonna die because of you."

Miko gritted her teeth at Danny. She stepped towards him in anger, but Shayla stepped in between. "Miko wait! Now this isn't all Danny's fault!"

Cody yelled. "Then why didn't he listen to me when I told him there was a storm coming?"

Danny defended himself. "How was I supposed to know how bad it was going to be?"

Eugene began to cry. "My… *sniffle* …cape… *sniffle* …is… *sniffle* …gone…" He let out a honking wail and fell to his knees.

"I'm sorry Eugene! I'm sorry Miko! I'm sorry everybody! I – I – I…" Danny couldn't find the words.

"Sorry doesn't bring back my $4,000 violin. My parents are gonna be pissed."

"I'll make you a new one." Danny tried to help.

"How Danny? How? You don't know a thing about making instruments! You don't know a thing about playing football, or planning an escape, or running away, or captaining a boat! I never should have listened to you in the first place. I'm going home."

Miko crossed her arms and marched away from Danny. She immediately cupped her hands to her mouth and shouted, "Help! Help! Heeeeeeeelp!"

And shortly after, Cody joined in the yelling. Then Eugene followed, leaving only Danny and Shayla. Shayla held Danny's hand.

Shayla looked Danny in the eyes and with a faint smile said, "I know you didn't do this on purpose. Don't worry, Danny. Everything will turn out okay. It always does."

This little act of loyalty gave Danny the extra energy he needed to take back control of the Castaway Kids. "Thanks, Shayla." He smiled at her then ran to the others. "I think we should look over that ridge."

Cody took a break from yelling to say, "I'm not listening to you anymore. You got us into this mess, I'm getting us out."

"Well the only direction we can go is up that trail towards the top of the mountain. Maybe from there we can get a sense of direction."

Eugene craned his neck back to look all the way up the mountainside. Sure enough, it was the only path going anywhere that wasn't water. "Way up there? Are you crazy?"

"We need to stay by the shore and hope another boat passes by," Cody sneered.

"We don't have any idea where we are," Danny shot back. "Maybe there's a city on the other side of these cliffs. Or at least some people. At the very least, we can figure out what's here and get a better vantage point."

By principle, no one wanted Danny to be right, but they didn't have any better ideas. "Fine," Cody gritted through his teeth, "follow me."

Cody led the way for the rest of them, up and around the Castaway Pointe Cave they had just spent the night in. As they climbed, the wind became warmer, and the rocks became more and more scarce. Plant life thrived as they ascended the mountain. At one point Danny realized they were all holding hands, guiding each other and helping when the terrain became harder to climb. Spider webs polluted their path and stuck to Shayla's long hair. Eugene picked up a snake that he thought was a wizard's staff. Luckily it was sleeping and was not disturbed by their presence.

After what felt like an hour or so, and with the sun in the middle of the sky, they came to a clearing of trees and saw a wooden sign poking out of the ground that read:

"Zactrala Island…" Shayla read. "Where is that?"

"I think we should be a little more concerned about the 'all trespassers being shot' part!" Eugene exclaimed.

Cody looked completely stumped. "I've never heard of Zactrala. Must be foreign…But it can't be, we were only out to sea for 5 days. We should be somewhere between California and Hawaii."

"So…we're not in the United States anymore? Oh jeeps…oh jeeps…oh jeeps…" Eugene's voice trembled as he suddenly became very suspicious and paranoid of his surroundings.

"I wouldn't be too sure. Look." Miko pointed to what appeared to be a little hut made of tree branches and leaves resting up against the mountain side. It was all natural, but there were glass windows. Other than the surrounding rocks and trees, it was the only thing up on the cliff. The plateau ceased there, providing no further path upwards or out around the mountain. Everything was sheer straight up or down save the path they'd taken. Despite it being the only feature this high on the cliffs, it certainly was well hidden from any other vantage point on the island. The Castaway Kids stepped closer to the shack. Upon further inspection, the materials used were actually a type of hard plastic. "Why would someone make a shack out of fake wood when they're surrounded by real wood?" Miko asked.

"Maybe they love the environment and didn't want to disturb its energy," Shayla suggested.

"I doubt it. See that?" Cody was pointing to an

American flag inside the hut. "This is an American Island. Look what else is in there." They all peered inside the window into the shack. There was a metal desk, an oscillating fan covered in cobwebs and rusted over, and various papers scattered on the floor. There was a pistol holster resting on a wooden chair, but the pistol was nowhere in sight. Cody pulled on the doorknob. "It's locked."

Miko was still staring at the American flag. "Do you guys see that? The flag? It only has 48 stars on it."

Eugene stood on his tippy-toes to see inside and counted. "There's supposed to be 50 stars."

"That's strange," pondered Miko. "That flag must have been made before the United States made Alaska and Hawaii official states in 1959. And, if you look at the cord coming from the fan, it's plugged into the rock of the mountain. Which means there's a power source somewhere on the other side of this rock wall."

"Hey! Look what I found!" Eugene squealed with excitement as he pointed to a spot on the mountain wall just to the left of the shack they had just found. He was pointing at what appeared to be an electronic keypad. It was mounted on the rock, but there was nothing else around it.

"What is it?" Shayla asked as she leaned closer and squinted at it.

"It looks like my mom and dad's security keypad for our garage back home." Eugene examined it by running his fingers over the buttons. "I wonder if it works. What do you think it does?"

"I've got a strange feeling about this island, guys," Cody said worriedly.

Danny noticed a patch of vines next to the mysterious electrical box. He approached it, and pulled down with all his might. All the vines ripped from the mountain wall and Danny tossed them aside. He revealed a boulder that appeared to be blocking the entrance to the inside of the mountain. He pushed and pulled on the rock, but it wouldn't budge.

"What the heck kind of island is this?" Shayla wondered.

"Now where do you suppose that goes?" Cody asked.

"I got it!" Eugene exclaimed. "The keypad opens the boulder to some sort of cave! And the hut over there is a guard shack!"

Danny and the other Castaway Kids looked at Eugene, thoroughly impressed. Danny asked, "Okay... that's an interesting theory, but we don't know the combination and there's no guard, so what good does that do us?"

For several minutes, they tried their hand at cracking the code. Every word and number and combination they tried had zero effect. "Password," "Zactrala," "Help-us." "12345," "America," and "this-is-stupid" all failed to work. Eugene even tried yelling "open sesame!"

The kids were suddenly startled by a low rumbling growl. "It worked!" Eugene shouted. But the rock still hadn't moved.

"No it didn't," Danny held his mid-section. "It was just my stomach. I haven't eaten anything today."

"Yeah, I'm pretty hungry too," Miko replied. "Do you think there's anything to eat around here?"

And just then, out of the tree directly above them, a small monkey-like animal fell down and dug it's claws into Danny's face.

...the 17th consecutive month of increased pirate activity in the Horn of Africa. Travelers are cautioned to avoid the area as major cruise lines have already canceled many popular voyages in these seas. There have been unconfirmed reports of a large, black vessel, undetectable by military radar, expanding the territory East in the Indian Ocean and Philippines with several fearsome attacks. A Naval spokesman would not confirm or deny any rumors about a military-type ship involved in piracy, but has informed us that they are looking into the issue. He also reiterated the warning to avoid sea based vacations in this area at this time. In other news...

9 FOOD & SHELTER

"Oh how cute! It's a bonobo!" Shayla's observation was lost on Danny who could only scream for help in getting the creature off his face.

Miko and Cody managed to pry the squirmy little guy off of Danny and set him to the ground. "Careful guys," Shayla warned. "You don't know what kind of diseases it might have."

Danny spit the hair out of his mouth and rubbed his face, "Somebody hit that thing before it attacks again!"

Eugene bent down to the bonobo and petted its head, "He didn't attack you! He was just trying to make friends. Look! He has a collar!" A little metal tag on an old leather strap around its neck was engraved with the name "Oliver."

Oliver and Eugene took an immediate liking to each other. Eugene picked him up and Oliver climbed all over him, checking his hair for bugs. "He must be somebody's pet, to have a collar like that," Cody commented.

"It probably thinks we have food," Danny was less impressed, holding a grudge for the fright he'd been given. "Shoo, go away, little guy!"

Cody stopped Danny from waving Oliver away, "Wait!

Don't you see? If he's somebody's pet, then he can probably lead us to that person. He can help us get out of here."

"I think he already has," Miko's eyes darted back and forth as she computed something in her head. "Look at the keys on the pad. Which ones are worn down?" Sure enough, the letters most rubbed off could be put into the order of "O-L-I-V-E-R." She punched in the code and, with a hiss, the rock facade dropped and the mighty steel door before them popped open.

Oliver darted through, like a house cat being let back inside. He stopped and squeaked back. "He wants us to follow him!" Eugene went in first, guided by his sudden trust for the bonobo. The rest followed, leaving Danny last. *Great, even the monkey makes a better leader than me.*

Behind the door was a long, narrow corridor. "Hello?" Cody's voice echoed around, but no response came. It was dark, but the light from outside cast upon a large switch that looked like something out of a mad scientist's lab. Eugene flipped it, giving life to the light bulbs above.

The bland, concrete walls were broken up only by the various pipes and wires strung along it. Occasionally stenciled numbers and letters would appear, but their meaning was lost on Danny.

Rounding a corner, they came across three doors. One was a great red imposing piece of steel, the others simple rectangles with windows in them. Oliver ran to the one on the right labeled "Galley." Eugene pushed it open for him.

The room was decrepit; dust covered the checkered linoleum floor. "Anybody here?" Miko's question went unanswered.

"I think this place is abandoned," Cody guessed. Long rows of tables and benches filled the space, looking like a cafeteria for a couple hundred people. Large windows let in the light from outside and gave a look at what lie on the other side of the mountains. It seemed that the island was shaped like a volcano with a vast pit in the middle of the steep-sloped sides. It was filled with small buildings, plants, and trees with the sheer cliffs on the other side of the mountain. The Castaway Kids surveyed the room and tropical view with discovery and wonder, but Oliver bounded with familiarity over to a closet.

He screeched and stomped with impatience. "Okay, Oliver, I'm coming, hold your horses," Eugene hustled to get there. "What do you want to show us?" He turned the knob and opened the door. Walls of canned and dry foods stretched out before them.

"Jackpot," grinned Danny.

Oliver swung himself up onto a high shelf where he pushed down a large jar of dried banana chips. Eugene caught it clumsily. "He's hungry!" Eugene opened it up and scooped out a handful for him. He snacked away happily while the others looked around.

The shelves were neatly ordered, each row stocked like a grocery store. Some sections were pretty well-picked over, leaving large gaps, but there appeared to be plenty of cream of mushroom soup and powdered eggs.

"Look! Whole bags of rice! We'll eat like kings!" Shayla celebrated merrily. "Canned fruit, cereals, you guys like cereal? There's unopened boxes on the bottom—" One of the boxes moved on its own accord.

Shayla jumped and screamed, all in one motion kicking at the box. It flipped over and revealed the source below: a very confused looking armadillo. "Are there armadillos out here?" Miko pondered in Shayla's general direction.

"I don't know. I mean, there's one right there," she replied helplessly.

Cody asked, "What do they eat?"

"Since when am I an expert on armadillos?" They left Shayla alone and went about shooing it out the small vent that it must have crawled in through.

Miko dropped a heavy box in front of the vent, blocking it off. "There, that should keep our supplies safe."

They finished exploring through the shelves and ventured into the kitchen. Eugene flipped another switch on the wall. Shayla tried the stove, "It works. We can cook here!"

The kitchen was old fashioned, but sturdy. It would need a thorough cleaning before they made anything to eat, but it'd certainly do for keeping them alive. Eugene pocketed some of the banana chips and put the jar away. "Come on, Oliver, that's enough for now." Oliver stuck with Eugene, knowing him to be the keeper of the food.

Back across the hallway was another door with the word "Berthing" written across it. Danny hung back as the others explored, curious about the red door. He knocked on it. It was so thick it scarcely made a sound. "TOP SECRET" was emblazoned along the top. *What could possibly need this much protection?*

Joining the others in the berthing, Danny found a row of discolored cots. The others had all claimed their own already, leaving Danny to take one in the far corner of the room. The springs supporting his mattress were considerably looser than the others, but it was still better than another night in the cave at Castaway Pointe.

"Who do you think lives here?" Eugene bounced on his bed, getting just a little bit of air.

"I'm not sure anybody does," Danny replied.

Miko had already lain down, answering with her eyes closed, "Of course somebody lives here, where would all this stuff have come from?"

"Well, sure, at some point," Danny clarified, "but look around. The food, the beds, all this stuff, the doors that say 'top secret...' don't you think somebody would have stopped us by now?"

A silence fell over the room as they pondered this question. "Maybe it's their day off," Eugene answered.

Cody massaged his still sore arm. "Tomorrow, we'll look around to find somebody. For now, let's try and get some sleep."

Danny laid his head down and shifted to get comfortable. No matter how he lay, there seemed to be something jutting into his back. Frustrated, he smacked the mattress and tried to smooth it with his hands. Then he noticed the conspicuous shape of the outline against which he was struggling.

Unzipping the mattress slowly as not to wake the others, he reached inside. He felt the cold touch of metal on his fingers. Pulling the object out, he discovered in his hand what looked like a laser blaster from some sort of science fiction movie. But this was no fake plastic movie prop, it was heavy and solid.

Danny decided not to wake the others. They all needed a good night's sleep. He quickly hid it under his pillow.

What is this place?

For Vasser

VERSE 2:

Half made of tin, half made of hate, he's less man than machine

Perhaps if they'd replace his heart, he wouldn't be so mean

Every ship whose path we cross will soon be overwhelmed

As long as we've got dear old Captain Vasser at the helm

CHORUS

VERSE 3:

Our bellies may be empty, but our pockets they are full

As more and more these treasures all keep filling up the hull

There is no man to whom our Captain ever has to kneel

After all how could he with a kneecap made of steel?

CHORUS

 To hear a recorded version of this song, go to our website: www.castawaykidsbook.com/music

Before the crew and the band were able to begin the final chorus, a glass shattered to the floor. Asad, a twelve year old Somali boy playing violin, jumped as his bow screeched across the strings. In a rage, the most massive, muscular pirate with a burly beard dyed bright red stood and slammed the table. The surly crew only knew him by his first name: Mu'mmar. Legend claimed that his beard was "dyed with the blood of his enemies." The musicians all came to a halt. The gigantic, thoroughly tattooed Mu'mmar gave a mighty punch to the singer, knocking him to the floor, then snatched the young Asad's violin.

"There will be no more music tonight!" He stormed out the back of the darkened mess hall amidst the silence of the other pirates. Before he reached the door, he slammed the violin down on the table where an unseen shadowy figure was seated. None of the crew had noticed the captain was sitting there.

Asad watched carefully as the ominous figure at the table picked up the bow. He twirled it once, then held it upright and quite still. A shaft of light fell across the figure's finger and thumb as he effortlessly snapped the bow like a pencil in his hand. He spoke Arabic in a calm, deep voice. "We drop anchor in the morning. Be prepared." He quickly stood and turned, disappearing from the room in a ghostly promenade.

Asad swallowed hard.

10 TOP SECRET

Over the following couple of weeks, The Castaway Kids explored all corners of the island. It truly was a massive fortress; the inhospitable, impenetrable outside was a stark contrast to the lush, cultivated land on the inside of the circle of mountains.

It was clear that whoever built this place had intended for it to be a long term settlement. Beyond the massive living spaces carved into the rock, there was ample garden space. Wild and overgrown, it had not been tended to in a very long time, but still several vegetables sprouted amongst the similarly untrimmed fruit trees.

Danny spent a lot of time with Shayla gathering these foods because everyone else was mad at him. The tensions seemed to ease once they came to realize that this island vacation might have been even better than the one they'd planned on. They had their own little paradise all to themselves. Within a couple of days, it seemed all was forgotten and relationships were back to normal.

There was a small lake bed in the middle of the island that Shayla made Cody use as physical therapy for his arm. This lead to a sort of daily swim meet for all of the kids that Eugene would judge from the water's edge. Whatever

Cody was doing must have worked because before long, his arm was better and he was winning every single race. It was more exercise than Danny had ever done, but he found himself enjoying it.

Oliver settled in as a regular member of the crew. He stuck with Eugene, mostly, who was the easiest to convince to provide extra snacks throughout the day. To his credit, though, Oliver's affections stretched beyond feeding time and he spent most nights curled up at the foot of Eugene's bed. Sometimes, in the middle of the night, however, Oliver could be found scratching impatiently at the large red door.

Throughout the mountainside were several carved openings. These lead to hallways and rooms of all kinds: offices, more bunk beds, bathrooms, and some large spaces that reminded Danny of a cross between his school's science lab and an evil villain's underground bunker.

Dotting the outdoors were several small ramshackle buildings. They were quite plain and weathered; the chipped, fading white paint indicated they had not been maintained in a very long time. Some were simple tool sheds, some empty, but three larger structures were far more interesting.

The first was discovered by Miko when she noticed it seemed to be the source of a constant, low hum. Opening the door she found a large turbine engine, spinning and churning. There were several pipes and gears that created a massive wall of machinery. With all of the wires feeding out of it, Eugene guessed it must be the power generator for the island. Even more impressive, there did not seem to be a fuel source. This bothered Eugene greatly until he saw giant pipes heading straight down into the ground. Though he couldn't be sure, he theorized that it must be running off of geothermal energy: heat from the inside of the earth.

The second building was much sleeker on the inside.

Long rows of metal tables divided walls of stainless steel freezer doors. Boxes and packing supplies were littered throughout the room like someone left in a hurry.

It was Shayla who identified these as containing the scientific Latin and common names of several plant varieties, many of which she'd never heard of. It was an enormous refrigerated room with plant seeds in it, just like the one built in Russia circa World War II she had once read an article about. Using the pictures on the labels as a guide, she went through it like a grocery store to shop for all the seeds she wanted to plant when she got home. She and Danny would hang out and explore the seeds for hours. They used jackets that were hanging on the wall because the thermostat was kept to around thirty degrees below zero.

The third building was completely solid. It didn't have a single window, giving it a monolithic and intimidating look from the outside. The door was locked tight and they had been unable to find a way inside. It had the most peculiar lock with a glass lens embedded where the keyhole would normally be.

Days upon days passed. Despite many questions still unanswered about the island, the Castaway Kids were able to form somewhat of a routine. They were very resourceful and used everything on the island to its fullest extent. For example, Danny made a wheelbarrow out of wood, pipes, and a large cog he found rusting near the garden. He and Shayla used it to get the "veggies of the day" as Shayla called it. Cody fished using the sharpened end of a broom stick as a spear. Miko made a bow and arrow to hunt small animals, but used it primarily to kill rats she found scurrying around the kitchen.

One morning, the smell of eggs frying in a pan woke Danny from his sleep. The room was empty. He must have been extra tired from yesterday's rock climbing along the cliffs and slept through everyone else waking up. Sitting up, Danny tightened the drawstring he had improvised into the belt loops of his pants. All of his clothes had become noticeably looser during the course of their stay. He shuffled into the galley where the others were already awake and sitting at a table.

"I don't know, maybe it's some kind of boarding school," Eugene guessed.

Miko rolled her eyes, "What kind of parent would send their kid to a school like this? All those beds crammed into one room. I still say it's a prison."

Shayla emerged from the kitchen with a giant pan of scrambled eggs. "Breakfast is ready! I mixed in some ingredients from the garden, but these powdered eggs still kind of taste like rubber. It helps if you just pretend they're real eggs that came from a rubber chicken."

She set the pan down on the table as everyone scooped out a portion. The eggs were definitely far from ideal, but the added ingredients compensated for it nicely.

"Sorry we're running low on cereal guys," Shayla apologized. "I think Oliver figured out how to get in the pantry. We had way more yesterday! I have no idea where he puts the empty boxes, though."

Between mouthfuls, Cody carried on the conversation, "Whatever this place was, they definitely had something to hide."

"I think it used to be a military base." Forks clinked against the pan as they considered Danny's statement.

"What makes you say that?" Eugene's eyes went wide.

"Doesn't it have kind of an army or navy feel to it?" Danny asked. "All the secret stuff, plus none of us have ever heard of it…" He trailed off as he remembered his find from the first night. "Oh yeah, I never even showed you guys!"

He bolted back to his bed and grabbed the gun he'd found, bringing it back to show the others. "Look what I found!"

The others froze, staring at it. "Is that a gun?" Shayla gasped. "I don't like guns."

"I mean, yeah, I think it is," Danny examined it closer. "It looks like one, doesn't it?"

"This is pretty serious," Cody's voiced lowered the way it did when he tried not to appear alarmed. "If you're right and this is some sort of military base with weapons on it, we could be in a lot of trouble."

Miko chimed in, "He's right. And if this place is a secret that we weren't supposed to find, they really won't be happy when they come back."

"Oh jeeps! They'll probably get us kicked out of school! And use a memory eraser on us! And make us move to Wyoming and change all of our names to numbers!" Eugene squeezed Oliver tightly. Oliver did his best to ignore this and continue picking pieces of egg off of Eugene's plate.

"Calm down guys," Danny reassured them. "We've already been here for a couple of weeks. If anybody was coming back, don't you think we would have seen them?"

"Danny," Cody looked him dead in the eye, "last time you wanted to be casual about a threat we faced, we almost died in the ocean." Everyone went silent. The unspoken truce on blaming Danny for their situation had been broken, but they all knew that Cody was right. He stood up, "Okay, let's go outside and find some high ground. We can light a signal fire, then maybe use some rocks to send a message to any passing airplanes. It's time we put all our energy into going home. Vacation time is over. We can't just merely survive out here anymore."

Everyone stood up but Danny, who slumped lower in his chair. Shayla offered her hand, "Come on, Danny, let's go."

"Nah, you guys go ahead," Danny muttered. "I'm still hungry." He picked at his food unconvincingly. Guilt always made him feel helpless.

Shayla bit her lip. She knew what Danny was feeling, but didn't know how to help. Cody and Miko were already almost out the door. "Come on, Oliver," Eugene had to use all his might to pull Oliver away from the food. Oliver stretched his hand back towards the plate in sorrow as Eugene carried him away. Shayla followed reluctantly, leaving Danny to his own problems.

Maybe I am an idiot. He rested his face on his palms, thinking about all the ways he'd let his friends down. *Maybe this isn't a military base anyway. I bet it's just some stupid old movie set.* He inspected the gun closer. He tried to imagine it in some cheesy sci-fi or James Bond movie.

Holding it out in front of him like an action star, he squinted one eye. "Freeze!" He must have been speaking to the oranges on the table because that's where the gun was pointed. He pulled the trigger, and to his surprise, a beam of light shot straight out of the end of it. He felt no recoil, but the orange he'd picked out glowed ominously for a moment as the energy from the beam seemed to dance around inside of it. It trembled slightly before settling back into place. Danny's jaw dropped open.

Questions raced through Danny's mind. He didn't know what to address first. His first instinct was to run and tell his friends, but he knew this would likely only further upset them at this moment. Unable to sit still, he went outside.

Now that he'd shaken off the self-doubt from earlier, Danny was able to clear his head. *We do need to get off this island at some point, but how?* He walked around the island's interior as he brainstormed for ideas. He looked to the trees and thought about chopping them down to make a raft. Without getting too far down that line of thought, he realized that if they had been unable to safely sail their seaworthy boat, an improvised raft on the open ocean was unlikely to perform much better.

Cody was right; they'd need help from the outside getting off the island. But what were the odds that a boat or a plane would get close enough to see their signals? There must have been some sort of communication system on the island that allowed it to talk with the mainland. Danny looked up from the path to realize he was standing in front of the solid building with the glass keyhole they hadn't been able to get into.

Looking at the gun, Danny had a thought. He backed up several feet, took aim at the door, and fired. Once again, the beam of light shot a glow around the hinges that burned brightly for just a moment before fading away. He tried opening it again. Nothing. The door was unfazed.

This gun doesn't even do anything! Frustrated both that some dumb toy had caused his friends to become upset with him and that he was unable to crack the lock, Danny threw the gun in anger at the building. When it hit the ground, he got a better view of the tip of the barrel. That was when he noticed that it looked just like the keyhole on the door.

Picking it up, he inserted the tip into the lock. It wouldn't turn in either direction, so he pulled the trigger. This time, the beam of light made the entire lock glow until a click came from inside. Danny turned the handle. He was in. *I guess that gun was good for something after all.*

His eyes still adjusted to the midday sun, he fumbled for the light switch before he could see anything around the room. Flicking them on illuminated an entire compartment filled with technical gadgets. Rows of work benches were littered with wires, scrap metal, and bits of machinery. The walls were lined with machine guns, swords, knives, grenades, dynamite…every kind of weapon Danny could imagine.

Dominating the center of a wall was a large map of Zactrala Island. Before he could process everything around him, Danny was sucked into this as it finally gave him some context to his surroundings. He noted the circle-with-a-bite-taken-out-of-it shape it had from this top view. He was able to figure out that the room he stood in was labeled as the "Armory." Sure enough, the other buildings were labeled as "Generator Room" and "Seed Vault." He located the trail from the island's main door down to

Castaway Pointe which went unlabeled. Finding a discarded ball point pen on the table below it, Danny took the liberty of filling it in.

Moving on, he scanned the well-organized weapon racks that lined the walls. He recognized many of the machine guns from video games, but several looked more futuristic like the gun he'd found in his bed. Landmines, grenades, and laser-triggered claymores were sorted from largest to smallest and ranged from bigger than a dinner plate to the size of a marble. Several similar looking mid-sized canister grenades had different colored labels on them that must have indicated some sort of meaning lost to Danny.

Looking down onto the tables he was passing by, he saw circuit boards with wires haphazardly soldered to one part and dangling off to nowhere. There were nuts, bolts, measuring scales, and all kinds of tools alongside empty plastic casings. *Incomplete projects*, it seemed. *I wonder what these were the beginnings of.* He picked up and flipped around a thick steel tube with wires sticking out of it. He couldn't guess.

Setting it down, he found a tube connected to a large tank. It looked like a fire extinguisher, but not one he'd seen before. He picked it up and pressed the trigger. Flames shot out across the room. The shock made Danny drop it, sending up a puff of smoke. *Oh, so that's what a flamethrower looks like.*

Armed with a new "no touching" rule, he looked only with his eyes until he reached the end of the table. Beyond it were a couple of desk chairs before a small stack of old fashioned computer monitors. The whole effect was something of an antiquated military arcade; joysticks, trackballs, and keypads littered the desk as a constant hum filled the air and lights twinkled about. Each of the screens had cameras pointed at different rooms of the island. He saw the empty kitchen, seed vault, and bedrooms. Some of the cameras pointed outside. He saw his friends walking down a path on the island's exterior. It reminded him of his purpose: to find a way to contact the mainland.

There was no phone on the desk, but all of these keyboards and joysticks were hooked up to computers of some sort. There was no mouse by which to operate them, though, and no cursor appeared when he moved the joysticks and trackballs around. Some of the cameras shifted their views, and this was all that Danny could muster. *What kind of high tech military base doesn't even have the internet?*

On the desk, amidst the useless old interface gadgets, was one thing that caught Danny's eye. A small, spiral bound journal with the title "Deck Log." *Maybe this will give me some answers.*

Leafing through, many of the entries ranged from quick notes about the weather to long, technical manifests. None of this was of any interest to him, so he skipped to the last entry, hoping for some insight.

Day 1,651 - Time: 1300.

Pressure from Washington growing serious. Feeling forgotten. Resupply ships coming less frequently. All non-essential personnel have been extracted. Likely that remaining crew will be left behind. The admiral has reclassified as survival mission, has promised to stay with crew on island to the end. The only job now is to stay alive and keep the weapon out of enemy hands. The experiment is over. May God have mercy on our souls.

The eerie passage unsettled Danny greatly, but it neither helped him call for rescue nor told him what was going on here. He closed the journal and looked back up to the monitors. It was then that he noticed that one of the cameras he'd managed to rotate was now facing straight out to sea. Rather than an empty sea stretching towards the sky, however, he noticed just the edge of an outline.

There was a ship out in the water.

He fidgeted with the controls more, but he was unable to manipulate the correct camera again. Looking back to the screen where the others were now passing directly beneath the camera, Danny knew he had to warn them. He sprinted from the room.

Up near the top of the ridge, Cody, Miko, Eugene, and Shayla were sparking their fire. Dry palm fronds, twigs, and spare bits of lumber were piled high as Miko encouraged her small flame.

"We'll need to keep this fire going around the clock in case any planes fly by," Cody explained.

Danny appeared from behind, screaming as he ran, "You guys! You guys!" Huffing and puffing, he kicked down the wood pile and stomped on the flames.

"What are you doing?! We need that!" Cody pushed Danny angrily.

Breathing heavily through his nose, Danny explained "I found a room full of cameras. There's a boat nearby. A big one."

Miko was excited, "Great! We're rescued!"

"I'm not so sure," Danny replied. "There were all these weapons and this journal about abandoning the base...I've got a bad feeling about this. We could be in a *lot* of trouble."

Cody paced back and forth. The others looked to him for a sense of guidance. Finally, he responded, "All right, so there's a boat. That's probably a good thing. But Danny might be right, we might be in trouble. Do you think you can lead us to where it is?" Danny nodded. "Okay, stay low behind the plants. We'll play it safe and lay low until we scope it out."

The Castaway Kids followed Danny as they blazed a trail around the cliffs to the opposite side of the mountain. They rounded a rocky bluff when Danny gave the signal to get down. Peeping through a crack in the rocks they caught their first sight of an imposing flat black painted naval ship with a name emblazoned in red on the side: "The *Mogadishu*."

A flat, thin, carbon fiber prosthetic pressed into the sand and flexed under the weight of its owner. He stepped out of one of the two power boats freshly run aground on the beach. In the distance, a massive, flat black painted naval battleship emblazoned with the moniker "The *Mogadishu*" sat anchored in deeper waters.

The long tails of a black coat infested with grime draped over the fake legs. Its golden buttons no longer shimmered in the light the way they used to, but had rather scratched and dulled their way to blandly clinging to the final threads of the garment. The wearer adjusted his belt from which hung a blood stained sword and a pistol. He next shifted the strap which held up the small camera positioned perfectly over his left eye patch. His right eye squinted as the camera aperture tightened. Taking in the long awaited sight of shore around him, a cruel grin crawled its way up his face. After just a moment of victorious reflection, he bellowed, "Set up the camp! Let's get moving."

A swarm of scraggly pirates hopped off the boats onto the land. They unloaded crates full of gear and supplies, bustling about their work. A thin pirate, sporting a gray beanie on his head and a well-manicured goatee nervously approached the man in the dark coat, "Captain Vasser? Sir, I'm very sorry, but I'd like to remind you that there were several injuries on the last raid." He sweated and tugged at his collar nervously. "I – I mean, of course – of course *you* know that. So, uh, perhaps, if – if it's all right with you, we could delay setting up camp for a day or two so that they could have a chance to heal and receive-"

Bang!

The man would never finish his sentence. The sound paused the other pirates in their work, causing them to stare at the Captain. He blew the smoke away from his pistol and pocketed it. "There will be no resting! Back to work!" The pace immediately resumed at double time.

Vasser shouted to his quartermaster, Mu'mmar,

"Round up any free men and have them set out upon reconnaissance of the island. I expect a full report before sunset."

Slinking from the crowd came Asad, the violinist boy. He was not big enough to help with the heavy boxes, so this would apply to him. At least reconnaissance would give him a chance to stretch his legs and poke around the island. He carried his instrument with him as usual, not trusting it to be left on the ship with dishonest men.

Rounding the shoreline away from the others, a wooden box bobbing in the water caught his eye. Upon closer inspection, it appeared to be a black violin case with the name "Miko Tanaka" inscribed on the side.

11 SEARCH PARTIES

"It's huge!" Miko exclaimed.

"Not as huge as the trouble we'll be in," Shayla lamented. "We've been all over their top secret base and now the Navy is gonna lock us up in prison for the rest of our lives!"

"I don't think that's the Navy," Eugene interjected.

Danny was confused. Surely the great, hulking fortress before him was a warship. "What do you mean?"

Eugene squinted towards it, "Well, that's a cruiser. It looks just like the one I took a tour of in the harbor one time. But they told us that the Navy paints all their ships gray so that they're less visible in fog. That boat's black."

Looking out into the water, Eugene had a point. The long, pointed bow of the ship had a flagpole at the front but no flag flying from it. The long, uniformly black body of the ship was intimidating and unusual, reflecting none of the mid-day sun back towards them. There were two massive guns on the front and back of the ship. Smaller machine guns aligned the sides and rear of the ship beneath a tall command deck high above the rest of the vessel. Squinting towards it, Danny could identify various radio antennae and riggings up and around the mast.

A sense of worry came over Danny, followed by a sudden worry, "So maybe it's not the Navy. You still think they're here to rescue us?"

Eugene grew cold, looking Danny right in the eyes, "That depends. Do you want to be rescued by people who stole a Navy ship?"

They scrambled as fast as their feet would carry them back to the base.

"What do we do? We're trapped here!" Miko paced the room.

Cody tried to manage as best as he could, "Well, hang on, now. There's no way they'll get up and over the ridge of the mountaintop, and if they don't have Oliver's code, they won't be coming through the door. We might be safe for now."

Eugene confronted Oliver very seriously, wagging his finger in his face. "Now Oliver, don't go out there and give them any clues to figure out the code, okay?" Oliver was mostly fascinated with his closed hand and disappointed when he opened it to find no food inside.

"They're going to get in eventually," Miko noted. "That ship is probably packed with tons of firepower, I mean did you see those guns? We're defenseless!"

Danny's eyes lit up. "Not entirely."

He took them to the armory he stumbled upon, sharing all the highlights of what he'd found there. Eugene and Miko were much less shy with the camera equipment than Danny had been. Flipping on more of the screens, they found camera feeds from all over the island. Cody was initially drawn to the flamethrower, but Danny advised against touching it. Underneath, however, Cody found a US Army pamphlet that was written as a field guide to booby traps.

He leafed through the diagrams when Miko called out.

"Look over here!" Miko pointed at a screen. A small band of men trekked along the outer rim of the island.

"I think Eugene was right, they don't look like military to me," Shayla squinted at the low resolution picture. "Too scruffy."

Danny saw a second group on a different screen. "What are they doing here?"

Eugene played with the controls, "I can't tell. The audio feed isn't working. I bet these speakers are blown. Can one of you guys read lips?" No one could. Eugene tried anyway. "I think they're saying... Purple clockwise watermelons marry vacuums."

Miko rolled her eyes. "No, Eugene."

"Worth a shot," he shrugged back.

"We'll have to go out there," declared Cody. "If we sneak up on them, we can figure out what they're up to."

Miko freaked out, "Sneak up on them? These guys? The ones with the giant guns? And do what? Ask them kindly to hitch a ride back to San Francisco?"

"Relax, Miko," Danny soothed her. "You and Eugene seem to have the video equipment figured out already. Somebody will need to stay back and be on the lookout."

"We can use these walkie talkies!" Shayla held up some radios she found in a box under a desk. Out of the corner of her eye, she saw Cody reaching up towards one of the machine guns on the wall. "Cody Chincey Nichols! Just what do you think you're doing?"

The sharpness of Shayla's chastisement stopped Cody

dead in his tracks. He still had his hands on the base of the rather menacing M-16. "Well, you saw the video. They have guns. We should be armed too."

"No guns! They only escalate dangers!" Shayla insisted. "What if they're nice people who have come to visit our island? It's very rude to point guns at your guests."

Danny and Cody looked at each other. "Shayla," Danny started, "I'm not saying we're going to have to shoot them, but it really doesn't seem very safe to go entirely defenseless."

"What if they don't speak English? They're just going to see your weapons and start shooting. Guns don't make friends. Peace offerings do. That's why I'm going to make a cake," Shayla turned her nose up at the boys.

"Do we have everything to make a cake?" Miko asked. "I don't think we have frosting or vanilla or anything like that."

Shayla was on her way out the door, "It'll be a fruit cake."

"Well now we're definitely going to get shot." Eugene's comments were lost as Shayla was already gone.

"She has a point," Danny said.

"But they have guns!" Cody countered.

"And they probably know how to use them really well," Danny rebutted. "So we probably don't want to show them a reason to use them."

"Well, we can't go out completely unarmed. It's one hundred percent legal to defend ourselves if necessary," Cody compromised. Danny nodded in agreement. Throughout the room, they picked out a couple items they thought would be the most potentially useful. Danny wrapped a rope around his shoulders while Cody snuck a hunting knife in his pocket just in case, but agreed not to tell Shayla about it. Danny followed suit and put one in his pocket as well.

One small ensemble of men appeared to be venturing the closest to their side of the island, so Miko suggested pursuing them because the cameras provided the best visual and audio coverage of that area. Danny and Cody waited at the secret boulder door for Eugene's "all clear" signal over the radio, letting them know it was safe to emerge.

Shayla met them at the door. She had, it seemed, been serious about that fruit cake which she carried with her on one of the baking trays from the kitchen. It definitely appeared a bit hurried, but the fact that it was shaped into a heart forgave any sloppiness amongst the toppings. With Eugene's go ahead, they crept out, staying low behind the brush as they headed towards their mysterious visitors.

As quietly as they could, they returned to the plateau where they had lit their signal fire to find a handful of men, all carrying AK-47 rifles, surveying the beach. A tall, dark man with dreadlocks bent down to touch the logs. "Still warm," he growled. Danny, Shayla, and Cody dared not even breathe from their hiding spot in the bushes. "This way," the man gestured, leading his gang down towards the beach.

"What do you think?" Cody whispered. "They don't look too trustworthy."

"Never judge a book by its cover," Shayla retorted. "I know several homeless men at the shelter back home who happen to be very charming."

"Yeah, well, we're not in Cali anymore," Danny added.

They still stayed a safe distance behind on the trek down the mountain, sticking to the brush and being careful not to be seen. Shayla grinned confidently. "I think they look like they could use some cake."

"Let's hold off on any cake judgments for the time being," Danny checked to make sure his knife was still in his pocket.

"Ack!" A yell came from the party ahead of them. A loud shuffling of sand and clanging of rocks followed. Popping up for a better view, Danny spotted the source: one of the men had tread too close to the trail's edge and had fallen to where the path switched back below about thirty feet down. The rest of the men hustled to his side while the Castaway Kids' search party used their momentary distraction to get a better position.

Danny, lying on his stomach, inched to the ledge just far enough for his eyes to peer over. Cody followed suit while Shayla kneeled, holding onto her cake. They had a clear view straight down on the party.

"Get him up," one man yapped. The injured man continued screaming and reaching towards his ankle. Judging by the angle at which his foot had turned, he must have broken it pretty severely on impact.

"It looks pretty bad, I'm not sure we'll be able to get him over the rocks and back to camp." A small, lean man with a bandana wrapped around his forehead, his hair tufting out above it, inspected the injury.

Shayla nudged Danny and whispered, "He's hurt! Maybe I can help him make a splint." Danny put his finger to his lips. Shayla's heart was in the right place, but he wasn't ready to give away their position just yet.

"Well, we can't leave a man behind," the dreadlocked man said coolly. He drew his pistol and fired it directly at the injured man's chest. Instantly, the crying stopped. "Grab what you need, then let's move out!"

Cody, Danny, and Shayla watched frozen in horror as the group took everything they could find on the now deceased man with speed and ease. This was clearly not their first time. His pistol, watch, rings, canteen, and shoes were all picked clean and soon they were on their way up the trail.

Danny and Cody had clamped their hands over Shayla's mouth to keep her from crying out until the men had moved on far enough for her to speak freely. "Did you see that? We have to get out of here!"

"I'm with Shayla," Cody chimed in. "We need to get back inside and hide right away."

"We can't," Danny replied.

134

"What do you mean 'we can't'? They just killed that guy!" Cody exclaimed.

"If we go back, they'll find us eventually," Danny continued. "How long did it take us to find our way in? Even if they don't figure out the code, they've got that giant boat full of guns. If we go back and wait for them to find us, we'll be sitting ducks. Right now, we have the element of surprise."

"Surprise who? The gang of murderous pirates?" Shayla was incredulous. "How is that going to work?"

"It might not," Danny scratched his chin, "but there's a whole boat full of them. If we can take them out in small groups like this, we might stand a chance." He got on the radio. "Eugene, which way did they go?"

"Down towards the water. You've got a clear shot back to the entrance," crackled the reply.

Shayla was rattled. "What do you mean 'take them out'?"

"They're headed down by the cave." Danny pressed the radio button again. "We'll be back in a little bit, we have to take care of something first."

"Take care of what? Danny! Get back here immedi-" Danny clicked his walkie talkie over, cutting of Miko's objection in mid-sentence.

"Switch to channel four," Danny said to Cody. "I've got an idea."

Danny blazed a trail along the rocks above the cave at Castaway Pointe. Staying low along the top, Cody tied Danny's rope around his waist. Shayla and Danny lowered him slowly down into the cave. "Oh my yikes… Oh my yikes… Please be careful," Shayla whispered after him.

"Find a good spot," Danny reminded him. "Not too far!"

Cody returned a thumbs up and disappeared into the cave.

The pirates were busy searching through bits of wreckage from the *Thug Life* that had washed ashore.

Inspecting the white paint chipping along the edges, a chubby pirate who was shirtless, save for the strap of his gun, ran his calloused hand along the edge. "How long do you think it's been here?"

The dreadlocked pirate scratched his thumbnail into his own piece. "Not more than a few weeks. Any bodies amongst the wreckage?" Grunts of uncertainty were the only reply. "Hmmm…"

Suddenly Cody's voice echoed out of the cave, "Help! Help! You guys, come quick! I need you!"

The pirates looked up from the shattered bits of the boat. "Did you hear that?" One gestured towards the cave, another chambered a round in his gun.

"Hurry up!" Cody's voice called again.

Walking as slowly and silently as possible, the pirate gang approached the mouth of the cave. Aiming their guns inside and seeing no one, they crept in. Not one of them spoke, staying low and communicating with hand gestures, they eased their way back towards Cody's cries.

"I think they followed me," Cody spoke again, but this time the sound came from within the group of pirates. Looking down, they found the source of the voice: an abandoned walkie talkie.

"Now!" Danny ordered. From atop the mouth of the cave, Cody put down the other radio and grabbed onto one of three large branches. He, Danny, and Shayla each pulled down hard on their own, leveraging them up and unleashing an avalanche of boulders. As each rock came free, more followed suit, giving way to the force of gravity and collapsing in the mouth of the cave.

Danny and Shayla jumped back from the edge, collapsing beneath their feet. Cody scrambled as quick as he could, but lost his footing. He yelped in pain, but Shayla was fast as lightning reaching out to pull him up. "Are you all right?" she asked.

"I'm fine. I think I caught my leg on something." Cody pulled up the cuff of his pants. A significant gash had just started to bleed from his calf, dripping into his sock.

"Can you walk?" Danny inquired. Cody nodded. "Quick! Let's get back to the base before someone else finds us!" Danny led the retreat back to the secret door, racing inside and to the armory.

Bursting in, Cody boasted, "Miko, Eugene! Did you see that? Oh man, we got those guys good!"

But neither Miko nor Eugene shared their enthusiasm. They only stared with horror towards the search party. Even Oliver was frozen in place. Miko started quietly, "Why didn't you answer us on the radio?"

Danny sensed the tension, "Oh, sorry, we never switched the channels back after we caved the bad guys in. Why?"

Eugene pointed behind them. Shayla, Danny, and Cody turned around to see what he was pointing at.

They had been followed.

"The cliffs are sheer all the way around the island," one of the many weary pirates reported to the fearsome Quartermaster Mu'mmar.

Another chimed in with his assessment, "No viable waterways or passages through. Is the captain sure there's anything here?"

Mu'mmar reached back his hand and let the insolent man's cheek know his opinion of the question. "If the captain says it's here, it's here! Now find a way to the inner part of the island!" In frustration, he ran his fingers through his fire-engine-red beard and into the damp bandana he'd fashioned around his forehead from a red sheet he'd found washed ashore. The water seeped out from the pressure of his hands and ran down his face, cooling both the heat of the day on his brow and his temper.

"Might be able to get a dinner out of one of these wild armadillos I keep seeing," a tubby pirate licked his lips in anticipation of fresh meat, but Mu'mmar hadn't noticed. He counted the men quickly.

"Was anyone behind you when you returned?" They shook their heads, shrugging their shoulders. No one seemed to have noticed any stragglers.

A shadow fell over Mu'mmar's back. Vasser had approached to receive his briefing. "How many are you missing?" The rest of the men scattered.

"Four, it seems. Deserters, sir?"

The Captain gazed upwards towards the mountainside, as though sniffing for a clue. He closed his eyes just for a moment. "Be wary. Something here is amiss."

12 FRIEND OR FOE

Leaning against the doorway stood a skinny Somali boy holding what appeared to be two small briefcases. He had a thin, cheeky smile and gazed at the Castaway Kids calmly. His short, black, curly hair had sand in it, and he sported a tattered t-shirt, a dapper vest, and long, cut-off jean shorts. He wore loafers with tall socks and a small bracelet that was made from rope. There was an easiness in his voice as he stepped towards the middle of the room. All five kids cautiously formed a semi-circle around him as he spoke.

"Hullo. My name is Asad Darzi. Pleased to meet you." His large, jet-black eyes stared at Danny, who was speechless. "You are American, no?"

Danny gazed at him in silence, hesitant of how he should answer. "Yes." Danny couldn't blink. He was still unsure of the intruder and his intentions. *Who is this kid?* Danny thought. "What do you want?"

"I come from the *Mogadishu*. The ship that bears the name of my hometown in Somalia. I'm not here to hurt you. I just-"

"If you're from Somalia, how come you speak English?" Danny questioned him. The other Castaway

Kids had their guard up, eyes darting back and forth between Asad and Danny.

"Please, I found something that may belong to you. I'm sorry I followed you in here, but I did not think you would have listened to me if I approached you while outside. I saw what you did to my shipmates in the cave. That was mighty clever of you."

Danny couldn't tell if he was upset or insulted. *He's so calm. I can't tell what his intentions are…*"Shipmates? So you're one of them. A pirate."

Asad set the cases down on either side of him. He then folded his hands and raised his head. "Sadly, yes. It is true. The *Mogadishu* holds many ruthless men you call pirates. It's not safe for you to be here."

Danny stepped right up to Asad's face until he was inches away. "Give me one good reason why we shouldn't tie you up right now."

Eugene yelled at the boy. "We have rope and Danny's not afraid to use it."

"There would be no point. They are coming in here regardless of what you do to me. Besides, you do not look like the violent type. The men on my ship, however, most certainly are. I'm not sure the best way to translate it, but they are a very…salty sort of men. Like dogs of the sea."

Shayla gasped, "Salty sea dogs?"

"Yes, something like that. What I mean is that they are a very ruthless sort and their intentions are not good. They say there is a very powerful bomb on this island and they will stop at nothing to find it. If we work together, then perhaps-"

"A bomb?!" Cody interjected.

"No way, kid! You'll just narc on us!" Sweat ran down Danny's forehead. He was growing upset that this kid wasn't at all intimidated, so he tried to sound tougher. "How do I know you're not a spy?"

"If I wanted to spy on you, I could have easily done so without revealing myself. Instead, I have stepped right into your home, unarmed. I may be able to help you. Please American, take my gift."

Asad bent down and picked up the nicer of the two cases.

"My violin!" Miko exclaimed. She ran forward and snatched the case from Asad's hands. She frantically opened it up and inspected the contents. Sure enough, it was her violin her parents bought her. "It's a little water damaged but otherwise good to go. Where did you find this?"

"It washed up along the rocks. No one on the *Mogadishu* knows I found it. It was in too good of shape to have been there for very long. When I saw you, I figured one of you may have lost it and would perhaps like to play with me."

"Wow, it's even tuned." Miko plucked the strings and inspected it from all angles. "Did you tune this?" Asad nodded. "I can't believe it. I never thought I'd see this again. Thank you."

"We are not so different, you and I." Asad then picked up the other briefcase. It was made of wood and worn out. He pulled from it his own violin. It looked homemade. "This is my most prized possession. My mother made this for me before I was born. It is all I have left of her."

"Would you mind playing us something?" Miko asked.

"I would love to. But alas, my bow was broken on the ship." Asad hung his head.

"You can borrow mine," Miko handed him her bow from her case. "It's the least I can do."

Asad smiled and took her bow, bowing as he did. He began to play a beautiful little tune. As the song progressed, Asad began to dance with his instrument. It crescendoed as he leapt around the room. He spun to his knees, playing faster and with an immense amount of passion. The five kids watched in awe of his performance, listening intensely and mesmerized by the show put on before them.

When he stopped playing, Danny thought he could see a tear in Miko's eye.

"That was beautiful," Miko smiled at him. "I've never seen anyone play like that."

Asad smiled back. "That's because most people play only with their hands. You must put your whole body into it, allowing the music to flow through you and burst out of your skin. And it begins here, " Asad pointed to his heart.

Shayla, Eugene, and Miko gaped with open-mouthed wonderment and curiosity at the Somali boy, as if hypnotized. "That's incredible…" Was all Miko could mutter.

"Hold on a second!" Cody interjected. "Before we get all 'buddy-buddy' with this kid let's think about who he's here with, okay? We still don't know anything about this guy. It's like Danny said, if he came from a pirate ship, that makes him a pirate, too! The others could be following behind him right now, and his violin dance was just a distraction."

"If he was bad," thought Shayla, aloud, "then wouldn't he have just stolen Miko's violin instead of returning it to her? I'd take that as a sign of peace. A sign of peace like this." Shayla made a grand gesture of presenting him with her fruit cake.

"Ah! Fruit!" Asad cried. "We have not had any on board for several weeks now. Thank you very much!"

Shayla turned to her cousin, "Look at him Cody, he's our age. How bad can he be?"

"You don't know what kind of upbringing he's had! He's not like us Shayla!" Cody was now yelling.

"And what are we, Cody?" Shayla wasn't giving up. She stood tall and didn't back down. "We're different, too, right? Isn't that why we're here in the first place? Isn't that why we call ourselves The Castaway Kids? We were judged too, by the clothes we wear, our body types, our race, where we come from, how much money our parents have. It's awful! It's not fair! And I'll be damned if I let you or anybody else here judge Asad before we get to know him. He said he comes in peace, so let's give him a chance to prove himself! Innocent until proven guilty. We're still on American soil, right?" She quietly waited for a response from the rest of the room.

Danny shrugged. "Yeah. I guess she's right."

"Yeah," Eugene echoed. "If Danny gives him a chance, then I will too."

"Agreed," Miko said. "Maybe he could show us a thing or two…you know, on the violin."

"This isn't a game you guys! We're not here on vacation anymore!" Cody recapped. "This is about our survival."

"I say we put it to a vote," Shayla said. "Whoever thinks we should give Asad a chance, raise your hands." Shayla, Eugene, and Miko shot their hands into the air. Danny stepped up to Cody, placing a hand on his shoulder.

"Look, Cody," Danny began. "I know you're just trying to protect your cousin and the rest of us, but this is something you don't understand. You don't know what it's truly like to be an outcast. We have to take a risk on this kid if we want any kind of chance of getting off this island alive. I'm voting with the rest of the Castaway Kids, and it would mean a lot to me if you joined us too."

Danny stretched his hand in front of him with his palm down. Shayla placed hers on top of Danny's, and Eugene and Miko followed. They all looked to Cody. He squinted at Asad, who stood calmly by. He begrudgingly placed his hands on the others. With his other hand, he pointed at and addressed Asad. "If you even think of betraying us, so help me!"

Asad placed his hand on top of Cody's. "You have my word." All six kids stood united. A smile and sense of excitement washed over them.

Danny said proudly, "I hereby make you an honorary member of The Castaway Kids, Asad." And right as he said that, Oliver leapt onto a nearby desk and placed his hand on top of Asad's. They couldn't help but laugh, even Cody. "You too, Oliver!" Danny rolled his eyes and smiled.

A huge smile grew on Shayla's face. "Guys, we had an awesome victory today and we just made a new ally. Before we get down to business, I think there's cause for a celebration!"

That night, the newly expanded Castaway Kids ate food that Shayla prepared in the galley and danced and laughed long into the morning. Her cake, which was surprisingly tasty, was the highlight of the menu. Eugene enjoyed teaching Oliver how to do a back-flip using banana chips as a reward. Miko switched off playing the violin with Asad until their fingers bled. Shayla cleaned and wrapped up Cody's calf wound. She made him drink some tea she made from Gotu Kola leaves she found growing outside. She explained how they had been used for many years to treat cuts and ordered Cody to stay off his feet while the scab formed. Instead of running around, Cody showed Danny receiver routes from the school football team's playbook using condiments as the offense and defense and a table as the imaginary field.

As the sun rose, Danny walked Asad to the secret door, punching in the pass code without him seeing it, or Asad asking to see it. He opened the door to let him out, both of their eyes groggy from the party. The others were fast asleep in the Armory. "Thank you, Danny," Asad said.

"For what?" Danny yawned.

"For showing me friendship. It is a luxury that I have never known." Asad put his hand out. Danny shook it, proudly.

"I think today was a good day," Danny smirked. "We all got to know someone new, which I think we needed. Tomorrow we'll talk about how we can stop these guys and get you away from them for good. Try and find out when they're attacking, where the bomb is, and anything else you might think will give us an advantage."

"Agreed," Asad responded. "I should get back to my ship before anyone notices I was gone."

"Will they be suspicious?"

"No. I will tell them I was scouting and got lost. The men on my ship are not concerned about the actions or whereabouts of a child."

"I know how you feel. You should meet my uncles someday."

Danny closed the secret door behind Asad after he left. He then strolled back to the Armory and laid down with the others on the floor. His thoughts raced about Asad and the encounter they just had. *What if he betrays us? No...he wouldn't. But what's stopping him? Does he see me as a friend? Impossible...I'm an American and he's a Somali pirate. But still...He could be the key to getting us off this island and back to San Francisco.*

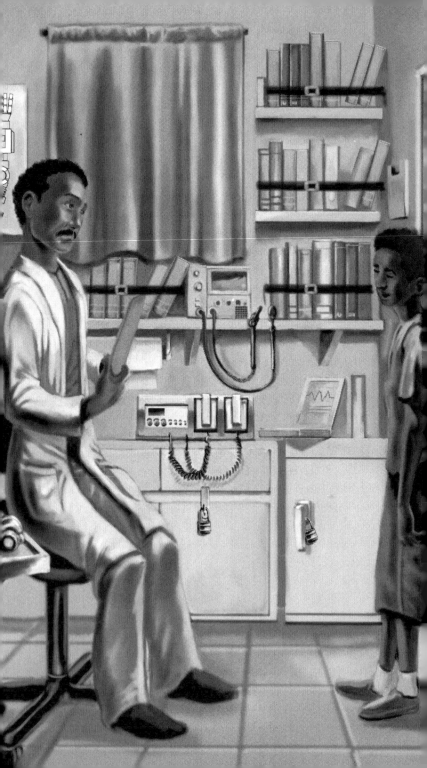

"Heave! Heave!" Barked Mu'mmar at a dozen pirates, straining to pull a giant crate up a plank and onto the flight deck of the *Mogadishu*. It contained the blades of the helicopter they stole only a month ago in a raid that involved a rather large explosion. The hijacking resulted in Captain Vasser losing both his legs, as well as the lives of several of the Somali pirate crew.

As the men pulled the large ropes, their palms bled and blistered. Mu'mmar had been given strict orders to finish the assembly of the CH-53E Super Stallion helicopter in three days, which was why he smacked a man who stopped pulling for a moment to rub his hands. The butt of his AK-47 hit the pirate squarely on the back of his skull. The man fell to his knees instantly.

"No resting on the job! Captain's orders!" He yelled at the rest of the men. "We have three days to finish the assembly, and until then, you will work twelve hour shifts, rest for six hours. Then work for twelve hours, and rest for six, and so on, until the job is complete! Now get these crates open!"

From behind the thicket of the jungle, Asad peeked through some boulders at the ship and all the men working by torchlight. A line of men brought garbage bags carried over their shoulders and marched them off the brow and onto shore. There, they took the bags of trash and threw them into a hole that several men had dug into the sand.

Asad needed to improvise a plan get back onto the ship without anyone noticing he was gone.

He stashed his violin in a crevice in the rocks. Surely if he had it with him, they'd know he hadn't been working. He waited for a few men to throw trash away, and then turn their backs. He quickly darted into the hole, grabbed a trash bag, and brought it out again. He ran behind the shrubbery and waited for more men to come back. When they walked by him towards the improvised trash dump, he casually marched in line behind them, as if he was following them off the ship the whole time.

He accidentally bumped into the man in front of him, who promptly turned around in anger. "Watch where you're going!" The man squinted at Asad. It was Yacoob, one of the older cooks who knew Asad well. He often gave him midnight snacks, which were not authorized by the Captain. "Asad? What are you doing?"

"Helping take out the trash."

Yacoob smiled back. "Your father must be very proud of you. Not too many men can handle long periods of time underway, so seeing you work hard with no complaints is quite inspirational. C'mon, let's keep moving. We mustn't let Mu'mmar catch us dawdling; his temper runs as red as his beard." They proceeded to the trash hole, then Asad continued back onto the ship with the rest of the men. None of the guards noticed or questioned his absence.

He wasted no time in running through the ship to his father's cabin, located below deck and away from all the noise going on outside. Acting as half living quarters and half office, the room did not have the sterile feel of most medical facilities. The volumes of books on the shelves made it feel much more like a cozy library. Most of these titles were medical journals, but the contents of the bookcases had also been Asad's education and upbringing. World history books, basic science, *The Adventures of Huckleberry Finn*, *The Iliad*, *Robinson Crusoe*, *Lord of the Flies*, and all sorts of classic literature had been his bedtime stories for as far back as he could remember. His father was tinkering with a prosthetic hand on one of his patients. Asad's father, Dr. Rasheed Darzi, was the ship's only medical professional. Since the raid of the military ship where they stole the helicopter, Dr. Darzi has had his hands full caring for the crew.

Asad quietly waited in the doorway. The patient was moving his hand at Dr. Darzi's command. It was working well. Finally, Asad's father noticed his son had entered. "You'll be fine, just no heavy lifting. I'll write a note suggesting light duties like cooking or cleaning around the ship," the doctor told him. "Hopefully Mu'mmar and the Captain take my advice, but no promises."

The man quietly nodded and passed by Asad without saying a word. Dr. Darzi waved his son in. "Close the door."

Asad obeyed. He then stood against the door, nervously staying away from his father. Rasheed simply sat on a stool and stared sternly at his son. "Where have you been?"

"I was helping with garbage duty," Asad said.

"I ask you again, Asad, and this time, don't lie to me." Dr. Darzi took his glasses off and looked him in the eyes.

"I just explored the island a little."

"I told you to never leave sight of the *Mogadishu*. No adventures!" His father scolded him. "This is not a pleasure cruise. Once the Captain gets what he needs here we can go back to Somalia. Back to where we belong and no longer in debt to the captain."

"Sorry, father," Asad hung his head.

"Come here," Dr. Darzi opened his arms to his son. Asad hugged his dad, who continued to hold him as he spoke. "I never wanted you to have this life. I always dreamed of giving my first born son the same education I received. I know you never met your mother, but she loved you very much. That is why she left you her violin. She dreamed that you would love music as much as her, and science as much as I."

Asad closed his eyes. He knew the story well. His father could not afford to take care of him and finish medical school at the same time after his mother passed. Captain Vasser discovered his breakthrough work in medicinal robotics, tracked him down, and had his crippling student loan debt paid off in exchange for his services on the ship. After two years of working for Captain Vasser on land, this voyage was supposed to be the final deed that Dr. Darzi owed the captain. The doctor continued, "I do not want you getting in trouble, getting hurt, getting lost…or else all of my efforts and your mother's life will be for nothing. So when I tell you not to wander off, and you promise me you won't, you have to keep that promise. I am very busy tending to many sick and injured men on this boat, so I cannot have eyes on you at all times. I am understood?"

"Yes, Father," Asad felt guilty about what he had done. "Why does the captain want this weapon?"

Rasheed cleared his throat nervously. Asad had never asked these types of questions before. "Well, the captain feels that the American government wronged him and that this will help him get their attention and get even."

"I thought you liked America," Asad pressed.

"I do. I enjoyed my time in university there very much. It was a wonderful place filled with many delightful people. If I wasn't living in Somalia, I'd live in America."

"So then why are we trying to hurt them?"

"Well, it's complicated. Insane, too. You see, Captain Vasser is going to kill tens of thousands of what he calls 'ungrateful civilians' so that he can then send a message to save millions. He thinks his former military brothers and sisters are being mistreated and ignored. Vasser sees himself as a hero to wounded veterans. As well-intentioned as he may be, he's a psychopath. I despise working for him but I have no choice. Thankfully, you'll never see him again after this mission. Why the sudden concern for all of this, my son?" Rasheed asked.

"Just curious," Asad sighed wistfully. *I shouldn't ask any more questions in case he begins to suspect something.* "Good night, Father." He ran to the other side of the room, kicked his shoes off, and laid in his hammock that hung above his father's.

"Good night, son," Rasheed turned the light off, keeping just a small desk lamp on.

That night, Asad dreamed of being with his new friends in America.

152

13 A NEW PLAN

Eugene awoke in the armory to find Cody tying metal gaffing hooks to the end of several ropes. Everyone else was still asleep. Oliver snored as his paws twitched and his tail whipped around from the dream he was having. Eugene rubbed his eyes and put on his glasses. "Awesome!" he exclaimed. This woke Danny up. He peeked out of his eyelids, listening to Eugene. No one noticed he was awake.

Cody took his eyes off his ropes for a moment to look at Eugene. "What's awesome?"

"It's been two months since we got stranded here and I haven't wet the bed *once*!" Eugene smiled at his pants with pride. He then noticed Cody had his hands full. "What are you doing?"

"I'm tying these ropes to these canteens that are filled with explosives."

"How come?"

"Well, if Asad comes back with bad news, then we have to be prepared to defend ourselves. Remember that booby trap field guide I found? Well, I also found *Volume II: Dirty Tricks to Stop Your Enemy Indoors*." Cody held the open book up to Eugene for him to see.

Eugene squinted at it. "Seems dangerous."

"It is. For the pirates." Cody very slowly and carefully held the canteen up and showed Eugene. "There. It's done. A bit of a crude design, but effective."

"This is kind of scary."

Cody sighed. "Yeah, it is. But I gotta do what I gotta do to defend my family." Cody stared at Shayla while she slept.

"And friends?" Eugene asked wide-eyed.

"Yes, Eugene, I wanna defend my friends too," Cody smiled at him with a sense of relief.

"Will it work?" Eugene drew his attention back to the explosive.

"Dunno. Never made a bomb before."

"How do you know you're making it right?" Eugene inquired.

"I can read. Plus most of the ingredients were here in the armory." Cody admired his work for another minute, then poured the water out of another canteen into a jar. He began filing it with explosives.

"Do you think Danny will like this?"

Before Cody could answer, Danny sat up in his sleeping bag. "Absolutely. I think Cody's got the right idea."

"Thanks, Danny." Cody gazed at Danny with an immense amount of respect. Danny couldn't believe how different things were now. If they were back on the football field, Cody wouldn't have cared what Danny thought of him. But here on Zactrala, Danny mattered.

And he felt like he belonged. He was accepted as the leader of The Castaway Kids, and even if they didn't last another day, Danny was blanketed with a warmth of accomplishment for a brief period in his life. It felt great.

That warm and fuzzy feeling soon went away when Miko woke up and asked what they were talking about. It wasn't long before Oliver was in Eugene's lap, nibbling away at banana chips, unaware of the impending dangers the kids discussed.

"Don't forget, Asad said they still don't know how to get inside the mountain. And that it'll be another day before the helicopter is assembled and they can go up and over. So as long as they don't find a way inside, we can barricade ourselves in and hope they don't find us," suggested Miko.

"I like her idea," admitted Eugene.

"No guys, we can't let that happen." Danny was a little furious at their cowardice. "What if they get their hands on whatever that weapon is that Asad said they were after? What if they use it to attack San Francisco? Or The White House? Or some innocent little farm town? What if they used it to attack your mom and dad? You wanna just hide and see what happens?"

Eugene felt like he shrank to just a few inches tall. "No...I've never fought anyone before though. And we're just kids. Those guys kill for a living."

"Hiding is not enough, Eugene," said Cody. "We took out some of their men already. They'll want revenge. They won't stop trying to find their way inside. And when they do, we'll be ready." Cody held up sticks of dynamite he had tied together with electrical tape.

"Besides," Danny chimed in. "Their boat may be the only chance we have to get off the island. We need to thin their numbers, then strike when they're most vulnerable." Danny pointed to the giant map on the wall. "Right now they dominate everything around the mountain. But *we* control everything underground and inside of the mountain. They want to get in the middle of the island, so we need to lure them inside here where we can take them out on our terms."

"It's settled then," Miko decided. "We have to stop these pirates before they kill us and take whatever's here on the island. I'll do whatever I can to help. But I'm not sure what I can do, since I'm more of an artist than a, you know, fighter. So there's that to consider."

"We'll figure something out," said Danny. "I'm tired of people telling us what we can and can't do. Sick of being told we're not thin enough, or brave enough, or too sensitive, or not old enough, or weird, or whatever. This is our chance to prove to ourselves and others what we're made of. This is a test of us, and we're going to ace it!"

"Yeah!" Eugene yelled. Oliver screeched too.

"I can't do this…" Shayla spoke softly. Danny hadn't even noticed she was awake. "I'm sorry. Excuse me."

Shayla stood up, crying, and ran out of the room.

"Shayla!" Cody called after her. "Shayla! What's wrong? Come back!" She was already down the hall. "I'll go after her," Cody headed for the door.

"Wait," Danny interjected, standing in front of Cody. "I'll talk to her."

"She's my cousin, I'll talk to her. She's probably just scared about all this pirate talk."

Danny put his hand on Cody's shoulder and looked him in the eyes very seriously. "I wanna talk to her Cody. I got us all in this mess. You show Eugene and Miko the booby traps you've been making and have them help you. I think I know where Shayla went."

"Suit yourself," Cody shrugged. He sat on the floor with Miko and Eugene and began explaining what motion sensing laser claymores were.

Danny peeked inside the Seed Vault. Sure enough, Shayla stood in front of the doors containing the different seed hybrids, arms crossed inside her jean coveralls, long blonde hair covering her face, hunched over and crying to herself. Danny proceeded inside with caution.

"Shayla?" Danny asked timidly as he slowly moved towards her. He was careful not to move too fast along the icy floor. Steam flowed from his hot breath and the only sound inside was the hum of the freezer motors whirring. "Are you okay?"

"Go away. Please," she sobbed. Trying to pretend she hadn't just been sitting there crying, she began leafing through the seeds. She dug out small packets of various types and tucked them into her pockets.

"Look, I know our situation is hard to accept. Believe me, I'm a little scared too."

"I'm not scared of any stupid pirates," she sniffled and wiped her eyes. "I'm scared of what I might lose."

"It'll be okay Shayla, Cody and I wouldn't ever let anything bad happen to you. We'll protect you." Danny grabbed a coat off a hook on the wall and wrapped it around her. "Come on, let's get out of here. You're gonna freeze."

"No, I wanna stay. I don't want everyone else to see me like this." Shayla tried to shrug the jacket off, but Danny persisted, and kept his arm around her. "Besides, I like looking at the seeds."

"Are you afraid you won't be able to take any seeds back home?" Danny asked as he stared at them too. Thousands upon thousands of different foreign names, species, sizes, hybrids. *Achyranthes atollensis...Melicope cruciata...Nesiota elliptica...Begonia eiromischa...*

Shayla started, getting comfortable being under Danny's arm. "When I look at these seeds, they represent hope that there will be a future. And hearing you guys talk about this attack like it's the last thing we'll ever do makes me think we don't need to have one. I mean maybe we're doomed to just stay here forever. Like these seeds." She picked up a few more she liked and found a pocket for them.

"Well, I think you're only partly right, Shayla,"

responded Danny. "I think these seeds represent us. And just like these seeds, our lives are just starting. And as situations change, they'll have to evolve to survive their environments, fight off diseases, climate, predators. Just like us. These seeds may represent hope for the future, but we are the future. And we need your help to preserve it."

Shayla backed away slightly, staring deeply at him. Danny had butterflies in his stomach, staring into her baby-blue eyes. He was shaking, but not from the cold. "That was beautiful, Danny," she said, her hands on his shoulders. "I'll do whatever I can to help the team out."

"Thanks, Shayla." Danny wiped the last tear from her face.

"You know…" Shayla leaned in close to Danny. "I'm also afraid I'll never see my parents again, work in my garden, go to school…but I'm afraid of losing someone too."

"Cody can take care of himself. He's a very capable guy."

"I wasn't talking about him." Shayla was now so close to Danny that the steam from their breaths danced with each other in the air. Danny put his arms on Shayla's hips. It was freezing in that room, but Danny felt warm all over.

They leaned in to kiss.

"Hey!" Cody yelled. "You okay?" He had run into the Seed Vault and was standing at the other end of the aisle. Shayla stepped away from Danny, embarrassed.

*So close…*Danny thought. *I almost had my first kiss…*He wasn't too happy with Cody's timing, but he tried not to show it.

"Yeah. What's up?" Shayla answered.

Cody continued, "We finished the sound blaster and found some rifles. I need to show you how to use them."

Danny was flustered. "Sure. Yeah. Okay. Everything's fine here. You two go ahead, I'll catch up."

Shayla stole a glance at Danny and whispered, smiling, "Thanks, Danny. I feel a lot better now." She handed back the jacket and marched out of the room past Cody. Danny and Cody stared at each other intensely.

"Nothing happened," Danny said defensively. He felt like Cody's death stare could burn a hole in him.

"You both need to focus on the task at hand. We need your head in the game."

"You're right, Cody. I'm sorry. It won't happen again."

Cody scanned Danny up and down, sizing him up. Whatever it was Cody decided about him at that moment, he didn't tell Danny because he turned and slammed the vault door behind him.

Now alone in that room, Danny suddenly realized how cold he felt.

Eugene, Miko, and Cody cleaned and loaded the automatic rifles with the instructions strewn out on the floor. Danny came out from the Seed Vault and rubbed his hands together. "All right, does anybody have any shooting experience?"

Shayla spoke up, "You guys, I have a confession to make. I've never even been in the same *room* as a gun. I still don't think we should use them."

This time, Cody was prepared for her objection. "You're right, Shayla. I don't think we should either. But now that we know these guys are heavily armed pirates, we might have to." He put his hand on her shoulder. "Hopefully we never use them, but if we have to, we need to know that we can."

Shayla exhaled heavily. "All right. But I *really* don't want to use mine, okay?"

Danny nodded understandingly. First, he showed them which eye to close and which eye to aim with when ready to shoot. "Put your hands together in front of you, and leave a tiny hole in between them like this so you can see a fixed object in the distance," he demonstrated, using a wall-mounted security camera as his focal point. "Now, close one eye, and if the object is no longer visible because it appears to shift, then that is your weak eye. Then, do the same but with the other eye open, and the object should appear not to move. That means that eye is your dominant eye. You want to aim using that one."

Miko and Eugene had their hands up, looking in different directions through the hole they created in between their hands.

"Oh, yeah!" Miko exclaimed. "That's cool! I'm left-eye dominant!"

"Mine's my right-eye!" Eugene was excited to learn something new about himself. "Where did you learn that from, Danny? You in the NRA or something?"

"Playing *Bullseye Bandits 5* online," said Danny. "I have the highest score in the U.S."

"I can't quite seem to get mine right," Shayla said, struggling a bit. Danny came up right next to her and re-explained what he said. Their faces cheek-to-cheek. "Okay, now put your hands like this, now close that eye…Now the other… See it now?"

"Oh, okay…Neat!" Shayla put her hands down and smiled at Danny. He smiled back, but felt Cody's protective stare on the back of his neck, so he quickly stopped and stepped away.

"We should probably finish setting the traps," said Cody sternly. "Danny, you go with Eugene. Miko, come with me. Shayla, go make some food. It's almost noon. It's only a matter of time before they find our secret entrance, so we have to act fast."

Shayla didn't seem to like the job her cousin gave her. "Jeez, Mr. Bossy, why can't I help set up traps, too?"

"We need food, Shayla," snapped Cody.

"I know but I wanna help with other stuff too!"

"Fine!" Cody gave up. "I got it, you're not my baby cousin anymore. Take this gun, and take Oliver to the front entrance. Grab a knife and cut down some palm fronds to help camouflage the door."

Shayla beamed and saluted him. "Aye aye!" She grabbed a gun and Oliver jumped on her back. Everyone split up. Danny and Eugene went over to the generator room, and Cody and Miko went to the cafeteria where the windows were still broken leading to the inner part of the island.

Shayla typed the pass code and cautiously stepped outside the door, rifle drawn. There was no one in sight. Their cover was still a secret. She leaned the rifle on a rock and began cutting low-hanging palm fronds from the palm trees. "Sorry trees," she whispered.

Suddenly, Oliver began screeching at something down the path at the shore. Shayla looked down and saw a group of armed pirates patrolling the area. "Shh! Quiet, Oliver!" The pirates looked up to the bonobo jumping up and down and making all kinds of ruckus. Shayla placed the last of the palm fronds near the entrance, typed in the code to get back inside, then quickly grabbed Oliver. She pushed the button to close the door behind her, then realized she had left her gun outside. She stuck her hand out and snatched it. However as she pulled it in, the barrel became stuck between the automatically closing door and the rock wall. She tugged and tugged on it as she heard the pirates making their way up the path.

"There's a path here!"

"Someone's up there!"

"It's just a stupid monkey, don't waste your time."

With one last pull, the gun accidentally fired three bursts into the air. "Oh my, yikes," Shayla whispered with an absolute look of terror on her face. She tugged with all her might and finally pulled the gun inside as the door shut behind her, but she knew it was too late.

Mu'mmar immediately whipped out his telescope when he heard the gunshot and pointed it in the direction from which it came. A crooked smile crept onto his face. "Samir! Form a search party! Investigate that noise! Mu'mmar collapsed and pocketed his telescope and thought aloud to himself, "We are not alone…"

Samir put the final magazine for his AK-47 in his vest. A tall, lanky pirate with a large broken nose and a unibrow, whistled to eleven other pirates standing by to get ready. They scrambled around, grabbing guns, knives, and loading up on ammo in preparation for a possible nasty fight. Samir was considered equally ruthless to Mu'mmar and the Captain. As a former Yemeni fisherman, he was a hard worker and fierce leader. He adjusted his worn-out headband to pull his thick, black-matted hair out of his eyes. "Mu'mmar, it appears this base is not as abandoned as the Captain hoped it would be."

"If their military was still here, we would not have been able to drop anchor near here. What I think we have here are more outsiders, like us. And they've just given away their position." Mu'mmar adjusted his focus to the lead mechanic building the Super Stallion. "Is the bird ready?"

The worn-out man lowered his wrench and wiped the sweat from his brow, "Another twenty-four hours, if we keep at it, but my team is under-fed, weak, and dirty. Some of us haven't slept since we arrived on the island."

"Well, keep at it, then! The sooner you finish, the sooner we can get the Super Nova and leave!" Mu'mmar allowed his anger to boil and then subside as the mechanic went back to work. Mu'mmar placed his nasty bear-like hand on the shoulder of Samir, handing him some C-4 explosives. "Take this and blast your way in. We must eliminate the threat *before* the helicopter is ready."

Samir cracked his knuckles, "And when we find them?"

"I said, *eliminate the threat...*"

Samir flashed his golden brown teeth through a gnarly smirk, "As you wish, Mu'mmar."

14 BREACH

Danny zipped hurriedly towards the main door. "Shayla!" He seized the gun from her, "What did you do?"

Cody emerged from the corridor holding a rifle of his own. "Is everything all right? Where are they?"

"They're right below us! On the cliffs!" Shayla was pale with fear as she quickly and submissively handed the gun over to Danny as if it were poisoned.

"Then why'd you shoot at them! Now they know where we are!" Cody gripped his M-16 with white knuckles.

Shayla's voice got higher as she held back tears of panic, "It was an accident! I didn't mean to."

"Nothing we can do now," Danny answered, "they were bound to find us sooner or later. Come on." Danny, Shayla, and Cody hustled back into the armory and shouted at the others. "Finish whatever you're working on! We have to move now!"

Samir ducked behind a rock with the rest of his men in the search party. They had located the hut at the top of the dirt road above Castaway Pointe. It wasn't long before they found the adjacent cave door, where Shayla's palm frond camouflaging did nothing more than serve as a nuisance to the pirates. After about ten minutes of frustrated keypad-mashing and arguing, one of the more scraggly pirates, missing several of his teeth and caked in grime, unrolled a length of wire leading from the C-4 on the door back to the detonator at Samir's feet. After connecting the wires, he offered to Samir, "Would you like to do the honors?"

Samir grinned and gripped the detonator, pushing it down with a grunt. A charge surged to the explosives and, with a resounding blast that echoed through the mountain, shook loose the rocks and boulders and decades of dust built-up on the giant land mass.

"Ready or not, here they come." Miko said wryly as rubble and dust fell onto her face. She finished placing the last claymore, a proximity mine that explodes when its laser sensors are crossed, and sprinted back to the others.

"Head out!" Samir barked. "Leave no man alive!"

No sooner had they charged the tunnel than a second, smaller explosion rang out. Two pirates were thrown against the wall from the detonation. Samir halted his men and examined the room. The smoke and dust from the explosion made it possible for them to see the small lasers emanating from scattered lumps of metal along the floor. "Claymores…hell. Grab rocks! Set off the others and keep moving!"

Miko pumped her fist and high fived Eugene as she rejoined the group, "Got 'em!"

Eugene beamed, "Think they'll run away now? I'd run away."

Danny kept an ear out, waiting for a signal. Several small explosions followed. "They're still coming."

"Through the land mines? They're crazy!" Eugene could hardly believe it.

Cody hooked the final trip-wire from his canteen bombs onto the galley doors, "Crazy enough I don't want to meet them. Man your stations!" The kids scattered to their hiding places and attack points.

Samir's men cleared the heavily fortified hallway and came upon the doorway leading into the galley. On his signal, two lead men kicked in the double doors.

A mighty bang blew the team back into the center of the hallway. The canteens filled with explosives had been rigged to the insides of the door with strings holding back the detonation. Grabbing them by their shirts and throwing them, Samir yelled, "On your feet! Get in there!"

Crouching low in the smoke, Samir followed his team into the galley, each one trained the sights of their guns to cover the spread of the room, but spotted no one. They stood into the clearing to examine the eating area when a tremendous hum buzzed over their heads. At once, the pirates' guns appeared to jump out of their hands and upwards, sticking to the ceiling with a clang.

"No, no, no, no, no!" A burly pirate, draped in several rounds of machine gun ammo, was lifted into the air and became stuck to the ceiling. The magnetic force overcame gravity and pulled him to the ceiling like a turtle in an upside down world.

"What the hell…?" Samir said aloud, baffled as to what

just happened. He looked to the others still waiting outside the room. "Don't come in here! We need to go another way!"

Little did they know that Miko and Eugene were watching them through the security cameras. They had hooked up a high-powered magnet to the steel beams in the structure and configured them to act as magnets themselves. "I told you they'd be too cheap to be using brass rounds," Eugene whispered to Miko.

"Okay, okay, you were right, and I'm glad you were," admitted Miko. "Now let's get out of here and get the speakers ready." They left their magnet and ran out of the room to their next battle station.

Several pirates began to climb onto the tables, jumping to grasp at their weapons as well as their comrade, but it was no use. Eugene and Miko had wired the magnet with enough amplification that it would require a rather hefty tow truck to release them from their resting places.

The windows crashed in.

Several rounds of gunfire broke through. The pirates hit the deck as the walls around them were sprayed with ammunition.

"Did you hit any?" Danny asked.

"I don't think so," Cody responded, "but I can't tell if the magnets curved the bullets or if I just missed." They were lying on their stomachs outside covered in leaves and shrubs. They reloaded their M-16 assault rifles.

"Same here."

Samir and the other pirates were subjected to crawling amongst the broken glass as Danny and Cody continued to scatter rounds into the galley. The pirates scrambled for a new plan.

One of the pirates panicked, "There must be dozens of them! Let's retreat!"

"That's what they'll want us to do," Samir called out. "You can wait here and die like rats, run back and die like cowards, or fight on and die like men!"

He waited for a lull in the gunfire. When it came, he knew the shooters were out of ammo. With grace, he pushed himself up from the floor and dove outside through a broken window towards Danny and Cody. Several men, emboldened with a new sense of courage, followed suit and rolled out into the shrubbery.

"Uh oh," said Cody. "Only one magazine left apiece. That's not going to be enough to get all of them."

"I say we run and shoot suppressive fire."

"Agreed. These guys are nuts. And we have terrible aim."

Cody and Danny jumped to their feet, throwing their camouflage down and blindly shooting behind them while they ran. They peppered the mountainside with bullets, but not with great accuracy. The pirates managed to make it to positions of cover, with only a few suffering minor wounds.

"Move closer!" Samir caught his bearings and ducked behind a tree. His courage gave him the adrenaline to push this far, but it had not helped his eyes adjust to the bright sunlight any faster. He scanned his surroundings for options. To his right was a wooden bridge over a stream hidden by a row of low bushes that may have provided sufficient cover to wrap around towards the direction the kids went. To his left was a small lake and a couple of irregularities in the rock face that could potentially have openings. He could not be sure.

Danny and Cody were finally out of sight and out of ammo.

Samir listened to the silence as more of his men dove behind trees. The babbling stream that led to the waterfall was the only sound they heard. Samir signaled them to move across the bridge. Just as the pirate in front stepped on the first plank of the bridge, a hidden hatch beneath the grass in front of them popped open. They immediately drew their weapons and pointed them at Eugene, whose head was the only thing the pirates could see, like a groundhog quickly checking for signs of winter. He was sitting on Miko's shoulders who strained to keep her balance in the secret tunnel below. They were wearing what looked like large, gray headphones. The pirates fired at Eugene, but just as fast as he popped up, he was back down the hole again.

Several pirates charged after him, firing wildly at the open hatch. Suddenly, a loud, high-pitched tone emitted from the hole. It was a giant amplified speaker designed to deafen large crowds from hundreds of yards away, and the pirates were only 20 feet from it. Grasping at their ears and collapsing to the ground, the pirates dropped their weapons and intermittently puked. One of the pirates felt blood coming from his ears, and the shock sent him falling off the bridge and into the stream, which took him over the waterfall that led back outside the mountain. Samir yelled directions at the remaining pirates, but to no avail. The sound blaster that Miko and Eugene turned on was too loud and deafening for any other sound to exist. Samir had no choice but to use hand signals to retreat his men back inside the galley.

The pirates ran back through the windows into the eating area. Their comrade, who had still been stuck to the ceiling, finally managed to release himself from his ammunition. With a thud, he collapsed onto several of the pirates. Getting up, they ran into the hallway and went inside a different door labeled "RADAR." Inside, there were dozens of old RADAR screens and electronic equipment that had long been forgotten. Luckily, the door was made of steel and suppressed the sound from across the hall.

Silence.

Relieved and frustrated, Samir and the remaining ten pirates collected themselves. "*Yela'an!*" Samir cursed in Arabic as he kicked a computer chair across the room. "Children! They are just stupid little boys! Radio the ship and give a status report! This situation is getting very annoying!"

One of his men fidgeted with the radio. "It does not work, Samir. The magnet, or maybe the sound blast, it must have broken-" Samir grabbed the radio and threw it into a RADAR screen with an angry yell.

"This fight ends *now*! We *must* win the day! Is that understood?" His men nodded and reloaded, catching their breaths and sticking their fingers in their still-ringing ears. As they did, they saw Shayla step out of the seed vault through the window. Surprised, she locked eyes with two of the pirates.

"Do you see that?" A bald headed pirate, covered in scars alerted his friend.

"It's just a little girl," he scowled. "We can take her." Together, the two of them charged for Shayla's position.

"Eep!" Shayla turned as fast as she could back into the seed vault.

Samir looked to the rest of the bewildered pirates. "What are you doing? Follow her!"

Still, the pirates froze. "What if it's another trick?" The bald-headed pirate asked.

The veins on Samir's neck pulsated with rage. "It's just a little girl! Move!"

Eugene quickly ran outside and chased after Shayla as she darted into the seed vault. The first pirate grabbed the handle to fling the door open but was instantly immobilized. Seizing and shaking, he fell to the ground with his grip impossibly tight around the handle, his arm locked straight at the elbow.

"He's being shocked!" His hand began to smoke before the bald-headed pirate could think to wedge him free with a nearby stick. Samir kicked open the door, jarring loose the wires Shayla had connected to the doorknob from a very large battery.

Inside the seed vault, Shayla was now ducking for cover at the end of one of the many long aisles of drawers which held the hundreds of thousands of seeds. When she heard the door open, she turned the lights off.

"Come out wherever you are little girl! We won't hurt you," the bald-headed pirate beckoned. Only he and one other pirate went inside, while Samir and the rest stood guard outside the vault.

Samir hissed at the pair, "Flush her out here if you have to, we'll be waiting." He closed the door behind them and posted outside with guns drawn.

Back inside the fault, the two pirates crept forward. "I give up! I'm scared," Shayla cried.

"Give us your gun, girly, we promise you'll be all right," the pirates smiled at each other.

"Well, all right, you promised," Shayla slid her gun along the cold floor to their feet. She stood with her hands over her head.

The bald-headed pirate grasped the gun and aimed it at Shayla. "I've never been very good at keeping my promises." He pulled the trigger and unleashed a mighty bang. The gun exploded in his hands, knocking him backwards and into a coffin-sized cabinet. Cody had rigged the gun to explode after someone pulled the trigger.

"Eugene! Now!" No sooner had the words left Shayla's mouth than Eugene jumped from a ceiling tile and delivered a flying kick to the pirate still standing. He too stumbled back into the open cabinet. Shayla dove for the door, slamming it shut and mashing the keypad with her palm to lock it. The two pirates screamed and banged on the door. It was reinforced steel, so they were not getting out of there anytime soon.

Eugene picked himself up off the floor, "Did we get 'em?"

"Soon enough, they'll be pirate popsicles." Shots rang out from the outside. "Oh my yikes! Come on, let's go!" Shayla grabbed Eugene's hand and dashed up to the ceiling tile to escape.

Meanwhile, back in the RADAR room, Cody and Danny were now laying down fire towards Samir and the eight remaining pirates who were still standing outside the seed vault building. The boys were shooting from behind a desk they toppled over to use as a barricade with their backs up against the wall. The lights were out and it was difficult for Samir's men to see inside the window. The temporary flashes from Danny and Cody's M9 pistols were the only light source. Samir and his men dispatched on opposite sides of the door. They entered the room, pointing their firearms at the metal desk. Both exits were now blocked by the pirates. The shooting stopped.

"You're out of bullets, little boys…" Samir laughed. "And nowhere else to run. Come out and make this easy for all of us."

"Boss," a short, stubby pirate spoke up, sniffing the air. "Do you smell something?"

"We've been at sea for quite some time. We're all a bit ripe," came a reply from one of the other men.

"No, stupid, in here." Guarded, they all grew silent and began to sniff. Stepping forward, the stubby pirate lost his footing and slipped, splashing into the layer of thin liquid on the ground. "An oiled floor? What do you think this is, some kind of game?"

"Oh, not at all," Miko's voice shot back from the door behind them. "This is survival." A scratch of sulfur on sandpaper broke the momentary silence as the flash of a match light illuminated the room. As though in slow motion, it flew, from where Miko's voice had been, in a graceful arc towards the floor where it bounced softly to rest, while she simultaneously closed the door, trapping the pirates inside. A noiseless, blue wave raced towards them, lapping up to a glimmering orange crest of fire and consuming the room back to front. Those that tried to run fell face first into the oil, unable to gain the traction to right themselves. Those that froze, quickly found their rubber soled shoes melted and trapped to the ground that would destroy them. While on fire, Samir crawled to the desk where Cody and Danny hid, only to find two pistols lying on top of a trap door, and no Danny and Cody in sight. He grabbed a gun, opened the hatch, and dragged himself inside, leaving the rest of his team behind to burn. Samir landed hard onto his back and quickly rolled around to put out the fire. He was the only one left.

When he stood, he pointed his gun around the room, cautiously checking for anyone. What he found was a series of large tubes, tanks, and engines. It appeared to be where all of the water was pumped throughout the island. A loud whir and hum filled the air. It came from a turbine that spun at a tremendous speed. He followed the sound of heavy panting where he found Danny hunched over with his hands on his knees. Samir pressed his gun firmly into Danny's temple. Miko, Shayla, Cody, and Eugene gasped. "Put down your weapons! Or your friend gets it."

Immediately, they complied. Samir was forced to yell over the sound of the machinery, "Back against the wall!" His skin was still smoking.

"Don't hurt him," Shayla cried, "he's really a nice boy."

"Nice boys don't kill a dozen of my best men! Now tell me, how many more of you are there?"

Shayla began to open her mouth, but Danny cut her off, "Don't tell him anything!"

Samir smacked him in the head with the magazine of his gun, "Let her speak! Or you all will die!"

"Let them go, I'll tell you everything you need to know," Danny pleaded.

With that, an evil grin crawled across Samir's face. "It's the blonde one, isn't it? Is she your *girlfriend?* Perhaps this will be the better incentive." He redirected his gun towards Shayla across the room. He put Danny in a choke hold with his free arm. "Now tell me what I need to know!"

"I'm not afraid of you."

"What did you say?" Samir seethed at Danny.

"I said, I'm not afraid of you."

"I hardly think this is the time to feign bravery."

"I'm not fakin' it. All my life I've been afraid of jerks like you pushing me around, but today we fought back for once. And you know what? We won."

"This isn't exactly a position a winner finds himself in."

"That's just because you haven't met all of my friends."

"What? What are you babbling about?"

"Oliver!" Danny glanced towards the loose grate between their feet which Oliver had popped through. Samir looked at Oliver, puzzled, and the bonobo waved back with a smile, dropping the rope he had tied around Samir's leg leading back towards the generator's blades.

With a swift elbow, Danny doubled Samir over. His gun fired once into the floor before Danny could strip it from his hands and kick it towards his friends. Samir grabbed at the rope dragging him, but he could not free himself.

"Don't look," Cody covered Shayla's eyes as they turned away from the horror.

The kids quickly regrouped in the armory, the lights flickering amidst the screams from the pump room. Then there was silence. It was finally over.

"Is that all of them?" Cody asked.

"I think so," Eugene interjected.

The other Castaway Kids hugged each other with relief that the attack was over. *But was it?* Danny couldn't help but think, *With half our base destroyed, no sign of the weapon the Salty Sea Dogs are after, food supplies getting low… should we really be celebrating?*

HOW MANY MEN?

At the base of the waterfall, a severely injured pirate staggered to his feet. Blood cascaded from his ears. He tripped over himself as he ran through the sand towards the *Mogadishu*. Sour sweat tingled his lips as he wiped his face with what was left of his shirt.

The world around him was muffled. He ran up to the *Mogadishu* pirates, and he could see that they were yelling in his face, but he could not hear them. He opened his mouth to speak, but could not hear what he was saying. He realized that he had fallen deaf from his exposure to the sound blaster in the battle. He pointed to his ears, miming to the other pirates that he couldn't hear. An annoying, high pitched ring was all he experienced.

Captain Vasser, smoking a pipe under a nearby tent, quickly marched over to the commotion. He immediately became impatient with the charades and pushed everyone crowding around the pirate away. He then brought the deaf pirate to his knees, and handed him a nearby stick. He pointed at the sand. The captain wanted him to write.

Vasser used his finger and wrote: HOW MANY MEN?

All the pirates on shore formed a circle around Vasser and the deaf pirate while Mu'mmar kept everyone back as a crowd controller. The deaf pirate shook his head. His shaking hand used the stick to cross out the word MEN with an "X" and wrote: KIDS.

The pirates standing around began murmuring. One of them spoke directly to Vasser. "I thought you said this secret island was deserted, sir?"

Vasser raised his bionic arm in the air and grabbed the throat of the pirate who just spoke up to silence him. He lifted him in the air, strangling him. The pirates' feet dangled as he choked and gurgled. "Are you questioning your captain, you filthy dog?" The man couldn't answer. Instead, he passed out. Vasser threw him aside like a rag doll.

He pointed to the deaf man, then made a gesture to the others to take him to the ship. They carried him away.

Furious, Vasser yelled as he strode back to his tent, Mu'mmar and the others in tow, trying to keep up with the captain's pace. Vasser's metal legs flicked sand as he moved, creating a cloud of dirt around his feet as he walked, giving the impression that he was almost floating. "Mu'mmar! Muster and arm fifty men! I want them ready to move by sunrise!"

"Aye aye, sir!" Mu'mmar responded.

"No one rests until the helicopter is ready! I want a full-scale attack on whoever the hell these kids are! I will not tolerate any more interruptions! Anyone with idle hands will be shot! Is that clear?!"

"Yes, Captain."

Vasser roared a loud yell as he pounded his robotic fist onto a table under the tent, smashing it in half. He proceeded to go on a rampage, flipping over a gun rack and kicking over a barrel of rice.

While this continued, Mu'mmar frantically began rounding up troops for the final attack.

Not far from the tent were three pirates and Asad, helping pour coconut milk into a bucket. Asad shaved out the flesh from inside the fruit with his knife. He saw and heard everything that transpired. He couldn't help but grin as he looked on.

Captain Vasser saw this and stopped his rampage. He glared suspiciously at Asad, who immediately wiped the grin off his face. Asad put his head down towards the coconuts, hoping the captain wouldn't further question why he was just smiling. Luckily, he heard the captain's carbon-fiber feet clank up the brow and onto the ship. Vasser whispered to Mu'mmar in passing, "Keep an eye on the doctor's kid. He knows something he's not telling us…"

Mu'mmar nodded.

He's starting to suspect something about me, Asad thought. *I have to warn Danny and the others about tonight's attack. It's the only way they'll have a chance. But how am I going to sneak away with Mu'mmar watching me?*

Asad hid his knife in his sock. He turned to Yacoob, the half Indian and half Somali cook who had earlier helped Asad get back on the ship. Due to his kind heart and long tenure aboard, he was more of an uncle to Asad than just another shipmate. Yacoob was drilling holes into coconuts to retrieve the milk inside. Asad stood to leave, "I dropped my knife by the trees, I need to go retrieve it."

Mu'mmar saw this and ran over to them. "Hey! Stop!" Mu'mmar towered over him, his biceps were the size of Asad's head. "Where do you think you're going?"

Yacoob stood up in Mu'mmar's face. "He dropped his knife in the jungle, he needs it to keep working." They stared at each other.

"Captain wants to keep a close eye on him," Mu'mmar grunted.

"He's just a boy," Yacoob protested.

"Captain's orders!" Mu'mmar growled.

"I'll escort him, then," the elderly cook suggested. "I'll need to gather more food to give the men energy for tonight's raid anyway."

Mu'mmar tossed the idea around his head. "All right, but if anything happens to him, I'll consider it an act of mutiny." Mu'mmar turned and went back to hissing orders at the men.

"Thank you," Asad expressed to Yacoob. Asad quickly heaved a rucksack onto his back that he had packed earlier with his violin and supplies. Yacoob didn't question it, but gave it a suspicious glance. They both grabbed a basket and began walking into the jungle.

"Don't thank me," the cook said. "You just make sure you warn your friends about the attack."

Chills ran up Asad's back. "But-but how did you know I-"

"You're not a very good liar, Asad. You never have been," He continued. "Besides, I can see your knife in your sock. Luckily Mu'mmar's beady little eyes didn't see it or else you'd be in front of the captain right now, wouldn't you?"

They stepped over vines and fallen logs. The sounds of the ship faded in the distance. Yacoob stopped to pick some mushrooms off of a tree's giant roots. "Look Asad, my restaurant was destroyed after the civil war. I was bullied into joining Vasser simply because I had no other choice. I want to see him stopped just as much as you," the cook continued. "So go warn whoever it is you were meeting with last night."

"They're Americans!" Asad said with a smile.

"Ah, interesting…" the cook pondered. "Not my favorite sort, but anyone's better than Vasser, I suppose. Run along now Asad, I'll cover for you as much as I can."

"What about Mu'mmar?"

"I'll deal with him. I am his cook by the way," he held up a wild spore he picked from a tree root and smiled. "And these *orellanine mushrooms* will make any man vomit himself to the bone within minutes."

Asad grinned. "Thank you!" He hugged him. Asad ran away, darting through the jungle towards the mountain entrance.

15 MIKO'S SONG

Danny squeezed icing over a carrot cake on the preparation table in the cafeteria's kitchen. Danny couldn't outwardly show how concerned he was that at any minute, their last meal might be interrupted by pirates bursting into the mountain to finish them off. Shayla chopped celery and onions on a cutting board near the stove, then used her knife to slap them like hockey pucks put them into a huge cast iron pot, resting atop a low flame. The water boiled a symphony of vegetables and spices in "Shayla's Island Stew," a recipe she was inventing as she cooked it. Cody and Miko twisted a corkscrew into the cork of a giant wooden barrel. They tugged on it, and red wine poured all over the two of them and the floor. They laughed boisterously at the mess they made. Eugene had found some pilot's goggles and a helmet, stuck his arms out to his side like a plane, then made engine noises and ran across the tables. He saw the wine spill and exclaimed, "Slip and slide!" He darted between the tables and slid head first across the wine-soaked linoleum into an open sack of flour.

They were still celebrating their victory over the Salty Sea Dogs. It didn't seem to faze any of the kids that they had just fought several men in the name of self-defense. Shayla was the only one to have a problem with it at first, but the more she thought about how vicious and deadly the pirates were to them, the easier it was to be de-sensitized to it. Danny looked on as his friends laughed at Eugene covered in flour and mused, *I guess it's true that laughter is the best medicine.* They had just finished cleaning up the bodies and mess from the aftermath of the attack. They dragged the dead bodies to the river which led to the waterfall. The galley, which earlier was full of bullet casings and a man magnetized to the ceiling, was now occupied with laughter and the smell of delicious food.

Danny found a remote TV that he wheeled into the room so he could continue to monitor the security camera at the front entrance, which was now more of a gaping hole in the side of the mountain than a formal entry. He decided not to share his lingering concerns for their safety with anyone else. It was late, the moon was out, and the Salty Sea Dogs were more than likely not going to attack anytime tonight. Regardless, he kept a vigilant watch over his monitoring station.

Shayla couldn't take the smile off her face. She was completely in her element when she cooked. When Danny and Miko did an inventory of their food supplies while the others finished cleaning up, they discovered they only had enough food for one more big feast. Shayla was happy to hear Miko say, "Cook everything we have Shayla, and have fun with it!" And so she did. She gathered everything she could from the plants outside the cafeteria windows and all of the dry goods in storage. She even opened the last of the canned desserts in the pantry, handing them to Danny and instructing him to make a cake. She was definitely breaking her own health rules when she tasked Danny to make dessert. He was clumsy at best, but she happily helped him.

The Castaway Kids all concluded that this would probably be their last meal. They took a vote on it, and because of the amount of men they fought to defend themselves, they determined the Salty Sea Dogs would be too upset to simply give up, and that they would most likely fight to the end. *This is it*, Danny thought. *I've finally killed us. I convinced everyone to come on an adventure with me, and now I've gotten us all killed.*

"We need music!" Shayla proclaimed. "Play a song, Ms. Tanaka!"

Miko and Cody were toasting and taking a sip of the wine. They both made disgusted faces as if they were about to throw up. They spit the wine out and proceeded to scrape their tongues with their fingernails.

"Yuck!" Miko gagged. "It tastes like vinegar! Why do our parents drink this stuff?"

"Yeah. It's ew," Cody agreed. "I agree with Shayla. Bust out the violin, Miko!"

"I would but, I don't really know any happy songs. All I know are the classical pieces my parents brainwashed me to learn. But…" Miko skipped over to her violin case. "I have been working on something rather personal lately. I was inspired by Asad's performance and his take on music. I haven't performed it yet, but seeing as how this is our last night together, I guess I've got nothing to worry about."

"Yay! Love you, Miko!" Shayla grabbed a pinch of spices and blew them off her palm and into the pot as if casting a spell over the food like a good-witch. She hunched her shoulders up and shook her fists with glee.

"This cake is going to be epic," said Danny. He was placing caramel-filled strawberries on the chocolate frosting.

"I thought that cake was supposed to be healthy," Shayla inquired.

"Well sort of….It's carrot cake, so that's healthy, I guess. But then I added a bunch of awesomeness to make it more of a dessert than a chore."

"Are you implying that my cooking is a chore, Danny?" Shayla jokingly poked him with a wooden spoon.

"No…but are you implying that my cake isn't healthy enough just because a fat kid is making it?" Danny asked. Once the words escaped his mouth, he immediately regretted saying them. He saw the look of horror on Shayla's face.

"No! Of course not! I just…" She searched for the words. "You've lost so much weight since we've been on the island, and-"

"Go on. Say it. I'm a fatty who only likes to eat fatty foods and you're worried about me having a heart attack and my corpse smelling the place up. My fat's going to kill me the same way it killed my parents," Danny said. "Well go ahead, I can take it. I've heard all the jokes."

"Danny, what are you doing? That's not what I was saying at all."

"Go on. Say it!" Danny was getting upset now. "You think I'm fat and gross."

"No! No, no, no, Danny! Stop it! Stop talking like that!" Shayla was fully upset and facing Danny, ignoring her food for the moment. At this point, Miko, Eugene, and Cody were all staring quietly at the quarrel happening. "It's just that I…"

Shayla took her apron off and placed her spoon on the counter. She stepped toward Danny softly, grabbing and caressing his hands as she said what she had to say. "I care about you, Danny. You're my best friend, and I'm really proud of you for losing more weight than you would have at the fitness camp your uncles wanted to send you to. But…I know how sensitive you are about it, and so I just want to cook healthy food for you so that you continue to lose weight and feel good about yourself, and most importantly stay healthy. It's not about me, it's about you feeling confident and good about yourself. Like you should."

Shayla fixed some of Danny's scruffy hair. All he could do was stare into her caring, baby-blue eyes. The freckles around her nose were more noticeable up close. She held his hands in hers. "Oh," was all Danny could say. "I didn't expect you to say that."

"Is that okay?" Shayla asked. "That I call you my best friend, and that I say that I care about you?"

"Yes," Danny said. "I'm sorry I got so upset. Force of habit, I guess. I didn't know… I just feel so bad about myself sometimes that I assume everyone else feels the same way."

"Well you're wrong, Danny." Shayla said with a smile.

They leaned into each other to try and kiss, but they were interrupted again.

"Heads up!" Cody threw a sleeve of crackers at Danny. He was caught off guard, so it hit him in the face and it fell to the floor. Shayla snapped out of her trance and went back to cooking. Danny, on the other hand, grit his teeth and flared his nostrils as Cody's over-protective behavior was getting tiresome.

Danny picked up the crackers and threw it back to Cody with all his strength.

"Whoa! A little hard there, don't you think, Danny?" Cody smiled coyly.

Danny tried to hold back his frustration.

"Hullo!"

The familiar voice of Asad both startled and excited them. He was standing at the entrance to the cafeteria. He was out of breath and leaning against the door. He had a rucksack over his shoulder.

"Asad!" Eugene announced. Oliver sucked on a popsicle while sitting on Eugene's shoulders. "What are you doing here?"

"I've come to warn you of an attack," Asad said.

"But we just got attacked," Eugene continued. "And we kicked their butts!"

"No, an even bigger one. More men. I overheard the captain talking about it. The helicopter is almost ready. They intend to use it to extract the weapon they call the Super Nova. They will most likely strike before daybreak."

Danny checked his remote monitoring device. *How did I not see Asad coming into the mountain? I need to focus…This is the second time I've been distracted by Shayla.* "We're aware that they'll attack, but we used most of our weapons and resources to fend them off earlier today. We can use the guns they had on them, but there's still only five of us. There's not much we can do, so we're celebrating being alive while we still can."

"Please," Asad said with such seriousness that everyone had stopped celebrating and was staring right at him. "I will fight alongside you! I cannot go back to the *Mogadishu*. Help me get my father and I off this island and away from those terrible men."

"How?" asked Danny. "We're out-numbered and over-powered. We can fend off *maybe half* of the men they have left. Then what? We're tired and this is the last of our food." Danny gestured towards the cake and stew.

"So that's it?" Asad began to get teary-eyed. "Y-you-you're just going to give up? You're just going to die here? I'm sorry, but that is unacceptable! We have the opportunity to change our lives forever and stop evil from moving forward! We have to do something!" Asad fell to his knees, his body limp and his head down. "I don't want to die here, and you shouldn't either…"

Miko went over to him, put her arm around his shoulders, and did her best to be comforting. "You can stay here, Asad," she whispered sweetly. "You're a Castaway Kid, too. For life. Okay?" A tear cascaded down his cheek as he gazed up at her. She smiled warmly and wiped his tear away. Miko continued, "You're so brave, Asad," Miko kissed Asad on the cheek.

"So does that mean you'll fight?" Asad asked.

Miko looked to the others. Danny nodded reassuringly.

"I have something for you." Miko calmly and confidently stood up, walked back to her violin and positioned it on her shoulder. She posed in the middle of the room, firmly grasping her bow. "But first, I hope this'll cheer you up." Miko closed her eyes, took a deep breath, and soaked in the silence.

She played.

Her song started off slow, a melancholy tune that was appropriate for the current mood. Everyone stared at Miko in the center of the room, who was completely focused on her performance. It was like a private concert. The rhythm became faster-paced and more intense.

She played.

The notes became higher, almost magical. The mood began to crescendo. Miko's eyes were closed tightly now, her face looked as if the song was hurting her. Then, her foot started tapping. She bent down and lifted her leg straight behind her like a ballerina and moved her body with the music like a snake.

And she played.

The rest of the kids witnessed the event. They stared mesmerized at the now twirling violinist, playing her ballad faster and faster. A cyclone of notes bounced off the walls of the bunker they occupied. Never had such a sad, dreary place heard such music or seen such a sight as Miko dancing like a forest sprite. The walls were getting stronger having heard such beauty.

Then she stopped.

She played a song with such heart and innocence that for just a brief moment, Asad and the other Castaway Kids forgot they were abandoned. Forgot they used to be mistreated back home. Forgot that this was going to be the last song they ever heard. Forgot that the fight of their lives was quickly approaching. They escaped into her violin and felt happy.

And then she stopped playing.

The wonderful distraction ended with a bold climax that was executed perfectly. Now with a huge smile on her face, looking right at Asad, she quietly caught her breath and stopped dancing. Asad stood, beaming back at her. And his thread-bare shoes glided him over to her. He placed his hands on her shoulders. "Thank you, Miko." He hugged her.

The rest of the Castaway Kids applauded. They whistled, yelped, and clapped as loud as they could.

"You taught me that music comes from your entire body," Miko said to Asad. "And I will proudly return the favor by fighting alongside you. Here. I made this for you." Miko reached into her violin case and pulled out a violin bow that she had made from extra wire and a tree branch. "It's not much, but I wanted to repay you for returning my violin."

Asad held it in his hands like a cloud, gently examining it as if it were a holy gift. "This is brilliant! This is the nicest thing anyone has ever done for me. Many thanks, Miko."

"Hey, what are friends for?" She gave him a playful punch in the arm.

The kids at last sat down at a table in the galley and ate a feast fit for six of the finest kings and queens. Asad had in his rucksack a velvet pouch with tea in it. He said the pirates stole a shipment of chai from an Iranian merchant vessel, and he and his father were given some of the finest tea in the world. He said he was saving his share for a special occasion, and so he divided the tea amongst all of them. It was warm, delicious and smooth. Shayla loved how good it was for them. Even Eugene, who said he wasn't a "tea-person," had three cups of it.

Shayla started the meal with what she called her "Tropical Mélange," which was a giant fruit salad served in a large mixing bowl. It consisted of chopped mango, kiwi cubes, cut-up banana, orange slices, pineapple chunks, and diced plantains, served with coconut shavings on top and a durian dip on the side. It was a juicy, delectable, healthy appetizer that didn't last very long. Everyone just stuck their forks into the bowl and ate straight from it.

Then, they passed around bowls of "Shayla's Island Stew," which had every vegetable that Shayla could get her hands on. Carrots, onions, bell peppers, eggplant, Kang Kong (water spinach), cabbage, broccoli, radishes, squash, cucumbers, snake beans, potatoes, and arugula. It was...interesting. It definitely gave them all the energy they lacked, but the taste was "acquired," according to Shayla. "Acquired by who?" Was Eugene's response. Asad, Cody, and Shayla enjoyed it more than anyone else, and Danny choked down as much as he could as to not hurt Shayla's feelings.

Finally, they ate Danny's dessert. His self-titled "Chocolate Carrot Cake With Strawberries and Awesome" was appropriately named. It brought the energy and mood up to a fever pitch. Shayla only had a thin slice of what she called the "sugar bomb waiting to explode in your stomach." Eugene and Oliver were jumping on their chairs while they were chomping theirs down. It was satisfying, and it filled them up. It truly was a fantastic last meal.

After they ate, Asad and Miko pulled out their violins and jammed together. They were even choreographing some dance moves. The others were still too stuffed to move.

Shayla took the next watch on the security monitor. Danny and Cody did the dishes. They protested at its pointlessness at first, but Shayla argued that if it was their last night on the island, and someday people found their dead bodies here, she didn't want people to think they lived in their own filth.

Eugene was trying to teach Oliver how to do the cha-cha, which his grandmother had taught him at his Bar Mitzvah. But Oliver was so stuffed with food and crashing from a sugar rush that he was not at all interested in moving. So instead it was just Oliver trying to sleep and Eugene continually waking him up to play, talking the poor bonobo's ear off about being a performer.

Cody washed dishes while Danny used a towel to dry and put them away. The tension between them was thick, but neither of them wanted to be the one to bring up

Shayla. "I noticed you didn't eat a lot tonight," Cody finally broke the silence. "Something bothering you?"

"You mean besides the fact that murderous pirates could walk through that door any minute?" Danny jested. "No, I'm fine."

"For the record, I totally agree with Shayla, I don't think you're fat."

"Please…You and your buddy tried to flatten me like a pancake at football try-outs. And not a day went by at school when you and Erik didn't make pig noises at me in the halls."

"That was Erik, not me," Cody tried to defend himself. "I never said those things."

"Yeah˙but you never stood up for me either, Cody, which in my book is just as bad. Not once did you say, 'Hey guys, leave Danny alone.' Or, 'Get off of him!' or 'Let go of his nipples, there's no milk in there' or anything." Danny snatched a cup from Cody and dried it furiously. "To me you're just as big of a bully as the rest of them. I wouldn't have had to start the Castaway Kids if it weren't for jocks like you and Erik."

"No, I'm not like him, I just-"

"Just what? Just happened to be standing next to that jerk every time he insulted my weight? Or picked on Eugene for being Jewish? Or called your own cousin a 'hippie-freak' just because she's into nature? Or thrown calculators at Miko and called her 'Ching-Chong?'" Danny tried to keep his voice down so as not to ruin the good time everyone else was having. This was between Cody and Danny, and the running of the dishwater masked the volume of their voices. "You're a coward Cody. You helped make us all feel like outcasts and pushed us to run away."

"Don't you think I know that! I feel terrible about myself." Cody said. "I just have so many problems of my own that I let him make fun of you guys so he wouldn't focus that attention on me."

"What? What would you know about being different? Mister Popular. Mister First String Quarterback. Every girl in school has a crush on you, and all you do is spend time with that jerk-face Erik. I'm supposed to believe you have it rough?" Danny scoffed, shook his head and went back to drying and putting away dishes. "You're unbelievable sometimes, Cody."

"I'm gay."

Danny accidentally dropped a stack of glass plates all over the floor. Miko, Asad, Eugene, and Shayla all turned and clapped for Danny's clumsiness. Oliver got scared and ran off, so Eugene followed him down a corridor. "It's okay, Oliver," Eugene called after him. "They're just plates! Come back!"

When everyone turned back around and continued what they were doing, Danny turned to Cody in bewilderment. "What did you say?"

"Only Erik knows. My parents don't even know. At least I don't think they know. And Shayla doesn't know either, so please don't say anything." Cody had a look of desperation and confession as he leaned in closer to Danny, making sure no one else could hear him. Danny could tell he was being sincere. "Erik is my boyfriend, and he said if I told anyone about us, he'd be so upset he would never see me again."

"So you let Erik terrorize us for being different, out of fear that if you stood up for us, he'd break up with you? Just for being yourself?" Danny asked in disbelief. "You're still a coward Cody, because at least we live out in the open with whatever makes us quote-unquote *different*. We live in the outskirts of the popular world, but not by choice, and at least we're true to ourselves. You put yourself in the spotlight to hide who you truly are, and just stand by as we get bullied day-in and day-out. That's unfair."

"You know what's unfair?" Cody retorted. "Wanting to just play football and be myself and normal at the same time. But it can't happen! You think this is a choice? While all other guys my age are looking at pictures of naked girls and going through puberty, I've already been through puberty and I'd rather look at my 49ers calendar.

"And my parents and coaches put so much damn pressure on me! I don't want to be who they want me to be. I know that people tease you for being overweight, but you can change that! And you have! And I think that's awesome! I can't and don't want to change this about me. I'm not just a macho jock, and it eats me inside that I can't be myself."

"We live in San Francisco, Cody!" Danny said. "If anyone's ever going to come out, that's the city to do it in. It's like the most open-minded city in America about this kind of stuff."

"I know! It's still hard though… It doesn't matter, it's too late now. We'll probably never see the city again, and I'll never get a chance to try being myself in my hometown." Cody turned the sink off and dried his hands on a dishcloth. "That's why I came with you, Danny, that night in the lighthouse. Yeah, I wanted to look after Shayla, but I've always really respected you and how smart you are, how tenacious you really are, what a good leader you can be, and that you put up with all that crap every day.

"I was hoping that by tagging along, you'd see there's more to me than just some jock. I'm a Castaway Kid too, Danny. And on the island, I want to be myself. I want to be myself around you. I've learned a lot from you, and I've realized that life's too short to hide from yourself. You've lost a lot of weight out here, and in a way, I've lost a weight, too. The weight that's been keeping me from coming out. I feel like it's been lifted now, and I want you to know that it wouldn't have been possible unless you came up with this crazy idea in the first place. I really want us to be friends."

Cody held his hand out as a peace offering. Danny was

skeptical. "What about Shayla?"

"I know she likes you, Danny," Cody said. "And I wouldn't want her to be with anybody else. She can make her own choices, so I won't intervene again if anything happens between you two."

"Thanks, Cody," Danny said sincerely. "That means a lot to me. I'm sure that was hard for you to say, and of course no one here will judge you for your secret. I think if we live through this, you should tell the others. And after that, you shouldn't hide it anymore."

"Remember that day we helped Eugene get off the bus? I told you I had something to take care of."

"Yeah. I remember," Danny said cautiously.

"That was mine and Erik's secret one year anniversary. We went and saw a movie, but afterwards I told him that I wanted to go public with him after football camp."

"Oh. I see." Danny cumbersomely grabbed a dust pan and Cody swept the broken glass into it with a hand-broom. Danny threw the glass away in a garbage can very slowly and ceremoniously, processing Cody's revelation. When he did, it was as if he just threw away his and Cody's negative history. He turned to Cody and smiled, "I'm proud to have you in The Castaway Kids. I'm lucky you came along and hope we can be friends if we survive this."

"Me too. Thanks, Danny," Cody agreed.

They shook hands, beaming.

"Guys!" Eugene yelled from down a long corridor. "Guys come here! Come here quick! Look at this!"

Danny, Cody, Asad, and Miko all ran down the hall towards Eugene's voice. Shayla was still at the monitor.

"Wait for me!" Shayla bolted down the corridor, too.

The six Castaway Kids stood in front of the Top Secret door that had been locked since they arrived. It was cracked open. Eugene held Oliver and stared into the darkness that was inside.

The crew of the *Mogadishu* plopped down in the galley to eat a late night dinner. They ached, they hurt, and were exhausted. This didn't stop men from standing guard over the others, jabbing anyone with the butt stock of their rifle who started to fall asleep.

Mu'mmar grabbed a plate with rolls and stew and sat at the head of a large table. He announced to the room before he began eating, "Fifteen minutes to finish your meal! Then back to work!"

He shoved all three rolls into his mouth at the same time, his jaw clicking with each chew. He threw his spoon aside and picked up his bowl of stew, drinking straight from it. His nostrils flared as he gulped down all of the carrots, onions, chicken...and mushrooms. He slammed his empty bowl back onto the table and wiped his mouth on his sleeve. He said to the entire galley, "See, men? It took me but two minutes to finish my meal! Perhaps someday you will be as disciplined as I! But don't hold your breath-"

Before he could finish, Mu'mmar grasped his mouth shut with his giant hand, dropping his dishes onto the deck. He was gagging. He ran to the nearest trash can and threw up. He wailed in pain as his food projected out of him. He sounded like a large dog trying to cough up a small cat, gripping his stomach and falling to his knees. "Poison! I've been poisoned!" Sweat dripped down his bald head as he tried to stand.

Mu'mmar burst into the kitchen where the cooks were hustling about. Mu'mmar raised his pistol in the air. "Who cooked my dinner?!" Everyone in the kitchen stopped what they were doing and looked at Mu'mmar.

Yacoob stepped forward and stood tall, lifting his chin to the sky. "I did."

Without hesitation, Mu'mmar shot him in the chest. The skinny cook flew backwards, knocking over several spoons and spatulas. Mu'mmar keeled over and vomited into a barrel of sugar. "The boy... Where is the boy?"

"We don't know sir. He never came back to the ship," said one of the prep chefs.

"I knew it!" Mu'mmar said to no one in particular. "Where is the doctor?"

"In the clinic, sir," said one of the dishwashers nervously.

"Clean this up," he pointed with his pistol to the vomit and Yacoob on the floor. He burped unapologetically, particles of food spraying in the air. Without saying anything else, Mu'mmar turned and left the kitchen towards the clinic.

Dr. Darzi was adjusting Captain Vasser's camera eye. He was putting a new lithium battery in it. The Captain waited for the doctor to finish when Mu'mmar swung the door open. Mu'mmar had never seen the Captain with his camera-eye out and no eye-patch. He took one look at the hole in his head and threw up again, this time in a nearby bed pan.

"Oh please, Mu'mmar, get a hold of yourself, it's not that bad." Captain Vasser commented.

"No sir, it's the boy. *His* boy," Mu'mmar pointed at Dr. Darzi. "The cook poisoned me and the boy has gone missing."

Vasser pulled his pistol out and shoved it in Dr. Darzi's ribs. "Where is your son, Doctor?"

The doctor was holding the Captain's device in both hands as he trembled, backing away from the pointed pistol. "I-I-I don't know sir, honestly."

Captain Vasser calmly pointed the gun at the doctor's leg. "Oh Rasheed, why would you make me do this?" He pulled the trigger, shooting Dr. Darzi in the thigh. He screamed in agony, dropping the camera-eye to the floor. Captain Vasser sauntered across the room, picked up his prosthetic, popped it into his socket and turned it on. "Did that trigger your memory?"

"I swear, Captain, please! Have mercy!"

Mu'mmar fell to the ground, grasping his stomach and

passing out in the doorway.

"If you don't find your boy soon, and I discover that he's been engaging in acts of mutiny, the next bullet will be in your head. Do I make myself clear, doctor?" The lens on his eye zoomed in at the doctor on the floor.

"Yes! Yes, Captain!" He pleaded. "Let me dress my wounds, please!"

"Permission granted, Doctor." Vasser holstered his pistol. "And do something about Mu'mmar, he's useless to me in this condition."

A running pirate stopped in the doorway. "Captain, your presence is respectfully requested on the flight deck. The helicopter is ready."

"Ah! Finally! Some good news!" The captain beamed as he stepped over Mu'mmar's body and down the passageway. "We will continue the attack as planned without Mu'mmar. The Super Nova is as good as mine…"

16 VASSER

"What did you do?" Miko gaped into the abyss. The mysterious top secret door was now ajar as if someone had just opened it.

Eugene stammered back, "N-nothing! It was just like this when I walked by! Oliver was the one who found it, actually. It's like he heard it open and ran in here."

"Well, it didn't just open itself," Cody said.

Danny squinted and peered down the gloomy staircase, disappearing into the darkness below, "It's almost as if someone *wanted* us to go down there."

"Then it's the last place we should go," Shayla turned back. "Come on, let's get out of here before whoever it is finds us."

Unmoved, Danny continued to stare, "Think about it: it's been closed the whole time we've been here. It was closed the whole time we fought those pirates. But now that we've beaten them back, it opens." Danny finally looked back at Cody. "I think someone down there likes us."

Skeptical though he was, Cody saw Danny's point. "I'm bringing a knife. Just in case."

"What if it's the Salty Sea Dogs luring us into a trap?"

Shayla asked.

"Doubtful," Miko chimed in. "They just barely found out who we are, and there's only one way in or out of the mountain."

"I haven't overheard anything about a secret tunnel," Asad added.

Oliver began screeching and jumping up and down, pointing down the stairs. He grabbed Eugene's hand and tugged him to follow. Eugene went with it. "Look! Oliver is trying to get us to follow him! Come on!" Down the stairs they began. There was no more discussion. Once Danny and Cody made up their mind, Shayla put all of her seed bags into Asad's rucksack and the rest followed timidly.

Any semblance of manufactured human settlement began to disappear as even the steps beneath them were no longer metallic, but carved out of the mountainside stone itself. Cody felt moss growing on the walls and Miko occasionally stepped into puddles of water. The path was only illuminated just enough by red light bulbs on the end of long, flexible poles on the walls. Shayla noticed something rather peculiar about them. The lights slowly tracked the movement of the Castaway Kids like spotlights as they wandered deeper into the cave.

As they descended, the dank scent of stale air and musk grew stronger until the path leveled out beneath them.

"Prrbt! Prrbt!! Blech!" Eugene spazzed, startling the others. "Sorry, some of the cave water dripped into my mouth. Gross." He brushed his lips and tongue against the sleeve of his shirt to clear any trace of the taste.

At the end of the long, meandering tunnel, they came upon a rock wall. "Dead end," Danny lamented. Just then, Oliver pushed a series of rocks into the wall in a specific order which activated a switch. The whole tunnel shook with a low rumble. The boulder in front of them began to lower into the ground with all the hesitation of an aging and underutilized machine.

Cody raised his knife, ready for whatever might greet them on the other side, when suddenly a booming voice, frail as it was commanding, called out from behind the door, *"Cody, put down your weapon. You'll not need it yet."*

"Who's there? Who said that? How do you know my name?" Cody asked the darkness, with a slight tremble in his voice. Just then, the boulder finished moving into the ground, revealing behind it what appeared to be a large dark void. The red lights went off. The kids' eyes adjusted to see that a large room with fluorescent lighting was indeed in front of them, along with the source of the voice.

"I feel like over the last couple of weeks, I've gotten to know each of you quite well," a very old man, his hair whitened and wisped by time, turned in his plush, purple, overstuffed office chair in front of dozens of old television monitors. The lights in the room blinded the kids at first, but once their eyes adjusted, they gazed upon an enormous cylinder-shaped room that looked like a combination science laboratory and a bee hive. The old man stroked his perfectly square, gray beard and faced them now, revealing each and every crag in his grizzled, wrinkly face as he smiled warmly.

Danny didn't understand how this man could claim to "know" them, but when he saw the video screens, it all began to make sense. They displayed security footage from around the island. Danny realized, *This old man has been able to monitor every square inch of the island in far more meticulous detail than any of us had access to in the armory.* "Allow me to officially welcome you to Zactrala Island," the mysterious man arose. "This is my Command Hub. I've been wanting very much to meet you since you arrived."

"Who are you?" Danny asked.

"Ah, how rude, forgive me," the man gently stood at attention and straightened up as best as his rickety body would let him. "My name is Admiral Vasser and I am the commanding officer of this Naval base. I am the last remaining personnel assigned to this mission known as Operation Super Nova. Well, I'm the last remaining *human* at least. I see you've grown quite fond of my bonobo, Oliver, haven't you, Eugene?" At that, Oliver let go of Eugene's hand and waddled up to the admiral, arms outstretched like a toddler greeting his dad after a long day at work.

Eugene's eyes grew wide, "Oliver is...yours? And this whole island belongs to you? Wow, you must be rich!"

"No, Eugene, Zactrala isn't mine in that sense. Technically, it's still the property of the United States Navy. But Oliver here...Well, I've raised him since he was a baby, after his mother and father were killed in an experiment gone wrong. He, too, was the runt of the litter, Eugene."

"So wait, you've been down here the whole time?" Danny asked. "You've been watching us, and listening to us...You watched us crash here...A-and fight those pirates? Why didn't you help us? Or at least try to contact us?"

"I wasn't sure if I could trust you," the admiral scratched Oliver's head as he coddled him. "After that nasty storm I thought for sure you were all dead, or as good as dead. But then I saw that you were just children, so I sent Oliver to do a little spying on you. Many of my outdoor cameras were damaged or limited in coverage, a complaint I've had for years, really. I was quite surprised to see him take such a liking to Eugene, as I am the only human he's ever really gotten along with. He's putty in your hands when you give him banana chips!" He chuckled a wheezy laugh and pulled some from his pockets. Oliver munched while the admiral continued. "Once Miko figured out the pass code to enter the mountain, I knew there was something different about all of you. So I decided I would keep a close eye on you and not retaliate like I would any other intruder. What started out as an experiment of distant observation, quickly turned into something else entirely.

"I locked the door leading down to this command hub merely because you are children, and I didn't want to have to kill you. There are many defense mechanisms built into the tunnel you just came out of, you see."

"But we've been here for almost two months," Miko said. "Why open the door now?"

"He probably ran out of food," Danny guessed.

"No, Danny, I have plenty of food down here. I periodically snuck out and took from the stores upstairs while you were all sleeping. I also have plumbing and access to potable water. And to answer your question, Miko, I only intended to observe you for a short period of time," the admiral continued. "And although I believed you crashed here merely by chance, I still couldn't risk exposing myself and this operation to you. If I were to help you, then my cover would be blown once you ran to your mommies and daddies, telling them about the island. I couldn't have that. So instead, I began documenting everything you said and did on my computer. I became fascinated in watching you acclimate to the deserted situation you found yourselves in. I, of course, continued my watch over the command, but also began keeping a digital log of all of your activities. Day in and day out. I missed interacting with Oliver greatly, but knew he was in good hands with you." Sure enough, there was a large computer with a holograph screen at a nearby desk. I tried bringing him down here once, but he refused to leave Eugene's side. He was already attached."

"You've been spying on us? That's kind of creepy," whispered Shayla. Danny was mesmerized by how cool the hologram was. It was a screen and keyboard made entirely of light that appeared to just be suspended in mid-air. He began to notice other oddities in the room as well. There was a robot that was crawling along the walls and cleaning them, an old gramophone playing songs from the 1920s, chemistry sets that were conducting tests automatically by themselves, and lots and lots of books. Tons of books, paintings, and statues from who-knows-when; artwork acquired by the military from countless wars and interactions from around the world. This command hub was like the distant past and the advanced future meshed into one giant cylindrical room. And in the middle of it stood the admiral dressed in dark blue coveralls holding his pet bonobo, a fresh cup of tea steaming calmly on the arm of his chair. He looked like a janitor with four stars on each collar, his hat resting on a bust of Albert Einstein.

"I was planning on staying down here, uninterrupted, continuing with my experiments, assuming that one day you would run out of food, try and swim off the island, kill each other, or something of that sort." The admiral continued. "And then, the pirates showed up, and my little TV show suddenly became much more interesting, but in jeopardy of ending once the entrance was destroyed. I certainly couldn't just stand by. I grew fond of all of you, your bravery, and ability to survive. So I made the decision that it was time to intervene."

"What happened to everyone else from the command?" Shayla inquired.

The Admiral wandered over to his towering shelves of dusty, old books. "It's been many, many years since someone else was here. This island was once an important stronghold for America during World War II, but in the years since it became one of the greatest, top secret laboratories for military and weapons research. This island isn't on any map, digital or print, in the world. We're a myth to the rest of the world. A conspiracy. The government slowly began cutting funds during the Cold War, until eventually it was deemed too important to stop but too expensive to continue funding. They gave us a choice: either stay with the base and protect it until funding picked up, faking your death, and never seeing your family again; or get re-assigned, hidden, and have a complete name and life-change. Well, everyone but me chose to be re-assigned. I occasionally interact with the absolute highest government officials via satellite, but other than that, I have devoted my time here to science and protecting the weapons and information here."

"We found a ton of those weapons upstairs," Miko grinned. "Thanks, by the way."

"A mere shadow of what we accomplished still remains here, Miko, for better or for worse. And any memories of who I was in the outside world is long forgotten." The Admiral ran his fingers along the layers of dust on the books. They clearly had not seen much attention recently. For just a moment, his mind was elsewhere, lost in the pages of his books or somewhere in a memory from long ago. "Well anyway, our funding was finally completely cut and the base was slowly decommissioned. Perhaps it was for the best…"

"You stayed all alone on an island for years and years because you *wanted* to?" Shayla's forehead formed tiny wrinkles as she struggled to comprehend why anyone would do that.

"One's duty is almost impossible to explain to outsiders, Shayla," the admiral sighed. "You may be aware that the best and worst of what we accomplished here was a mighty weapon. A bomb so powerful, that the possessor could tip the scales of world power with it. It was deemed too dangerous to move as every army in the world would lust for it if they knew it existed, and too critical to simply disable. And so it has remained here in its chamber with me as the guardian. Behold: the Super Nova." He pressed a button which opened up an overlapping deck in the center of the room. From underneath it arose a bomb the size of a RV. It had a bubbling, blue gel encapsulated in what appeared to be a glass tank, surrounded by a stainless steel case and buttons and lights alongside it. "The blue gel is a deadly chemical agent that makes napalm feel like sun tan lotion. The tip contains two triple-enriched uranium explosives which, by themselves, could wipe out the entire population of the state of Florida, but, combined with the gel, the effects are unpredictably genocidal. The back of the Super Nova contains ten computerized rockets that use accelerometers to hit its target within inches of where it's programmed to attack from miles away.

"Which leads us to our current situation with the pirates. There's only one other person on the planet who knows about the Super Nova and who knows about the existence and location of Zactrala Island. And he is the one who has lead the pirates here, no doubt."

"Captain Vasser," Asad gasped. "He is-"

"My son," Admiral Vasser hung his head in shame. "The last time I saw my family, Kerry was still a boy. I went into his bedroom when he was sleeping, and I told him goodbye for the last time. He tried following me to work the next day by hiding in my car, and I'm afraid he saw some documents regarding the island that he wasn't supposed to see. Over the years, I thought surely he would have forgotten. I was sorely wrong. I don't think he ever believed the story that the Navy put out about my death. He must have a deep seated hatred for me because I abandoned him and his mother, and I knew he would someday seek revenge. I'm sorry you were dragged into this."

Danny asked, "So what are we supposed to do about him? Can you talk to him?"

"I'm afraid not," the admiral admitted. "He is a Vasser, and we have a tenacity and drive to never give up. If he has come this far, it is safe to assume he is not to be reasoned with. And this is where I need your help." The Admiral turned to an old, wooden chest and began to fiddle with the lock. "You succeeded in stopping a few of them, but can you stop them all?"

"We can try," Danny gulped.

"Trying will not be enough," he managed to get one of the locks loose. "If my son and his men manage to get through, I will have no choice but to take extreme measures to prevent the weapon from leaving this island."

"What kind of extreme measures?" Eugene was terrified.

"If they find their way down here, then nothing will escape. Not the bomb, not any of you, and not even me." The Admiral finished opening his box, carefully lifting the lid. "So you have to make a choice: fight them off, steal their ship, and return to your homes, or give up now and be destroyed with me and the rest of the island."

"What if they kill all of us and take the weapon?" Cody asked.

"I have installed a pacemaker in my heart that wirelessly communicates with the self-destruct button. If anyone kills me and my heart stops beating, Zactrala Island will be destroyed as well. It's a measure that the government is unaware I have taken."

Asad voiced his uncertainty, "My friends, I must warn you, this will be extremely difficult. *Captain* Vasser arrived here with nearly one hundred men aboard the *Mogadishu*. Surely we are outnumbered."

"We'll fight," Danny said confidently. "The Castaway Kids never give up."

The admiral smiled. "I thought you might say that, Mr. Herrera. And that is why you'll need to take these with you." The admiral opened the chest and revealed three ball-shaped metallic objects. "I knew that you would need help, so I took the liberty of finishing development on some of our experiments for you to use. I hope they serve you well. This is for you, Shayla."

He handed Shayla the chest which had a name-plate on it with the word 'Goo-nades' on it. "What are these?" Shayla stared in awe.

"These are non-lethal grenades that use a tiny camera and face-recognition software to identify the location of its target. When activated, it explodes onto the faces of whomever is in a twenty-five foot radius. It produces a sticky, slightly toxic green goo that is a hybrid of hundreds of rare plant secretions. It quickly hardens and restrains its victim when exposed to oxygen. It is a great way to disable a group of enemies in a hurry with extreme accuracy. Just make sure your face is hidden when you detonate it. I call them Goo-nades."

"Neat!" Shayla exclaimed. She took the chest, which had two clips that hooked onto the back of her belt. "Thank you, sir."

"Next, I have something for Cody," the admiral walked over to a refrigerator size cabinet and pushed a button. Two doors opened with a hiss and smoke emitted from within. Inside was a black and green suit of armor. "This is a bullet proof performance-enhancing super suit. It is made of a material which is stronger than Kevlar and as flexible as a wet suit. It holds a six hour charge and its batteries are powered by micro-solar panels checkered throughout the suit, which is where it gets its green glow. It will stop bullets, go under water, and won't catch fire. It is my attempt at making a suit of armor that most resembles that of the mythological dragon, so I call it my 'Dragon-Skin Suit.' Oh, and it is custom fit and tailor made for you, Cody. I hope I got your measurements right. Go ahead, try it on."

Cody slowly stepped up to the cabinet. He ran his fingers along the chest and arms. "It feels like a snake," he said. He stepped into it, zipping it up with a long zipper-string in the back, like a surfer's wet-suit. "Cool!" He exclaimed. "It fits great!"

"Go ahead, try it out," the admiral handed him a crow bar. "Try and bend it."

Cody grabbed either end and tried with all his might to bend it, his face turning red. He grunted and gave up. "I can't..." He panted.

"Press the button on each shoulder," the admiral directed. Cody crossed his arms over his chest and simultaneously pressed both buttons. The suit made a slight electrical charge-up hum and the green micro-solar panels lit up under the exterior of the suit just enough to indicate that the suit was on. "Now, try it again."

Cody picked up the crowbar and easily bent it as if it were a golf club. The admiral picked up a magnum and pointed it at Cody. Oliver, still being held by the admiral's free-hand, covered his ears. The admiral pulled back the hammer on the pistol and took aim at Cody's chest.

"No! Don't!" Shayla screamed. It was too late. The admiral fired a controlled pair of shots right at Cody's sternum. Cody stepped back slightly, as if someone gently pushed him. He looked at his chest and inspected it with his hands.

"Not a scratch," he said in awe.

"Good," the admiral smiled and put the gun down. He picked up a pencil and wrote in a notebook, speaking out loud to himself what he was writing. "First...operational... test...satisfactory."

"That was your first test?!" Shayla yelled.

"Yes, I've been busy." The admiral said matter-of-factly. "It's over now, let's not dwell on the past. Pressing on. Miko, I have something for you. But might I first add: I thought your song was wonderful."

"Thanks," Miko blushed.

Admiral Vasser put Oliver down and pulled on one of the books on his book shelf. It was actually a switch that activated a nearby wall panel. The panel spun around to reveal what appeared to be a gun from a sci-fi convention. He took it down and presented it to Miko.

"What is it?" Miko asked.

"I call this a 'Laser-Tazer,'" the admiral beamed. "It uses light to electrically shock enemies from a distance. Simply turn the laser on, point it at your target, and pull the trigger. This knob on the side controls the power. It is extremely accurate from a very long distance. It, too, is powered by solar technology."

"Freakin' sweet!" Miko exclaimed. "I'm going to make some pirates dance!" She aimed the laser around the room. She accidentally pulled the trigger while it was pointed at a painting. It shook the frame and burned a line through the canvas. She pulled the weapon to the side, rattling books and shaking them off their shelf, setting some of them on fire. The admiral quickly grabbed a CO_2 bottle and put the fire out.

"Please be careful, Miko," the admiral put the fire extinguisher down.

"Sorry," Miko squeaked. "I figured it out now though."

"Okay, so where were we?" The admiral wiped some sweat from his brow.

"Does Oliver get a weapon?" Eugene asked.

"No," the admiral said. "But you do, Eugene. And you can use it to protect Oliver. Follow me." The admiral walked around the Super Nova to a separate glass room with a strange object on a pedestal. White smoke filled the room. Air from the device blew it ferociously out of the way, creating a column of clean air in front of it.

"Is that a blow dryer?" Eugene asked.

"In a way, yes," the admiral stated. "But a blow dryer with a small jet-engine equipped inside it. I call it an 'Air Blaster.' It's a hand-held cannon that pushes air with enough force as a focused mid-western tornado."

"It doesn't seem *that* powerful," Eugene said smugly as he nonchalantly walked in front of it.

"No, Eugene-!" The admiral tried to stop him, but Eugene flew violently against the wall on the other side of the room and was smashed face-first against the glass. He stayed stuck to the wall like a bug on a windshield as the air pounded against his back. The admiral dashed to the air blaster and removed the lever that was pulling the trigger. The air stopped blowing. Eugene was still stuck to the glass.

He said with his face still smushed into the wall, "Okay, you win. It's awesome." He fell hard to the floor. He walked back to the weapon and pulled it off the pedestal. He held it in his hands, still checking it out. "Thank you, sir. I promise to protect and serve Oliver and my friends with this if it's the last thing I do."

"Very well, Eugene." The admiral fixed Eugene's hair, which was standing up. "And now for you, Asad. I figured you would want to help with this fight as well."

"Of course, Admiral," Asad stood tall. "I know your son, and forgive me for saying this, but he has become an evil, evil man. I too have decided that I will do whatever it takes to stop him."

"I understand, Asad." The admiral said. "I have seen your dedication to your newfound friends, and I know that you are strong at heart. You are making a difficult choice to defend your beliefs, which is why I developed this for you." The admiral opened a briefcase labeled "B-KEMS." Inside resting in packing foam were what appeared to be a set of brass knuckles.

"Brass knuckles?" Danny asked. "My uncles have a pair of those. They say they're only for gangsters and New Jersey bouncers."

"To the untrained eye, yes, they appear to be the blunt instrument of force commonly known as brass knuckles," said the admiral as he put them on Asad's hands. "And they can absolutely be used as such. However, their main purpose is revealed when the user presses a small switch hidden where the fingers are. Stand back, and push the button, Asad."

Asad held his hands out in front of him with the brass knuckles on and pressed the small button on either one. When he did, a round force of energy created a honeycomb-like circle of light around it. The admiral explained, "These are 'Brass-Knuckle Electromagnetic Shields,' or B-KEMS for short. When objects, such as bullets or knives, come at you from one direction, they block it instantly. If you want to throw something at them or deliver a punch from your direction, the sensors re-calibrate themselves to allow the object through. For example-" The admiral picked up a small propane torch and fired it at Asad. The B-KEMS repelled the fire with ease. The admiral quickly fired the flames from Asad's side of the shield and they flared out with no resistance. The admiral then threw the torch at Asad from the front part of the see-through shield, and it, too, did not penetrate the circle of light. "Press the button again, and the shield retracts."

"Thank you, sir," Asad said. "This is truly the third best present I have ever received. My mother's violin and Miko's bow being the first two."

"I'll take that as a compliment," the admiral grinned. "Which brings us lastly, but certainly not least, to Danny. I have a very special gift for you, my boy." The admiral led them back to his chair where his tea was now cold. He walked around to the front of his desk where a cutlass rested on a display stand. He gently picked it up and held it out to Danny.

"Cool! A cutlass!" Eugene exclaimed excitedly. "Everyone in the military used to have one of those! Does it shoot out flames or glow in the dark or something?"

"I'm afraid not, Eugene," the admiral said. "This is my cutlass that was given to me by my father when he first became a chief petty officer in the Navy. When I eventually became an officer, I held onto it. My superiors wanted me to use the standard issued officer sword, but I preferred the cutlass. I have modified it significantly over the years."

Eugene pressed his face up close to it. "Does it fly? Or is it voice-activated? Or is made of kryptonite? Or adamantium? Or unobtainium?"

"The blade is pure diamond," the admiral continued. "But not just any diamond. It is diamond that was made from the ashes of my fallen colleagues who served bravely on this island. When they were cremated, I processed the ashes to make an extremely sharp diamond, which now edges the blade. So not only is it very powerful, it reminds me of those who have given the ultimate sacrifice for their mission. I carry them with me always. I now pass it on to you, Danny Herrera. This weapon only belongs to true leaders."

Danny slowly grabbed the gold hilted handle of the sword. He examined it as he rotated it in front of him. It felt comfortable, light, and strong, like an extension of his body.

"Thank you, sir." The light glimmered a speckled rainbow onto Danny's face. "I won't let you down."

Captain Vasser watched from his helicopter as dozens of pirates stormed through the blasted door into the mountain. Once they were all through, he gave the command to the pilot, "Fire the rockets!"

"But, sir," the pilot countered, "your men are in there."

"Seal the exit. We escape with the weapon or no one gets out alive." The pilot fired and caved in the side of the cliff, trapping the pirates and everyone else inside.

The ground shook above Danny's head. The Admiral checked the monitors and saw the men storming the entrance. "It appears the time to act is now."

17 THE RAID

The Salty Sea Dogs were now trapped inside the Zactrala mountain base, but continued to storm down into the tunnel that led to the command hub where the admiral and the Castaway Kids were hiding. This time, however, the admiral activated a computer. On the screen was a layout of the tunnel. The admiral then turned to the kids and asked, "Which one of you has exceptional hand-eye coordination?" Miko and Eugene both pointed to Danny.

"Danny's the best video game player out of all of us," Miko declared.

"Yeah," Eugene nodded. "He's won every video game tournament we've ever had. He wins at pretty much every contest that involves sitting down."

"Well then, sit in my chair and activate the booby traps as the pirates traverse the tunnel. Use your hands on the holographic keyboard to control the defense mechanisms. The red dots represent foreign objects in the tunnel. Those are the pirates," the admiral spoke quickly and feverishly. He was flipping switches on a nearby control board. "I have an idea in case they get through, but try and stop as many of them as you can. Godspeed, Danny." The admiral quickly moved up some stairs and began fiddling with a large white floor pad overlooking the lower deck.

"You can do it, Danny!" Shayla put her hand on his shoulder and smiled warmly.

"It's all you, bro," Cody gave a thumbs-up.

Danny took a deep breath and let out a huge sigh. Red dots began to appear on the screen, rushing down the stairs into the tunnel. The TV screens behind Danny showed images of what was happening in real time. Danny didn't dare to look. *This is just a video game...This is just a video game...*he told himself. *I'm just at Miko's house, on her couch, hanging out and playing video games. You got this, Danny, you got this...*

As the red dots finished swarming down the stairs, his friends crowded around him anxiously watching the pane of glass that was the computer screen. Danny stuck his hands into the holographic keyboard, gripping the virtual controls.

"He's not holding back, Danny," Asad whispered, a tremble in his voice as he stepped back from the screen, wide-eyed. "He is sending almost all of his men. You must stop them."

"Let's make something happen," Danny punched his right fist towards the two red dots in the lead. In the tunnel, a mechanical arm burst out of the rock face and punched the two pirates against the adjacent wall. Danny slapped his left hand, which moved the wall outwards, pushing the two pirates into the middle of the tunnel, where he again used the mechanical arm to punch them, knocking them out.

"Nice one!" Cody patted Danny on the shoulder.

In the tunnel, the pirates were both surprised and horrified at what they saw. The pirate who was leading the raid, Waled, a gangly Somalian with one ear, shouted, "The walls are alive!" They fired their assault rifles at the mechanical arm, shooting it in half. Waled threw a grenade behind the wall that was pushed out, and when Danny retreated it, the grenade exploded and destroyed the gears controlling it.

"Damn!" Danny shook his head. He scanned the screen as the red dots pushed forward. He twisted his hands as if he were turning a faucet on. "Let's see what these do."

The pirates were now on alert, and a panel of sprinklers opened from the ceiling and sprayed a cloud of pepper spray onto the group of pirates. Coughing, crying, and eye rubbing quickly ensued. "Cover your eyes!" Waled ordered. "Back up! Back up!" The pirates retreated slightly, but a dozen of them had been temporarily blinded, and one of them even accidentally fired his gun at other pirates. Waled quickly shot him to stop any further damage. He then ordered two of them to fire at the ceiling panel. Just then, Danny punched the blinded pirates with two more mechanical rock arms. After taking out a dozen of them, the remaining pirates destroyed the pepper spray sprinklers and the rock arms.

"Yeah, yeah, yeah! Awesome!" Shayla jumped up and down excitedly. "I know I should probably feel bad when others get hurt, but I don't! Yay, Danny!"

The admiral was still up one level typing furiously into a computer and clearing off a white platform. "Good show, Danny!" He yelled without looking up at them. "Keep it up!"

Danny began tapping his fingers in the hologram, like playing an invisible piano. This fired lasers inside the tunnel with each tap of his fingers. He was hitting pirates left and right. Some of them took cover behind the robotic arms they shot down.

Waled threw a smoke grenade towards the lasers.

"I can't see..." Danny was frustrated. "The sensors...they stopped working. The dots disappeared."

Miko was staring at the TV monitors behind him. "They threw a smoke grenade, Danny! Just keep shooting!"

He did. He wasn't very accurate though. The smoke

screen gave the pirates enough time to aim their shots and destroy the laser guns. They quickly kept moving down the tunnel.

"They're halfway here, Admiral!" Asad shouted.

"I'm almost done," he yelled back. "Try the pit, Danny!"

Danny opened up the floor which exposed a pit into a large spiked hole in the ground. Several pirates fell in, and Danny used another robotic wall to push five more down. He closed the pit and retracted the wall quickly so that he trapped two more pirates behind it. He was punching again, using the last two robotic arms.

Waled swung his assault rifle sling behind him and put a knife in his mouth, biting the blade. He ran straight towards the arms, jumping and dodging to avoid Danny's blows. Like an acrobat, he ran up the arm and straddled it like a wild bull. He grabbed the knife from his teeth and cut the hydraulics, shutting down one of the arms. He then jumped onto the second arm and did the same thing. He reloaded his gun as he yelled, "Forward men! We're almost there!"

Danny pulled out a few more walls, but the pirates anticipated them and were too quick. Danny then used the flamethrowers to pick off a few more. "That's it!" Danny called out. "I got nothing left! They're about to breach the command hub!"

The admiral ran down to where they were and placed a hockey puck sized electronic device on the floor and said, "It's ready. Grab the weapons I gave you and follow me."

At the end of the tunnel, only twelve Salty Sea Dogs remained. Waled spoke into his walkie talkie before entering. "Captain Vasser, Breacher Team 2. We've taken heavy losses… We are about to enter the command hub…Hullo? Captain, this is Breacher Team 2…" There was no response.

One of the other pirates, panting, chimed in, "There's no signal down here… We must continue with the mission. We have five minutes until contact."

After Waled's string of C-4 explosives shattered open a man-sized hole into the door, the pirates swiftly entered the command hub with their assault rifles drawn. There, the admiral and the kids stood up against the wall near the computer with their hands in the air.

"Don't move!" Shouted Waled, while the other eleven pirates pointed their weapons at the silent, unarmed kids and the admiral.

"Please don't shoot us," pleaded Shayla. "We surrender!"

Waled craned his neck to admire the Super Nova. He smiled a toothless grin. Into the radio he reported, "Captain, if you can hear me, I have eyes on the Super Nova. Commencing opening of the ceiling." He then moved to the control panel and, after some trial and error, he found the right button. There was a loud hydraulic hissing sound.

The ceiling to the command hub opened slowly like an aperture of a camera to the tropical skies above where Captain Vasser's helicopter was hovering.

Waled sauntered over to Asad. "You chose the wrong side, boy. Should've stayed with us."

Asad looked back at him with a cocky smile and responded, "You sure about that?"

On the radio, Captain Vasser spoke up. "Status report!"

"Captain, we found Asad and a group of kids! There's an old man with them!"

"An old man...?" There was a moment of silence on the captain's end of the radio. "Kill them. No time for prisoners."

"With pleasure, Captain." Waled jammed the barrel of his rifle into Asad's face and fired. He was surprised, however, that his bullet went right through the boy with no resistance. The pixels of the hologram that projected from the small round object on the floor became fuzzy. He stomped the device with his boot. "Bloody hell..."

His realization that he had been tricked was too late. The kids jumped down from the white platform located above and behind where the dozen pirates stood. Danny used his cutlass to take out two of them right away, slicing their assault rifles in half. Eugene used his air blaster to roll a heavy roman pillar, with a Julius Cesar bust on top of it, off the platform and onto three others, crushing them instantly.

Cody jumped on two others, punching them with the extra force his dragon skin suit provided for him. He fought with them, bent the barrels of their guns and knocked them out with two elbow hits to their temples.

Miko dropped to one knee and used her laser tazer to electrically shock the remaining five pirates, one of which was Waled. She grabbed onto Eugene's back, who shot his air blaster downward to propel the two of them into the air, and then down to the level where the pirates were. Miko pointed the laser tazer at them. "Don't even think about moving." Asad detached a coiled up rope from the wall and used it to tie up the pirates. He cut off the remainder and tossed it into his rucksack with the violins.

Shayla held her goo-nade up like a baseball. She scanned the room, trying to decide if and how to throw it. *Cody seems to need help, but so does Danny.*

Asad ricocheted rounds back at some pirates with his B-KEMS. Cody kneed one in the face, knocking him out. Then, the .50 caliber machine gun turret on the helicopter began shooting at Cody. He ran across the command hub dodging the bullets and pulling the attention away from the others, his dragon skin suit giving him extra strength and speed to maneuver through the space. Asad used his shield to protect Miko and Eugene from the flying bullets, many of them bouncing off carelessly and hitting the pirates who were tied up on the ground.

One of the rounds from the turret grazed Danny in the leg. He screamed.

Waled used this moment of weakness as his

opportunity to disarm Danny of his cutlass and cut his arm with a hunting knife. He did so with such speed that Danny didn't even see it happen. Danny let out another scream and dropped to the floor. Just as Waled loomed over him, about to finish him off, Oliver jumped on his head, clawing his face. Shayla saw this, panicked, and threw her goo-nade at the last remaining pirate.

With a loud 'splurt' sound, the goo-nade exploded, splattering Waled and Oliver with an extra strong, green goo. They both became stuck to the walls with the pirate getting the bulk of the explosion. The goo covered his mouth and nose, suffocating him. Oliver could breathe through his nostrils, but his mouth and body were completely plastered to the wall in what looked like a slimy cocoon.

Danny grabbed his arm and leg, putting pressure on his knife and bullet wound.

"Danny!" Shayla and the admiral ran down the stairs from the hologram platform. She kneeled down next to him. "Oh my yikes… Oh my yikes… Are you okay?"

"Yeah…I think so." Danny winced. "This sucks…"

The admiral ran to the other side of the command hub, taking cover from the bullets still being fired at Cody from the helicopter. Miko aimed her laser taser at the machine gunner, firing it into his eyes and blinding him instantly before falling to his death below. Captain Vasser barked orders at his pilot, "Lower! Lower! Get as close as you can! But don't shoot the Super Nova!" He turned to the six others in the chopper. They were his team of engineers who came along to properly hook the Super Nova to the helicopter. "Get the crane ready!"

"This way, kids!" The admiral gestured to an old oil painting of Odysseus tied to the mast of his ship. He positioned his eyes in front of the retina scanner. A green light momentarily illuminated his face and then the painting moved to reveal another passageway. The whir of the helicopter blades blew his hair violently, as well as papers and everything else not bolted down in the command hub. "This tunnel leads to shore. It's the only way out! Hurry!"

Asad kept his shields up, defending Eugene and Miko as they moved together as a unit towards the opening. Eugene looked back at Oliver, who was struggling to squirm free, still stuck in goo on the wall. "Oliver! I have to get Oliver! I can't leave him!"

"No, Eugene! There's no time!" Miko held him back, pulling him towards the secret exit behind the oil painting.

"No!" Eugene cried. "I have to save him! He's my best friend! I love you, Oliver! I'm sorry!" Asad and Miko yanked him into the tunnel.

Chaos...thought Danny in between breaths. *This is total chaos. This is exactly what Captain Vasser wants.*

Cody grabbed Shayla's arm and pulled her away from Danny. "Let's go!"

"Wait! What about Danny!?" Shayla pleaded.

"I'm fine. Just go!" Danny crawled under a stainless steel lab table for cover. His wounds left a trail of blood behind him. Cody carried Shayla over his shoulder into the tunnel, her outstretched arms in Danny's direction.

"Danny!" A tear fell from Shayla's eye as she faded down the dark tunnel out of sight. Danny was now alone in the command hub with a dozen dead pirates and the admiral hiding in the corner. The blades of the helicopter became increasingly louder, continuing to blow papers, beakers, vases, books, and other objects in the command hub into all sorts of directions like a wild tornado.

Captain Vasser and the rest of his team repelled from climbing wires into the command hub. *He doesn't see me*...thought Danny. *I have to keep fighting. I have to. My friends need me. They need time to escape.* Captain Vasser pointed an ivory-handled pistol at the admiral while the rest of his team began securing the Super Nova to the harnesses at the end of the helicopter's crane.

18 REUNION

"Stay right there!" Captain Vasser shouted. Bang! A shot rang out. Danny clenched his shoulders and froze. *Is the admiral okay?*

Creeping out from underneath the heavy table, Danny spied the admiral, who was nursing his now bloodied hand. The other pirates pulled ropes down from the helicopter and began fastening them to the Super Nova.

"Back away from the machinery, old man, or I'll put another hole in you." Undeterred, the admiral reached again towards the console to close the ceiling, but the captain knocked him flat on the ground with his robotic arm. His prosthetic leg pushed very firmly into his chest, breaking one of his ribs. He aimed his pistol directly at the admiral's forehead. "This is for what you did to my father."

"Kerry...? My god, it *is* you." The admiral struggled to form more words, but this was all he could muster. His lips and hands quivered as the captain lowered his weapon. "I almost didn't recognize you."

"Where did you hear that name?" Leaning closer and zooming in with his camera-eye, he examined the elderly military man in more detail. "Father?"

"That's right my son," the admiral whispered. "What on Earth happened to you? Your legs…"

"Never mind my legs, you're supposed to be dead! I thought you were dead!" Captain Vasser lowered his weapon slightly. "You're the reason I'm here..."

"Am I *truly* the reason you're here? Or have you gone completely mad, and tell yourself you're here for a nobler cause?" he asked. "I chose to stay behind when others abandoned their post. No one could possibly know I was still here. Except you..."

"Abandoned your *post*? You abandoned me! And mother!" The Captain swallowed hard. Water began to form on the lower part of his eyes.

Could this evil terrorist really have feelings? Danny thought. *Or is it just an act?*

"I'm sorry…truly. For I now see the results of my actions have made you more monster than man." Admiral Vasser sat up, still holding the gunshot wound on his shoulder. He winced. He gently put his hand on his son's pistol. "Then perhaps, I *am* the reason you're here. But now, you and your men need to leave."

Danny inched his way on his hands and knees to make a move and took cover behind a bookshelf. *This is my chance*, he thought. *The captain is distracted and the pirates are busy with the Super Nova.* He tried to roll over to spring himself up to his feet, but had to bite his tongue to hold back a scream. The pain was too great, he'd never make it to the captain without being shot. Or the exit. *I'm trapped… I'm going to blow up with the island and the admiral and these awful pirates…*

"Don't you see what your country has done to you, Father?" The captain pleaded, "Whether you realize it or not, they left you here to die. They destroyed our family. They deserve vengeance! Come with me and we'll take our lives back together!"

Danny spotted Oliver, still stuck to the wall. Only his bloodshot, scanning eyes and flaring nostrils were visible, the epitome of panic painted across his face. Danny grabbed his cutlass off the floor. He had an idea.

"No, son. You have it all wrong. This is what I chose, Kerry. I chose to stay and stand guard and devote my life to research, so that you and your mother could live in a safer world…then maybe we could have reunited on better terms. I was a fool because in my pursuit to rid the world of evil-doers, I created one in you."

Extending his fingers as far as he could, Danny dragged himself silently across the sleek, white floor. He pressed his wound against the cold deck to temporarily feel relief.

"You were my hero!" Captain Vasser shed a tear, gritting his teeth. "I wanted to strike the government back and make it hurt for taking you away from me! For taking my eye! And my arm! My *life*! And now…now I realize that you are *them*. You are part of the machine that made me who I am! You're responsible for more lives lost than I am! So which one of us is truly less human?"

Oliver spotted Danny's approach and watched him carefully.

"Innocent lives will be lost, Kerry! Can't you see? It's *my* responsibility. It's *my* burden, not yours. And I followed through with my choices, even if it meant hurting those I love. I created the Super Nova, and now it's my duty to keep it out of the hands of men who would use it for evil."

At the base of the wall, Danny reached up with his cutlass. He carefully cut away around Oliver's head. The goo had hardened, but it cut clean through with the point of his blade like butter.

"Step aside and let me finish what I came here to do!" The pirates tugged on the ropes and gave the signal. The bomb was secure.

"Never!" The admiral shot daggers with his eyes at his son.

The captain stood, coldly wiping the tear from his one good eye. He turned and joined the rest of the pirates, grabbed onto the ropes tied to the bomb, ready to be lifted up and out of the hub. "Then I have no father." Captain Vasser raised his pistol, aiming at Admiral Vasser.

Just then, Oliver jumped and latched onto Captain Vasser's face, biting furiously. He fired wildly in the air, losing his grip on the ropes. The helicopter began to rise. The pirates drew their weapons and aimed at Oliver, but could not fire at a target that was so close to their beloved captain in the event that they accidentally missed.

The captain pried Oliver loose and threw him across the room. He fired blindly at him but missed as Oliver quickly scurried behind a giant marble globe.

The scratch marks on his face were bleeding as he returned his attention to his father. The veins on Captain Vasser's neck pulsated with fury. Once more, the admiral reached for the button to close the ceiling. Captain Vasser gritted his teeth, "Good-bye, old man." With that, he shot the admiral twice, slumping him to the floor. "You fool, you've made your own tomb."

Danny's eyes widened. *He's dead…He killed his own father. There's no chance he's going to have mercy on me.*

With the bomb very near escaping out the top of the hub, Danny abandoned his stealth and leapt to his feet. In a moment of panic, he did the only thing he could think of: he hurled the cutlass like a boomerang towards the bomb. Up it sailed, spinning like a propeller flown loose from an old plane. Just above the bomb it went, slicing through the cables connecting it to the helicopter above. It froze in air for just a moment before hurtling downward. A couple of the pirates tried to jump clear, but they fell to their death instead. Captain Vasser, who was down below the bomb and watched Danny throw the cutlass, sprang out of the way on his prosthetic legs. When the Super Nova came down in a mighty crash, parts of the laboratory were crushed beneath it. The men who had held onto the bomb fared no better than those who jumped, their lifeless bodies contorted onto the cold floor. Only Captain Vasser remained standing on a surgical table, the helicopter losing its equilibrium above from the sudden weight shift.

"You!" The captain bellowed, pointing his pistol right between Danny's eyes. "You and your stupid little friends have been a pain in my side since we arrived. It's time I put you in your place." Danny gulped. Unarmed, he was helpless.

A radio crackled on the lapel of a crushed pirate. "Sir, we lost the cargo and the cables are snapped. We're having stability issues. Is everything all right down? Should we get the back-up ropes and cables from the ship?"

He snatched the mouthpiece off the shoulder of his fallen crew member to reply, still grinding his teeth together. "Yes! Just get what you need to get the Super Nova! I have some business down here to take care of!"

"Aye aye, Captain." The helicopter slowly rose and flew up and out the top of the command hub. Debris was everywhere. Now Danny and the captain were the only ones left. Oliver was nowhere in sight, and Danny's knife and gunshot wounds were beginning to take all the energy out of his body.

Where's Oliver? Danny's thoughts raced. *Maybe he's passed out somewhere from being thrown by Vasser...I doubt he can surprise attack him again, he'd be expecting it now. I have to stop Vasser before the helicopter returns. This is it. Kill or be killed.*

I wonder if everyone made it out of the tunnel okay...

19 THE TUNNEL

While the reunion between Captain Vasser and his father transpired back at the command hub, Asad and Miko ran the fastest down the long, musky tunnel that the admiral revealed behind the painting. There were only small work lights, no brighter than candles, strung up along the walls every twenty feet or so. Cody carried Shayla over his shoulder, who was still inconsolable. She cried into the back of Cody's dragon-skin suit. The floor was cement for the first hundred yards or so, but now it was coarse gravel and dirt. Eugene was the furthest behind, wheezing heavily.

They could hear a gentle lapping of water ahead, and distant sounds of the rumbling ocean. The cave was otherwise quiet.

"How much longer?" Eugene panted.

"I don't know," Miko called back. "Just keep running."

Cody stopped. He swung Shayla down from his shoulder so that she was standing and facing him. Without the suit, there would have been no way he could have carried her and run this far. "Shayla...Look at me Shayla..." Cody pleaded. Her blue eyes oozed tears that ran down her red face. "You need to concentrate. You need to run."

"I liked him, Cody," was all Shayla could say. "I really liked him. He's the first boy I've ever liked."

"I know. He'll be fine. We need to hurry."

"Guys!" Miko's voice echoed. "It's a dead end! This tunnel leads nowhere!"

Cody and Shayla ran to where Miko and Asad looked into what appeared to be a small lake. Hard rock lead up to it and walls surrounded it.

"Maybe we should swim across," Miko suggested.

"We can't. Look, there's a wall," Asad pointed out. Sure enough, at the surface of the water, about twenty feet away, was the wall of the cave.

"Why would the admiral lead us to a dead end?" Eugene asked.

"The same reason he'd make us leave Danny behind. He's a jerk," sniffled Shayla. "He doesn't care about us. He just doesn't want his son getting that super-bomb thing. He's going to blow up the island and we're all going to die. It's useless." Shayla laid face-down in the dirt, slowly running her hands along the surface of the ground.

"What's her deal?" Asad asked.

"Shayla, you need to snap out of it!" Cody yelled.

"Let's just go back," Eugene suggested. "We can get Oliver and Danny!"

"It's too dangerous. We have to get out of here." Miko ran her hands along the walls. "Maybe there's a trap door or a switch or something…"

Cody joined Miko feeling the walls for something. Anything. Eugene joined Shayla on the dirt, lying on his back and hopelessly staring at the ceiling. "I know how you feel, Shayla," Eugene said. "I miss my best friend, too."

Asad continued to stare at the water. "Do you hear that?" He asked.

"Hear what?" Miko responded, kicking the cave to test for false walls.

"The ocean…I can hear the faint sound of waves crashing over here." He said. "I think if we swim to the bottom of this water, it will take us outside into the ocean."

"That looks pretty deep, Asad," Cody said while he looked into the water. "There's no way to see where we're going. It's too dark. What if we get trapped down there?"

"I have a rope," he said, as he pulled it from around his waist. "I will go first. Then, if I reach the other side, I tug on the rope three times. If I need air, I will tug on the rope two times, and you can pull me back up."

He was already tying it around his waist before anyone could object. "Are you sure about this?" Miko asked.

"What else are we supposed to do?" Asad said. "Wait here until the admiral makes this our grave? Or Vasser follows us? My father would kill me if I die here." He handed the rope to Miko and Cody, who nodded to him.

Asad took a deep breath and jumped head-first into the water. Cody and Miko held onto the rope, giving him enough slack to swim deeper, but not too much to where they might let go of the rope.

The water was getting warmer. *Good*, Asad thought. *That means this is most-likely ocean water.* That realization gave him the confidence boost to swim a little harder. He reached the bottom, which was about sixteen feet from where he dove. His ears hurt from the water pressure.

Asad kicked hard off the cave wall at the bottom of the small lake towards the opposite side, hoping there was a way up and out. He did so blindly, as no light made its way down there. He let out a small amount of air, bubbles tickling his face as they surfaced.

Like he had hoped, there was no wall in his way as he paddled to the other side. He opened his eyes. Up ahead, there was a bright light coming down from the surface of the water. He couldn't see how high up the other side went, but swam frog-style towards it. *Sunlight!* He thought, *That has to be sunlight!*

More air escaped between his bulging cheeks. He began to feel light-headed. His hands, feet and face were numb. He pushed and pushed. His body began drifting upwards, his back scraping against the cave above him.

Suddenly, a school of fish swarmed him. Like a cyclone, they encompassed him. His body wriggled around. He turned and flipped and tried however he could to get the tiny fish away from him. They nibbled his skin and blocked the light from the sun. Asad lost his direction.

The rest of the air in his mouth escaped. The school of fish swam away. Asad re-aligned himself. He felt weak and dizzy. The rope around his waist wasn't tugged during the foray. *I can still make it…*

He twisted himself upside-down and pulled along the ceiling of the cave through the water. He grabbed onto seaweed and jagged rocks to pull himself faster. The light was just a few feet away, the sounds of the ocean dominating.

He made his ascent towards the foamy white ocean surface, kicking with every last ounce of strength he could muster. Closer…Closer…He gagged on swallowed water. His eyes began to close…

"Why is he taking so long?" Miko asked Cody, who was transfixed on the rope in the water. "He's been down there for a while now. Maybe we should pull him up."

Shayla was now pacing back and forth. "Oh my yikes…Oh my yikes…We're doomed! We're going to die!"

Eugene was in the fetal position on the ground, rocking back and forth. "I wish I had my cape back…I wish I had my cape back…"

"Just wait," Cody said to Miko. "Give him just a little bit longer…"

A moment later, there was a tug at the rope.

"Asad!" Miko exclaimed. "He's alive!"

Another tug.

"Pull him back!" Miko yelled. "That's two tugs!"

"Wait!" Cody insisted.

Another tug.

"That's three!" Miko hugged Cody and jumped up and down, still holding the rope. "He made it!"

Cody turned to Eugene and Shayla. "Come on, you guys, we have to keep moving. Pull yourselves together."

Eugene and Shayla sighed heavily at the same time. They looked to each other for guidance. "I guess it's time to be strong, Eugene. For our friends," Shayla lamented.

"Yeah, I guess you're right." Both Eugene and Shayla stood up, embarrassed. "Sorry for freaking out there for a bit, guys," Eugene apologized.

"You're right, Cody," Shayla said boldly with a sudden surge of confidence. Cody recognized this body language whenever Shayla would get really mad, which was rare. "If they think they can take Danny from me, they've got another thing coming." There was a glimmer of determination in her eye. Deep inside, something had changed. "Come on, Eugene, this is what Oliver would have wanted."

"I'll go next," volunteered Miko. She handed the rope to Eugene and Shayla, who now held onto it with Cody. She took a deep breath, pinched her nose and jumped in feet-first.

The cold water gave her goose bumps. Miko grabbed the rope and easily pulled herself along it down and under the cave tunnel, the temperature getting warmer as she neared tropical waters. She pulled herself quickly to the other side, the school of fish bothering her a bit, but not slowing her down. Seeing Asad's hand reaching into the water, she grabbed it. He yanked her up hard as she gasped for air.

"You all right, Miko?" he asked. She didn't realize it at first, but she was on top of him. They were lying on a jagged rock that had a sewer-cover size hole that Miko just came out of. Asad had tied the rope to a nearby piece of broken pier that jutted from the rock. Waves crashed up against them. They were on the shores of Zactrala.

"Yeah…I'm good…." She was trying to catch her breath. An inch away from Asad's face, she was staring into his deep, dark eyes. His dimples were revealed in his cheeky smile. She gazed upon him renewed, like he was her hero. "Hello…" Was all she could think to say.

"Hullo…" He laughed back. After an awkward moment of ogling at each other, Asad spoke up. "Perhaps we should let the others know you're here."

"Oh. Yeah. Uhhh…right." Miko was flustered and embarrassed. She tugged the rope three times.

"She made it!" Shayla exclaimed at the other end of the rope.

"Good," said Cody. "You're next Shayla."

"Let's do this." She pinched her nose and jumped in.

"Cody?" Eugene asked.

"Yes, Eugene?"

"I'm scared."

"Don't be." Cody reassured him. *Eugene, now's not the time to be scared*, he thought. "Asad and Miko made it to the other side just fine. Shayla will go, and then you, and then me."

"I'm still not a very good swimmer."

"It's not swimming, it's more like underwater pulling," said Cody.

"Oh." Eugene bounced this idea around his head. "Hey Cody?"

"Yes, Eugene?"

"I stink at pulling, too."

"Well, Eugene, I don't know what to tell you." Cody was getting impatient, trying to focus on the rope. "You're gonna have to learn real quick 'cause it's almost your turn."

The rope was tugged three times.

"All right, Eugene," Cody stepped aside and placed his hand on his back. "You're up."

"I can't…I can't do it!"

"Why not?"

"I can't hold my breath for more than fifteen seconds.

My doctor said I have the lungs of a guinea pig."

"This is maybe a minute. Tops," said Cody. "C'mon Eugene, you can do this."

"No, I can't! I'll drown! Just… Just leave me behind."

Cody threw his hands in the air with frustration. "Damn it, Eugene!" Cody stood there, pondering. "All right, I have an idea. Come here. I'm gonna tie the rope to the both of us, and I'll use my dragon-skin suit to swim us both to the other side."

"But it'll take too long, I can't hold my breath for a minute."

"It'll only take fifteen seconds using the suit. I promise."

"Promise?"

"Yes."

"Promise-promise?"

"Yes, Eugene! Come here!" Cody grabbed Eugene and in one swift movement, tied the rope around the two of them, grabbed Eugene's air blaster from his back, and jumped in the water.

The moment they got under, Cody aimed the air blaster upwards and fired. The blast propelled them downwards like a water jet. They bounced onto the cave floor, then Cody re-aimed it at the wall and fired, blasting them at an intense speed towards the other side.

The school of fish couldn't keep up with them, and they even cut through some seaweed. Cody then aimed the air blaster downwards for the final shot, pulled the trigger, and like a dolphin surfacing to catch a jumping fish, the two of them flew eight feet over the surface of the water and crash landed hard on the rock. They had flown over the others and smacked down clumsily, Eugene landing on Cody. They both coughed up water.

Cody asked Eugene, panting, "How long was that?"

"Eleven seconds…"

"See?" Cody exhaled. "I told you."

The others ran over to the two of them, smiling and cheering at their awesome entrance.

"Wow! That was so cool!" said Miko. "Great job, Eugene! Way to use your head!"

"Thanks," Eugene answered. Cody rolled his eyes and put his arm around Eugene. The celebrations quickly subsided, however, when Cody realized what was just fifty feet away in the water.

The *Mogadishu*.

The ship was moored by huge nylon lines to rocks and stakes in the ground, as well as an anchor that had chain-links the size of hula hoops. It towered over the kids. The brow leading to the ship was being pulled up by several pirates on the other side, their backs turned to the five kids.

They craned their neck up to look at the ship. Waves smashed up against its hull, barely swaying the monstrous structure. "This is it." Eugene said. "There's no turning back, is there guys?"

"No, Eugene," answered Cody. "This is the only way."

"This is a big ship…" Muttered Miko in awe.

"I'll tear them to pieces! How do we get in there?" asked Shayla.

"I know the way," said Asad.

"Then what do we do?" asked Eugene.

Cody took his eyes off the *Mogadishu* and planted them on Eugene.

"We kill us some pirates…"

20 SHOWDOWN

Back inside the command hub, Captain Vasser checked the magazine of his pistol. He was out of ammo. He tossed the weapon aside and unsheathed a sword of his own. Danny dared not move from under the fallen lab table.

He still doesn't see me yet...

The captain scanned the rubble of what used to be the command hub. He moved quickly and purposefully, like a snake searching for a wounded mouse in tall grass. His prosthetic legs gave him a bouncing rhythm, like a boxer bobbing and weaving in the middle of the arena. Vasser yelled to the whole room, "All right, kid, so you've managed to keep the weapon here a little bit longer! The Stallion will be here shortly with another crane and your efforts will be for naught! You've simply delayed the inevitable! So why don't you just come on out and make this easier for the both of us?" The captain waited. He listened for a response.

Silence.

Danny was trying to think of a plan. *I need to get to the tunnel entrance behind the painting. I can barely move with this damn bullet wound bleeding all over me and this cut on my arm.*

Danny peeked around the table at Vasser, but quickly retreated so as not to give away his position. He was sweating profusely and trying not to whimper in pain.

"Very well then, you can die here along with your friends." Captain Vasser continued to search the command hub, swishing his sword coolly in the air as he proceeded. "Your friends, dear child, are most likely already dead. I hired some of the most desperate, ruthless, loyal men Somalia has to throw away. They have lives and families they want to go home to and they'll be damned if some snot-nosed punks try to stop me from achieving my goal and safely returning them from whence they came.

"Why don't you come out from wherever you are hiding and let's chat, shall we? Let's get to know each other. You've only got a few minutes left to live anyways, we may as well make your last moments pleasant. I promise I won't kill you, I'll simply abandon you. It's much worse." The captain circled the desk from which Danny earlier controlled the booby traps. "Were you the one who controlled this clever death machine my father invented? If you were, I can only assume that you're American. I know Asad took an awful liking to you, and I know he has a soft spot for the good ol' US of A. It's a shame he'll never see the states…You see, I, too, am an American. Just like you. A proud one at that. Which is why I must get revenge on the US military for wronging me and so many others like me. Poor medical attention. Lying day after day after day. Taking my father from me. Something he himself was too blind to realize. A nice shock to the system is exactly what the government needs to restructure their broken empire. If an evolution will never occur, a revolution is the next natural step."

If he keeps talking, Danny thought, *then maybe he won't hear me crawl over to the secret exit.* Danny began inching towards the painting, being careful not to make any sudden moves and staying in the shadows.

"I'm not exactly what you picture when you think of a

pirate, am I?" Vasser stopped for a moment to examine himself in a cracked mirror. "I am the *faceless* enemy within. Today's pirates aren't from the Caribbean and have swashbuckling romantic adventures. Far from it. It's ugly. It's struggle. It's survival of the fittest."

The captain jumped onto the computer table. He faced the cables coming in and going out of the back ports of the control unit. "You know, if I were to incorrectly slice these wires, there's a very good chance I could get electrocuted. However, if I strike quickly and in the right spot with enough force, I can cut them all without feeling a thing." The captain leaned back and raised his sword with his bionic arm, a mechanical whir purred as he did. He swished his sword once at the large bundle of cables in the back of the computer. They fell to the ground, cleanly cut. The computer's holographic screen, having now lost power, flickered out. "There we are."

Danny used this opportunity of the captain being distracted to hustle behind a statue of Zeus holding his Aegis shield. He was now only feet away from the painting and the door that hid behind it. He noticed something sparkling in his peripheral vision: his diamond cutlass. He gripped it, and waited for the right opportunity.

The pirate captain jumped down from the computer desk. He continued to stroll about the round room swinging his sword as if he were swinging a cane on a nice sunny day in the park. "Permit me to tell you, as we continue to wait for the return of the helo, a sea story about the day I came to realize who I was truly meant to be. One day on the ship I was stationed on, the USS *Montebello*, or the 'Mighty Monty' as we nicknamed her, we were cruising about the middle of the Atlantic Ocean in a common shipping lane. I was on watch as the officer of the deck at the time, and it was an unusually hot February afternoon. It was an uneventful watch, as most of them are, until suddenly a quartermaster claimed he saw something floating in the water up ahead, port side. I peered through the binoculars and sure enough, I saw hundreds of cows floating in the waters ahead.

"As you can imagine I was as confused as anyone would be at such a sight. As we came closer, we slowed the ship to about two knots and observed what appeared to be the wake of a recently passing cargo vessel. An operations specialist received a message that said a merchant vessel was having issues staying afloat, and was forced to jettison some of its cargo. Apparently their cargo was bovine in nature. What I found interesting is that some of the cows were swimming, which you would be surprised at how skilled they are at doing so. Other cows were already dead. Did you know that dead cows float? I didn't. I found it terribly fascinating and couldn't help but smirk a little. For you see, it wasn't all bad news, because right as our bow passed the animal graveyard, I saw large, dark shadows moving towards the cows under the surface of the water. They were sharks. Dozens of them. And they came to feed.

"The sharks saw the perfect opportunity for a feast and took it. It must have been the luckiest day in their lives. The conning officer, had the audacity to say, 'Those poor cows! How could the sharks do that to them! Shouldn't we help them?' I tried explaining to her that there was nothing we could do at this point, but some people have more trouble accepting fate than others. I ordered that the Mighty Monty change course and plow through the cows, cutting them up in our propellers. That way they didn't have to suffer the pain of being eaten alive or drowning to death. So we did, and a trail of red blood mixed into our light blue wake. The conning officer called me a *monster*. I suggested we instead be happy for the sharks, who I like to think are still alive today, oh so many years later, thanks in part to the beef we helped put in their stomachs. And after many years of thinking back at that event, I finally realized the importance of that day. *I am a shark.*

"I feed off of those who have fallen victim to those

they trust. When I see the weak, I see opportunities. When others feel sympathy, I laugh. I am strong when need be, but know when to work smarter, not harder, just like the sharks. Does anyone in their intelligent mind blame the shark for doing what's best for their survival? Why should the demise of hundreds of stupid cows be a hindrance on those destined for greatness? I am a shark, boy, and you're just a castaway cow, waiting to be chopped up and eaten."

At that, Danny leapt from behind the statue and pointed his sword at Captain Vasser. "Nobody calls me a cow and gets away with it!"

Taken aback, Vasser stopped in his tracks and examined the sight before him. "Well, well, well! It seems as though I've struck a nerve!" The captain smirked a crooked smile as his eye-lens focused on Danny and he raised his own sword. "Surrounded by some of the most advanced technology America's Navy has developed, and here we are holding blunt instruments of olde. Now be a good lad and stand down, boy. You won't win this fight."

"I'm not afraid of you," Danny growled. "You're nothing but a bully. I've got news for you, Cyclops, I've been bullied my whole life. And you met me at a real bad time, Captain. Since I've landed on this island, I feel really good about myself and my friends and who I am, and I'm not going to let bullies tell me what to do anymore! Even if I die trying…"

"Is that right?"

"Yeah that's right! I'm not going to let you take that bomb and hurt anyone else!" Danny sidestepped around the captain, limping a bit on his bad leg. The adrenaline pumping through his body masked the pain. Danny winced but kept his posture.

"Don't wince, boy! Wincing is a red flag to the enemy that you're weak!" Vasser hissed. "Besides, you can't even begin to imagine the meaning of the word pain!" Captain Vasser leapt forward and kicked Danny hard in the chest with all his might, his prosthetic leg bouncing Danny into the air briefly before smashing through a glass display case full of Egyptian artifacts.

The added strength of the captain's leg alteration flung Danny twice as far than if he were kicked by an ordinary man. "You see, boy, you stumbled upon an opportunity to become great merely by stupid chance," Vasser continued. "Your pain is a symptom of something that happened at random. Whereas I *created* my opportunity. Pain is the driving force of what I do, not the effect of poor timing on your part. You're in the way of my plans, boy, and I intend to move you and your little friends out of my way by whatever means necessary!"

Vasser raised his sword and swung it down on Danny, who was still recovering on the floor covered in glass. In a flash, Danny blocked Vasser's attack by raising his cutlass above his head and striking his sword against the pirate's. Danny would have been dead if he waited just a half-second longer to react. "My name is not 'boy!'" Danny yelled. "It's Danny! Danny Herrera!"

Danny stood tall, covered in glass and cut all over. He screamed what he thought was his war cry as he charged forward at the ruthless pirate, swinging his sword clumsily like a tennis racket. Captain Vasser chuckled lightly as he walked backwards, blocking every advance Danny made towards him. "Fencing team, Naval Academy, two years." Vasser boasted. He jumped up and over Danny like a kangaroo, flipping and twisting in the air like a gymnast. He landed behind Danny, and quickly proceeded to disarm him.

Danny now stood facing the captain without a weapon.

"You show a lot of courage, Danny Herrera." Vasser admired. "But now you stand unarmed and hopeless in a fight that isn't even yours."

"When you came to my island, and messed with my friends, you *made* it my fight," Danny retorted.

"Danny!"

From the opposite side of the command hub, the

admiral had sat up and was pointing a grappling hook gun at his son. He fired. A metal hook and wire flew towards the captain and knocked his sword out of his hands. Danny took this opportunity to tackle Vasser. He couldn't help but recall his football training he had with Cody as he bent his knees and charged up towards the captain's torso, following through with his motion forward and wrapping his hands around his waist. He slammed the captain back into a large Greek vase, which caved in and broke into pieces, dust flying everywhere.

The captain grabbed Danny by the throat with his robotic arm. He squeezed hard, attempting to choke him to death. Danny tried pulling the captain's hands away, but to no avail. Vasser lifted him up so high that Danny's feet were now dangling off the ground. He grabbed Vasser's camera-eye and pulled it out of his socket. Wires flailed from the hole in his head as Vasser screamed in pain. He used his free hand to cover it up and apply pressure. Danny's face turned red and purple as Vasser squeezed harder with his bionic arm.

As Danny's eyelids began to close, he saw Oliver emerge from a pile of rubble. And in his hands something sparkled.

It was his diamond-edged cutlass.

Oliver tossed the weapon to Danny and with his last ounce of strength, Danny reached up and caught the sword, then brought it down as hard as he could on Vasser's bionic arm. It sliced right through it. Danny collapsed to the ground, tearing the still-gripping hand from around his neck and tossing it aside. He gasped for air as he watched Vasser drop to one knee and scream.

"Ahh! You little devil! Look what you did to me!" Vasser examined what remained of his now missing arm with his one good eye and a horrified expression on his face. Danny towered over him with his cutlass extended just inches from Vasser's face.

"It's over, Vasser," Danny rubbed his red throat, his

skin color slowly restoring itself. "Radio your men to give up the ship and let my friends go."

"And what are you going to do if I don't? Kill me?" Vasser growled from between his grit teeth. He then laughed at Danny. "You are the spawn of an America more concerned with its own comfort than real progressive action. You're too soft to take a life."

"I'm also a proud member of the video game generation," Danny raised the cutlass back. "And I'm desensitized to violence."

A look of horrifying realization came over Vasser's head as Danny swung the cutlass at his neck. Vasser quickly ducked and swept Danny's feet out from under him using the hook of his prosthetic leg. Danny fell to the ground and Vasser ran to the oil painting, jumping over rubble, tables, and more artwork. He turned back to Danny and the admiral one last time. "Farewell, Father. And Danny," Vasser stared Danny right in the eye. "You've succeeded in delaying my plans, but you will only be remembered as a speed bump, and nothing more."

Danny sprinted towards him but it was too late. Vasser ripped the retina scanner off the wall as he went into the tunnel and the door closed behind him. Danny tried pulling on the painting door, but it was hopeless. He spun around and scanned the command hub.

I'm trapped...

Oliver stood in the middle of the room, clutching his hurt arm. Danny scooped him up and rubbed his head. "Good boy, Oliver, good boy." They hugged. Danny then turned his attention to the admiral, who was lying against a control panel, barely moving. "Admiral Vasser, are you okay?"

"No Danny..."

"You saved my life," Danny bent down and held his hand.

"I know, Danny, which is why it breaks my heart to do this-" The admiral slowly closed his eyes and grew still.

Two beeps emanated from the admiral's pacemaker. Alarms and red lights went off.

"What did you just do?" Danny panicked. "What did you just do?!"

A female's voice came over a loudspeaker: *"Attention Zactrala Island personnel. Super Nova self-destruct sequence initiated. Please exit the vicinity of the island in accordance with emergency evacuation plan Delta 24601. Ten minutes remaining."*

"You can't do this!" Danny shook the admiral's body, but it was no use. He was already dead. A single tear rolled down Danny's cheek.

I'm doomed.

21 THE *MOGADISHU*

While Danny and Captain Vasser had their duel in the command hub, Asad had huddled the others in a circle and laid out a plan to take over the *Mogadishu*. There were sentries standing guard, but luckily most of the crew was concentrating on receiving the Super Nova back aft on the flight deck. The element of surprise was on their side.

After they went over the plan, the kids split up. Cody powered-up his dragon-skin suit and jumped from rock to rock, plunging into the water while making a very little splash. He set his sights on the anchor chain leading into the "bull nose," a fairlead on the bow of the ship that guides the anchor's chain into the ocean. He swam smoothly across the marine, his eyes protruding like a crocodile stalking its prey. He waited at the point where the chain met the water.

Meanwhile, Asad and Miko ran along the shoreline, tracking a small speed boat with two armed sentries aboard, circling and patrolling the *Mogadishu*. Miko hid while Asad waved his arms and jumped up and down, yelling to the small boat, "Hey, over here! It's me, Asad! I give up! Please, take me back!"

The two guards, guns pointing at Asad, turned the

motor so they went straight towards the surrendering boy. "Well, well, well…" One of the guards scoffed. "Look who's come crawling back."

"You have a lot of nerve showing your face, Asad. The captain will be most displeased," the other guard said.

"Displeased with *me*?" Asad said. "He'll be more displeased with *you* for abandoning your post."

"What?" they responded, confused. "We've done no such thing!"

"Not yet."

At that moment, Miko jumped up from behind a rock and fired her laser tazer beam at the two guards with perfect accuracy. They convulsed and stiffened up, writhing in pain before falling off the boat and into the water.

Asad turned to Miko with a beaming smile. "Brilliant!" They hugged. Miko held onto him a little longer than perhaps was appropriate at the moment. Asad cleared his throat and backed off.

"Hehe…sorry…" Miko laughed nervously.

"It's okay. Let's go." Asad jumped in the boat, helping Miko get in as well.

While this happened, Shayla and Eugene were positioned across from four guards on the forecastle (front of the ship). They watched the armed guards who were smoking, and guarding the only ladder that hung over the side and down the hull of the *Mogadishu*. At that moment, however, the ladder was bundled up on the deck, only feet away from the Salty Sea Dog sentries. "We need to get rid of those guards," Eugene whispered.

He pulled out his air blaster and positioned it on his shoulder, aiming at the guards. They were way too far away to hit them with any accuracy from the shore, and the air wouldn't be strong enough to knock them out by the time it traveled such a distance. Instead, Shayla pulled out her box of goo-nades. Two left. She grabbed one and closed the box. "Ready?" she whispered to Eugene. "There's only a five second delay before the facial recognition is activated, so this has to be perfect."

He nodded once in response. Shayla activated the goo-nade and tossed it in the air towards Eugene, like a coach lobbing a softball to a player for an easy hit. Eugene pulled the trigger and shot the goo-nade as it fell in front of his air blaster. The goo-nade launched towards the four guards. Eugene and Shayla watched as it soared high into the sky, then descended onto the deck in the middle of the guards. There was no time for them to respond because the instant the goo-nade landed, the facial recognition locked onto them and the goo exploded onto their faces. They hopelessly grabbed at the sticky substance and hit the deck, suffocating within a couple of minutes.

Eugene and Shayla high-fived. They gave a thumbs-up to Cody who was still waiting in the water. He gave a thumbs up back and pulled himself up the anchor chain. He moved with the speed and agility of a ninja assassin. Once he pulled himself through the bull nose and onto the front deck, he ran to the ladder and released it over the side.

Miko and Asad steered the speed boat over to Shayla and Eugene, picking them up, and driving the four of them to the ladder that Cody had just put down on the starboard side. Cody began stripping the outer clothes off the pirates, and putting them on himself as a disguise. One by one, Shayla, Eugene, Miko and Asad ascended the ladder and came aboard the *Mogadishu*. Cody handed pirate disguises to everyone except Eugene.

"How come I don't get a pirate costume?" Eugene asked.

"Because, there are only four here," Cody said. "Besides, even if there were enough, you're too short to pass as a pirate from far away anyways."

"Aw man," Eugene moped. "Can I at least get a gun?"

"No guns," Cody answered firmly. "They're too loud. We can't draw attention to ourselves. No one knows we're on board, let's keep it that way."

"Follow me," Asad said as he activated his B-KEMS, crouching down and moving forward. Miko, Shayla, Eugene, and Cody followed, respectively.

They moved inside the "skin" of the ship as they swiftly and quietly traveled aft. There weren't many more Salty Sea Dogs hanging around, as most of them were awaiting the arrival of the helicopter on the flight deck.

Asad led the way, using his shields as a first defense. Miko fired her laser tazer at pirates roaming the decks. Shayla held tightly to her one remaining goo-nade. Asad and Miko continued to take down the rest of the crew one-by-one, while Cody stealthily ran around beating up and choking out any and all lingering pirates. Eugene fired his air blaster at anyone who ran up behind them. When they passed the galley, three pirates snuck up on them. Eugene blasted them like dominoes. The kids moved smoothly and methodically throughout the ship. They moved as one and stayed close.

Cody was the only one who went rogue. He moved on the port side while the others were on the starboard side.

The whole ship smelled of dank, musty algae and salty body odor. There were still some remnants of when it was a military ship, such as some of the orange life vests that had a US flag on them, the dinner plates with the Navy emblem on it, and the "Loose Tweets Sink Fleets" propaganda poster. The pirates had otherwise made it their home. There were random clothes drying on pipes and overheads, folding chairs stolen from a cruise line on the mess deck, a large blue Somalia flag with a white star in the middle painted on the floor of the quarterdeck. Trash and alcohol bottles were stuffed into angle irons and scattered throughout. Pots and pans and cups were tied to strings, random hatches, pipes, and handles throughout the boat. Shayla almost screamed when they moved through one passageway that was covered in fish heads, bones, lobster shells, blood, and all sorts of other animal body parts. That was where the pirates prepared their live catches before bringing them into the kitchen for cooking. Light bulbs flickered eerily and as the boat gently swayed and bobbed in the water, it creaked loudly like un-oiled gears grinding against each other.

Cody, on his solo mission to find stragglers, followed the sound of the engines rumbling. It led him down to the bottom of the ship where he came across a lone door with a wooden sign on it. On it were words crudely etched in with a knife:

Cody very slowly and carefully opened the door to the room. Inside was a hammock with a bear-sized, bald, red-bearded man sleeping in it. On the floor was a wooden barrel that had vomit bits around the rim. The room smelled like a hospital inside a dumpster. There was a toilet out in the open and a sink with a mirror above it. Greasy coveralls and exercise weights were piled into a corner. A ceiling fan whirred and wafted the scent of vomit towards Cody. A dart board with knives in it was screwed into the bulkhead.

Cody decided that this sick man posed no threat to

their mission at the moment, so he grabbed a nearby rope. He tied the rope to a pipe outside the room, and grabbed the doorknob to close it and tie the other end of the rope to it. That way, when the man did wake up, he'd be locked inside his room. However, as Cody was pulling the knob towards him to close it, he noticed that on the mirror in the man's room hung a red cloth.

"Eugene's cape..." Cody whispered in disbelief. He tiptoed towards the cape and gently lifted it off the mirror's corner. The whole time he did, he was monitoring Mu'mmar's snoring. He took long, slow breaths. He sounded like a pig with asthma. Cody was gently tiptoeing to the exit with the cape in hand when a voice came over the radio resting on the sink.

It seemed to be Captain Vasser yelling at the helicopter pilot.

"Yes! Just get what you need to get the Super Nova! I have some business down here to take care of!"

Cody froze. The captain sounded angry. Mu'mmar awoke at the sound of the radio. He rolled over to his other side, reaching for it and mumbling something that Cody couldn't fully hear. "Damn mushrooms...If I was on the island...I'd show 'em...Home by now."

Mu'mmar lowered the volume on the radio then rolled over to return to his slumber.

Phew! Cody thought. *That was too close...*

He started again towards the door when he heard a voice grumble deeply. "Where do you think you're going?" Mu'mmar spun around in his hammock and threw a hidden dagger at Cody all in one quick movement. It stuck to the back of his armor, but only a little. It didn't hit skin and Cody pulled it out pretty easily.

Damn! He did see me! Cody pulled the pirate disguise he was wearing off and tossed it aside. *No use trying to hide now...*

"What?" Mu'mmar looked stunned. "That should've killed you!"

"Dragon-skin suit," Cody said confidently. "Sorry, but this cape isn't yours. It belongs to my friend Eugene, and I'll be taking it back to him now."

"I'd like to see you try," Mu'mmar was standing now. "That's my favorite sweat-rag. I use it to wipe the sweat under me armpits."

Cody shoved the cape in his back pocket, then got into a fighting stance, putting his fists up. "Fight me for it."

Mu'mmar let out a thunderous laugh. "You've got to be joking! I'd squash you like a bug!"

"No joke. Let's do this."

Mu'mmar sobered up and examined the boy in front of him. "Okay, suit yourself. But I'm not going to go easy on you just 'cause you're a kid. You've killed a lot of my men, and it'll be a pleasure throwing your corpse overboard!" Mu'mmar lunged at Cody with a haymaker punch. Cody put his hand up and caught Mu'mmar's fist in the palm of his left hand. "What the hell?"

"My turn." Cody punched Mu'mmar square in the jaw, who leaned back from the force. Cody pulled Mu'mmar back towards him and punched him again. He then let go and rained a flurry of left and right elbow hits to the sides of Mu'mmar's enormous head, followed by multiple left and right hooks to his kidneys.

Mu'mmar stumbled back and bumped into the wall. Cody had him trapped. He jumped up and wrapped his hands around Mu'mmar's head, pulling it down and repeatedly kneeing the pirate in the stomach, chest, and face. He then threw the burly pirate down to the ground behind him, returning to his fighting stance.

Mu'mmar spit out a tooth onto the deck. Cody caught his breath while monitoring the damage he had just inflicted. Mu'mmar staggered to his feet, dizzy, grunting, and in a lot of pain. "You little weasel...I'm going to kill you."

"Ready for round two?" Cody smirked. Just then, the lights on his suit began to flicker. The hum of electricity faded. Then it turned off. Cody smacked the shoulder buttons a few times.

Nothing happened.

He looked down at his forearm display: LOW BATTERY.

"Uh oh..." was all Cody could think to say.

Mu'mmar laughed maniacally. "Not so strong without your little gadget, are we?" He wiped blood from his mouth and put his fists up. "Now, let's try this again."

This time his right-handed haymaker launched Cody backwards. He blocked it, but the force was so strong it still made him hit the wall with enough force to break a valve off a fire main pipe. Sea water sprayed everywhere. Mu'mmar grabbed Cody's wrist with one hand and the back of his suit with the other and tossed him into the sink, breaking it instantly and spraying more water all over the deck. Cody threw pieces of the porcelain sink at the approaching pirate. Mu'mmar kicked Cody in the ribs. Hard.

Then Mu'mmar wrapped his banana-size fingers around Cody's neck and began to choke him. Cody flailed his legs at him, kicking and squirming. He reached for anything around him he could use as a weapon. He grabbed a nearby wrench and smacked Mu'mmar in the head with it. The blow sent the man crashing onto his back. He released his grip on Cody and rubbed his head.

Cody saw a pipe labeled "steam" along the bulkhead. He jumped on top of it and smacked the pipe with the wrench, spraying hot steam into Mu'mmar's face. His skin turned red and blistered as the large man screamed in horror. Cody quickly ran around him, pulled out Eugene's cape, and used it to strangle Mu'mmar from behind. He pulled tighter and tighter as the massive pirate struggled to breathe. Eventually he gave up and slumped face-down onto the wet deck.

Motionless.

Cody turned the water off with a wrench before he left

the room and continued towards the back of the ship, Eugene's cape in hand.

The others finally made it up to an aloft part of the weather decks, overlooking the flight deck, where the remaining eight Salty Sea Dogs awaited the return of the helicopter. Cody regrouped with the rest of them. "That's everyone," he reported. "Hey, Eugene, I got something for you." Cody tossed the wrinkled up cape to him.

"My cape! Thanks, Cody!" Eugene put it around his neck. He sniffed the air. "Why does it smell like booze and gym socks?"

Asad kept his focus on the remaining men on the flight deck. "Miko, can you hit them from here with your laser tazer?" Asad asked.

"No," she said. "They're too far down there. How about you, Eugene?"

"Negative," he answered.

"I can try and run up to them," Cody suggested. "But my suit ran out of power, so I don't think I'll make it."

"It's too risky," Asad said.

"Where's Shayla?" asked Cody.

"What do you mean, she's right here-" Miko said, cutting herself off as she looked around the bridge. Much to everyone's surprise, Shayla was not there.

"Did she get separated?" Asad asked.

"She was right next to me a moment ago," Miko said concerned and baffled.

"Look!" Eugene pointed down to the flight deck. Everyone peered down below. There, in the middle of the helipad, where a large circle with an "H" was painted on it, was a small hatch that led below deck. It opened, revealing Shayla's hand and head as she popped up and onto the flight deck.

"What the hell is she doing?!" Cody panicked. "They'll kill her!"

"She must've just snuck down there," Asad said.

"Hold on guys, they don't see her," Miko pointed out.

Shayla quietly pulled out her remaining goo-nade. She activated it and placed it on the deck, right in the middle of all the armed pirates.

"Hey, losers!" she yelled. They turned and ran towards her, two of them shooting. Shayla closed the hatch and ducked below deck. The pirates ran up and curiously inspected the goo-nade. Five seconds later, the facial recognition software identified all eight faces of the Salty Sea Dogs and exploded onto them. Each one of them suffocated on the goo that shot out of the explosive, some of them even falling overboard, the others simply falling to the deck, taking their last breath.

Shayla emerged from the hatch, saluting her friends with a hard-nosed scowl still stretched across her face.

Cody grabbed his chest and let out a huge sigh of relief.

"I must admit, Cody," Asad said. "Your cousin is quite impressive sometimes. It must run in the family."

"I think I'd be happier if it didn't," Cody said.

At that moment, all of the loudspeakers on the island emitted a female voice saying, *"Attention Zactrala Island personnel. Super Nova self-destruct sequence initiated. Please expedite exiting the vicinity of the island in accordance with emergency evacuation plan Delta 24601. Ten minutes remaining. Ten minutes remaining."*

"Uh oh…" Eugene said, wide-mouthed.

"There's no time to celebrate" Asad said. "We have to cast off."

"What about Danny?" Miko asked. "He's still on the island!"

"And Oliver?" Eugene's lower lipped quivered.

Asad answered somberly. "If we don't leave now, the explosion from the island will take out the *Mogadishu* and all of us on it. We need to get underway immediately. It's what Danny…and Oliver…would have wanted."

"What about the helicopter? I heard on one of the radios downstairs that it's coming back to the ship." Cody asked. "Can we use that gun on the fantail to shoot it?"

"No, we'll never hit it. They weren't designed to take down helicopters," Asad said. "Here's what I suggest: They will attempt to land on the flight deck, and so we will *greet* them. As their shipmates." He pulled the robe across his face, covering it.

"Right…" Cody said.

"Now, I think I know enough about the landing equipment onboard to use it to our advantage," Asad scratched his chin as he was figuring out a plan. "That platform on tracks over there is called the RSD, or Rapid Securing Device. It's part of the RAST system, which stands for Recover, Assist, Secure, Traverse. They used it to move the frame of the Stallion and will need to use it again to safely land on the flight deck. If everyone does *exactly* what I say, we should be able to destroy this helicopter without a single shot being fired."

"I like that kind of plan," Shayla responded.

"Okay, so listen carefully, because we have to act fast…" Asad pulled the others in to a huddle and whispered his strategy.

Moments later, the kids were in position and ready. The Super Stallion was in the distance and steadily approaching the *Mogadishu*. Asad was up above in the air traffic control tower with a radio headset on. When the pilot of the Super Stallion asked in Arabic for clearance to land, Asad did the best he could at making his voice sound deeper than usual. "You have clearance to land," he answered. He was eye-level with the pilot at this point as they hovered above the flight deck.

So far, so good, Asad thought. *They don't suspect anything yet.*

The helo began to descend as Miko, her face covered with the pirate's clothes, directed the craft to lower using the hand gestures that Asad had just taught her. Standing guard next to her was Cody holding an AK-47. The wind from the rapidly spinning blades blew their robes violently. All they could hear was the whir of the engine.

Asad switched channels on his radio and gave an order to Eugene, who was in the Landing Signal Officer (LSO) shack, which was just below the flight deck and had a window that allowed him to give hand signals to the others. "Tell Shayla to move in."

"Roger dodger!" Eugene replied. He then gave Shayla a hand signal to move towards the RSD platform.

Shayla was crouching near Cody when she nodded to Eugene. She ducked as she swiftly ran under the still hovering helo. The chopper lowered a cable that Shayla attached to another cable that she pulled from the RSD. Once there was a firm click and positive connection, Shayla ran back to her crouching position near Cody and gave Eugene a thumbs-up. Eugene returned one and spoke into the radio excitedly. "Asad, connection confirmed! Repeat, the helo is connected to the RSD!"

I have you now, Asad celebrated in his head. He couldn't help but smile. "Copy. Give them the evacuation signal."

Very hurriedly, Eugene flailed his arms around. Miko, Cody, and Shayla saw their cue in the LSO shack window and ran around the corner. The helicopter pilot saw this and asked Asad over the radio, "Hey! What's going on?"

Before he could respond, he gave Eugene the next command on their secondary radio channel. "Now, Eugene!"

Eugene grabbed the joystick controls in the LSO shack and jerked it hard all the way towards the hanger bay. The RSD pulled the helicopter forcefully forward, its tail propellers hitting the flight deck and breaking off behind it. The blades on top of the Super Stallion hit the massive bay doors of the hanger. They flew off in different directions as the rest of the aircraft was pulled to the deck in a fiery explosion.

Asad and Eugene had ducked in their respective control stations, but were now standing to witness the damage. Their plan had succeeded.

Miko, Shayla, and Cody emerged from the side of the ship and surveyed the burning rubble. They let out a joyous cheer, jumping up and down and hugging each other. Eugene was fist pumping the air as he climbed out of the shack to join the others. Asad simply sat back, taking off his sweaty headset and let out a sigh of relief.

"That was awesome, Eugene!" Cody yelled.

Eugene shrugged. "It's the cape!"

Asad stepped down from the control tower and broke the mood, "You all were brilliant, but we still have to cast off." The others knew the jubilation couldn't last.

Miko asked sternly, "What do you need us to do?"

"You and Shayla need to cut the mooring lines. There should be axes near each bollard," he directed.

"You got it!" Shayla called back. She and Miko ran down to the fantail.

"What about us?" Cody asked.

"I need you two to raise the anchor. I'll show you how, then I need to go to the pilot house to steer the ship."

"We're on it!" Eugene stuck his arms out like Superman and ran towards the front of the ship Cody started to follow when Asad called after him.

"Wait! Cody!" Cody spun around and looked at him. "Down below, did you see my father? The doctor?"

Cody shook his head. "I'm sorry. No sign of him."

Asad nodded and swallowed hard. He fought showing too much emotion. "We should hurry."

22 A NEW COURSE

"Nine minutes remaining."

The clock was ticking. Danny ran first to the control pad. He scanned the rows of buttons and levers for anything that might cancel the self-destruct sequence. Nothing was labeled in any way that made sense to him. "You wouldn't happen to know how to stop the island from blowing up, do you, Oliver?" Oliver looked just as panicked and confused as Danny. The evacuation sirens and warning lights were scaring him.

Danny began pushing buttons and turning knobs until he finally gave up and just ran his palms over the entire board of buttons. Useless. *The self-destruct probably overrides everything else.* Danny searched the admiral's pockets for a key or a card or a badge or something. Nothing. His job was complete, the weapon would be destroyed, and so he just continued to lie there. Dead. Unaware that Danny's life was on the line. *I have to get out of here!* Danny was getting angry now.

"Eight minutes remaining."

Desperate, he sprinted across the room. He used his cutlass to cut the lock off the trunk full of weapons to see if anything could blow open the door. He pulled out a flamethrower similar to the one he had found in the armory. He pointed it at the door and squeezed the trigger. A wall of flames rocketed across the room and engulfed the door, but it had no effect. He threw it to the floor.

The next thing he found in the box resembled what would have passed for a laser blaster of the future from a 1950s comic book. "Check it out, Oliver!" Danny exclaimed to the bonobo who helplessly followed Danny around. "Maybe this is a laser that will cut through the door. Cross your fingers. Or your...whatever you have." He took aim and fired, but rather than a laser, bullet, or some other destructive element, it let off a tiny radar ping. Its robotic voice responded, "THE TARGET IS TWENTY-THREE POINT TWO FEET A-WAY." He chucked it at the door, which was equally ineffective.

"Seven minutes remaining."

The last item in the crate looked like an ordinary, dried out sponge. It was a yellow, squishy rectangle topped with a green, rough textured surface. "What does this do?" He tried to bend it, and it crackled slightly as its stiffness refused to comply. "Maybe it's a plastic explosive!" He banged it on the side of the box, but nothing happened. Throwing it didn't seem to help either.

"Maybe it has to be wet to work," Danny spit on it, hoping it would provide a clue. The yellow section swelled slightly under the moisture of his spit, but nothing followed. Danny pressed his thumb into it, gushing a small amount of the liquid back out and onto dryer parts of the object. "It's just a regular sponge..." Oliver grabbed it and put it in his mouth, promptly spitting it out in disgust.

"Six minutes remaining."

There were no other weapons in the trunk. "There must be some other way out of here!" Danny tried looking around the command hub with new eyes. He cleared his mind. *The books. There were hundreds of books on the shelves. Maybe one of them was a secret lever.* He pulled the books, one by one out of the shelf. Each plopped to the floor with no rumbling movement of a wall or any sign that it had been anything other than a book on a shelf. Oliver did the same, mimicking Danny's movement's. He began to remove as many as he could grab with both hands on the higher shelves.

"Five minutes remaining."

Furiously now, Danny cleared rows and rows of shelves with sweeping motions of his arms, making nothing more than dust in the air and a mounting pile of old literature littering the ground. He climbed up to where Oliver was, checking even the higher rows.

"This is ridiculous," Danny decided. He gave up on the book-door idea and scrambled for a new plan. Scattered around the room were various storage lockers. *Certainly one of them would have something that could help.*

Flinging open the first set of doors, he revealed a pantry full of non-perishable foods. Sugary cereals, Twinkies, and all kinds of snacks that would have set Danny's chubby little heart aflutter just several weeks ago now brought him only disappointment. Oliver lunged for the snacks, but Danny slammed the doors shut. "No, Oliver! I never thought I'd say this, but there's no time for Twinkies!"

The next cabinet over was a large supply of spare circuit boards, wires, and electrical components that perhaps he could have used if only he had more time and knew anything about electrical engineering. He dug through, emptying the shelves in hopes of finding some kind of tool, but came up empty.

"Four minutes remaining."

"Shut up, lady!" Danny threw a circuit board at one of the loud speakers. It landed on a large, unopened crate. Danny approached it, hoping for a miracle. He used the hilt of his cutlass to pry open the box and all sides of it fell apart as Danny backed out of the way. After the dust settled, he saw it. His way out. His miracle.

In bold letters across the top of a typically plain

government issued manual read "C-351 Model B Jetpack."

"Jetpack. Awesome." Danny tossed aside the manual and dug through the packaging to produce a shiny metal backpack. He wrapped the straps around his shoulders and found the trigger near his right thumb. "Time to blast off, Oliver!"

He pressed the button. Nothing happened.

Danny stood crouched, depressing the button as hard as he could, but still his feet were firmly planted to the floor.

"Three minutes remaining."

He flipped it over looking for an 'ON' switch. Nothing. "Is there some assembly required or something?" He dug back through the box, producing a few metal poles, thumb screws, and a circular, metal disc. "Oh, you've got to be kidding me! Where did that manual go?"

Oliver was chewing on the corner of the manual. Danny tried to pry it from his hands. "Let go, Oliver. Let go!" Oliver pulled it away from Danny. "I know boy, I know, I'm a nervous eater too. I'll get you out of here soon and buy you all the banana chips you want, just LET GO!" So he did, and Danny flew back on his butt. Opening the manual, he hurriedly leafed through the diagrams. He was too rushed to read closely, but he got the gist of what he needed to assemble.

"Two minutes remaining."

Before long, he had a fully assembled jetpack, but not like one he'd seen before. The circular disc went on the floor, made for standing on. The underside contained the actual propulsion device, and running up from it were rigid metal tubes to the backpack. Danny guessed that this must be how the fuel got from the backpack to the engines. He adjusted it to his height and strapped in.

Flipping the footswitch, it hummed to life.

"One minute remaining."

"Let's go, Oliver!" Oliver jumped onto the jetpack and latched himself to Danny. Danny squeezed his thumb on the button again, only this time he felt a surge of motion upwards. *Too fast! Too fast!* He thought. He veered off to the left, clanging into the cabinet full of snacks and letting go of the button. Falling, he squeezed again. Twinkies and candies spilled onto the floor. Oliver jumped off the jetpack and began shoving food into his mouth. "Oliver! No! Get back up here! Bad boy! No food now!" He had rotated somewhat in the descent, so now he was flying straight for the other wall.

Instinctively, Danny covered his face with his hands. It may have prevented a black eye, but it left him completely out of control of the jetpack.

"Thirty seconds remaining."

"Oliver!" Into the wall he went. Realizing his mistake, Danny grabbed the handles again, squeezing the trigger much more lightly. With some clever shifting of his weight, he found a spot where he hovered almost gracefully about six feet above the ground.

"Sweet! Oliver! Let's go!" The bonobo wouldn't budge. He was in a sugary heaven. "Let's go get Eugene! You want to see Eugene?" At the sound of Eugene's name Oliver's ears perked up and he leapt up towards Danny, grabbing a dangling strap. "Good boy!"

Less than twenty seconds to go! Steadying himself, he slowly let the trigger down further and further. Before long, he was accelerating upwards like a rocket for the hole in the ceiling.

"Ten, nine, eight, seven…"

He burst out the top of the command hub. Fresh air. He squinted into the night sky, adjusting his eyes to the darkness and attempting to maintain control. Without a watch, Danny had no idea where the timer was at, but his mind was working at about a thousand times its normal rate so each second felt like forever.

"Oliver, are you okay?" Danny looked down. The strap dangled still from the bottom of the jetpack, flapping furiously in the wind. There was no Oliver holding on anymore. "No! Oliver!"

Up and up he climbed until he heard a great blast from below.

Boom! Beneath him came a spectacular yellow flash followed by several gigantic fireballs. It illuminated the mountain below him as he could see that he was just cresting the peaks of the rim. Rocks, dust, and debris scattered everywhere, flying towards him at great speed.

Squeezing as hard as he could, Danny was at full throttle. The glowing blue flames beneath his feet caught several boulders nearly catching up to him as he shot up higher and higher into the heavens. A hunk of flaming metal flew right by his head. Finally, he was out of range of the debris. And for a brief moment, he thought:

I wonder if Captain Vasser ever escaped the tunnel...

On the *Mogadishu*, Shayla, Eugene, Miko, and Cody were all standing on the fantail of the ship, watching the island explode. Shayla had just tended to everyone's wounds, wrapping them up with the pirates' clothes they had been wearing. And even though they were over a nautical mile away, they could still feel the heat that the explosion emitted. The *Mogadishu* was cruising away, leaving a long, jagged wake behind her.

Asad came down from the pilot house, where he had just put the ship on auto-pilot. Shayla burst into tears, burying her head into Cody's chest. Eugene sniffled. His lower lip quivered as he began to cry, hanging on the ship's lifeline at the end of the deck. Asad hugged Miko, who was as white as a ghost.

"I can't believe it...He's gone." Miko said in a breathy whisper.

"Danny and Oliver," Eugene choked on his own words. "They were m-m-my best f-friends."

"Danny changed our lives," Cody said. "He's a hero. And his sacrifice will never be forgotten."

"I can't do this." Shayla let out a painful cry and ran behind the large cannon, crouching into the fetal position.

Cody tried to break the silence. "We should probably do something. Say something. Right?" He looked to Asad. Asad put his rucksack down and pulled out his and Miko's violins. She wiped her nose on her sleeve and dried her tears. They played a sad, beautiful requiem as a funeral song. Eugene slowly pulled the rope on the flagpole down. He removed the Somali flag and threw it in the ocean. He took his red cape off and raised it in its place. He then lowered his head and listened to the song. Cody did the same.

Free as a bird, Danny soared higher and higher on his jetpack, screaming into the night. *I can't believe I made it! I've never felt so alive!* he thought.

Suddenly, he became keenly aware of just how high he was flying. He had no idea how much fuel he had or how much higher this contraption could take him. He veered right, banking a turn to get out and away from the center of where the island had been. The now barely rising sun gave him just enough light to see the land falling into the sea.

Lights below. A ship. The *Mogadishu*. Danny had no

idea what or who would greet him on the deck. Scattered fires from the helo crash continued to burn on the flight deck. *I wonder if everyone's okay...What if they were captured...or worse? Maybe I'll have to fly in circles around the ship until I run out of fuel or get shot down. Hopefully nobody sees me landing onboard.*

He slowed his approach, pulling up more and more vertical until he was nearly hovering in place. When he saw it, his heart lifted. There, hanging from the flagpole was the one sign that could tell him his friends had taken the ship: the Somali flag was gone and in its stead was Eugene's cape waving boldly.

Spotting the flames from the jetpack, Asad recoiled, "What's that up there?"

"Is it Vasser? Did he escape?" Cody made a fist, adjusting his stance to be ready to charge.

Danny floated closer, slowing his descent as he came nearer to the deck. "Wait, guys," Eugene called out, "It's Danny! It's Danny!"

Setting down gently on the fantail, Danny flicked off the footswitch and let go of the handles, "Sorry I'm late everyone, but I hope you don't mind me dropping in anyway."

Miko ran to him first, embracing him tightly, still holding her violin. "How long were you working on that one?" Miko cracked.

"The entire time I was up there. What's with the doom and gloom? Is everyone okay?"

"We thought you were dead!" Cody hugged him, still in shock.

"I missed you, Danny." Eugene hugged him next.

"Hullo, Danny. It's very good to see you alive." Asad beamed and hugged Danny.

"Where's Shayla?" Danny searched the deck.

From behind the huge gun, Shayla slowly stood. She walked cautiously towards Danny, her hair covering her face. They fell silent as they watched her approach him.

She finally glanced up at him through her hair.

Revealed behind her long blonde locks were tears of relief, "I thought I lost you," she whispered. She hugged him hard. They pulled tightly into one another.

"I thought I lost you, too." They pulled back and looked into each other's eyes. Danny held her tight and wiped a tear away with his thumb, then made the slightest lean forward...when Eugene interrupted.

"Umm, Danny? Is there any chance you happened to bring Oliver back with you?"

The mood sank.

"Ah, geez, Eugene. I...I tried to, but-"

"He's right here!" Miko had been inspecting the jetpack when suddenly, a terrified and trembling Oliver covered in soot and checkered with singed hair, clinging to the back of the jetpack, jumped onto the deck.

"Oliver!" Eugene bubbled over, grabbing his friend and cradling him to his shoulder much as a mother burps her baby. "You're okay now, everything is safe!" He patted Oliver's back whose eyes were still wide with disbelief. He coughed up a puff of smoke.

"Asad..." said a deep voice from behind them. Everyone jumped. The kids had thought they were alone. Turning towards the door leading below deck stood a tall, dark, shadowy figure.

23 BEST SUMMER EVER

Cody's solar-powered dragon-skin suit was now recharged, so he activated it and got into a fighting stance, facing the mysterious passenger on the ship. Asad placed his violin on the deck next to Miko's and activated his B-KEMS while Danny pushed Shayla behind him to protect her as he raised his cutlass. Eugene and Miko each dropped to one knee on either side of Asad's shield and aimed their air blaster and laser tazer respectively.

"I thought you said you got everyone on the ship," Asad asked Cody through the side of his mouth.

"I did, I swear!" Cody defended himself.

The man leaning in the doorway stepped into the daylight. It was Rasheed, Asad's father. "Papa!" Asad shouted excitedly. He retracted his shields and ran straight towards him. He leapt into his father's embrace, wrapping his arms around his neck. Rasheed leaned down and hugged his son, ruffling his hair.

"How are you, my son? Are you hurt?"

"No, Papa, I'm fine. And so are my friends." Asad turned to the others. "Everyone, this is my father, Rasheed Darzi. He's the doctor of the *Mogadishu*. Papa, these are my American friends." Slowly, Danny gave the nod to everyone else to lower their defenses.

"Hullo everyone, nice to meet you. Thank you for taking care of my son."

"It was him who helped us," Danny said. "We should be the ones thanking him."

"The ship is ours, Papa!" Asad said. "We can go home now! No more pirates!"

"That's right, Asad. No more pirates." He hugged him again.

"Where have you been this whole time?" Cody asked. "I searched the whole ship, even the medical room."

"Ah, good question. How about instead of telling you, I'll show you?" Rasheed smiled as if he were hiding a secret. "Come. Follow me. I will tend to your wounds, although it looks as though someone with skill already has." Shayla blushed. "I also have a gift for all of you. Come! Come!" He waved the kids to follow him into the ship. He and Asad walked in first. The others turned to Danny. Danny shrugged and limped after them. Shayla helped him keep his balance. *What on Earth could this be about?* Danny thought.

Rasheed led the way five decks below. He finally took them to what appeared to be a dead-ended hallway. There was a large aluminum sign on the bulkhead that read WARNING: HIGH VOLTAGE. Rasheed pulled it off the wall to reveal a hidden hole leading into another compartment. "Come on now, watch your step," Asad's father said reassuringly. "The sign is just to keep others out."

"I definitely did not find this room," Cody said.

When the last of the Castaway Kids entered the space, Asad's father turned on the lights. "This is where I was hiding when I noticed the light-haired fellow running around attacking the crew." Before them were crates and crates of treasures and money and art and electronic devices worth millions of dollars.

"Whoa," Danny said, bewildered. "What is all this?"

"This is the Treasure Room," Rasheed began to stroll between the crates. "This is where the crew of the *Mogadishu* hid all of the riches they stole from ships across the Pacific. Everything they plundered on our travels went to Mu'mmar, who was the only one besides the Captain who knew about this place, and was put into these crates to be divided up later. The captain kept this room guarded and hidden so no one tried to take their share early and abandon the mission. The only reason I know about it is because the captain used this place as a physical therapy room to try all of the alterations I made to his body."

"Why are you showing us this?" Miko asked.

"Because, this belongs to the crew of the *Mogadishu*, and that's you."

"No freakin' way!" Eugene's eyes lit up.

"Really? Seriously? This is for us?" Cody's legs became wobbly.

"Well, hold on now," Shayla interjected. "Doesn't this belong to the innocent people from whom it was originally stolen? It's not ours to keep."

"Sweetie," Rasheed said softly. "I'm not sure how to put this, but Captain Vasser didn't allow those he stole from to live. All the rightful owners are dead. And to track down and trace the source of all this would be...well, it would be practically impossible. And if we turn it in to authorities it would go unclaimed or go into the hands of the wrong people. You could assure the use of this money is for good."

"Oh. Okay." Shayla said. "Well, if you put it that way."

The kids began rifling through the spoils. Gold, jewels, bond notes, diamonds, traveler's checks...an absolute fortune the likes of which the Castaway Kids had never dreamed to own. Miko and Shayla went straight for the jewelry, digging through and sizing them up. Cody and Danny leafed through the stacks of bills, their eyes glazed over as if they expected to wake up from a dream. Eugene nearly passed out seeing the massive haul of electronics.

Asad's father left the kids to play and count the riches. After showing Shayla how to bandage up Danny a little better in his medical office, he went up to the pilot house to take control of the ship. But before he left, he asked, "Where shall I set our course to?"

The Castaway Kids thought about it.

"Well, guys," Miko offered, "we're safe and it's still summer. And not only that, but we're fabulously wealthy. What do we do now?"

"I think it's obvious," said Danny. "We started on this trip to go to Hawaii. I say we see that through."

"Yeah!" They all cheered.

"Hawaii it is," Rasheed said with a smile.

"Sir?" Danny asked. "Do you think you could show me how to steer the ship?"

"Sure," Rasheed responded. "How about you all come up to the pilot house. You can tell me more about your adventure. I love a good story."

And so they did. Rasheed showed Danny everything he knew about piloting a ship, including some of the evasive methods Captain Vasser had used to avoid the Navy and Coast Guard. Although the ship itself was covered in paint that made it invisible to radar, that wouldn't stop a lot of questions from being asked when a stolen battleship rolled into a Hawaiian harbor. So when they reached Hawaii, they had a plan to stay inconspicuous.

The *Mogadishu* was left anchored over the horizon with the seven of them taking a much less conspicuous power boat (called a RHIB, meaning Rigid Hull Inflatable Boat) onto shore.

They stayed on the island of Kauai with abundant style. Everything was first class from the moment they set foot on land. They booked the entire top floor of the fanciest hotel they could find. Danny found a water park that he rented for the day so they could go on every ride without any wait. Shayla visited a wildlife reserve and convinced the keepers to allow her to hug every single animal in the park. Cody and Miko managed to rent dirt bikes so they could do some extreme off-roading while Asad and his father spent most of their time doing absolutely nothing but lay by the pool and keep a constant supply of the finest food coming from the café. Eugene bribed a security guard and gave Oliver the best day of his life when he snuck him into the fields of a massive banana plantation.

After their week of vacation, they packed up their new wardrobes and souvenirs and jetted back to the *Mogadishu* on the RHIB. They now set their sights on Somalia to bring Rasheed and Asad home. Along the way, Eugene got it in his head to rename the boat and took a large supply of paint over the edge. He was very secretive about it and only allowed Oliver to help him. When they finally arrived at the Horn of Africa and set down anchor, he showed his pride and joy: a somewhat sloppily written moniker "The Friend Ship," followed by two crudely drawn smiley faces. Miko groaned at the pun, but the others were supportive.

They split the treasure evenly between the six of them (Rasheed insisting that he not receive a separate share), and dropped Asad and his father off to be exceptionally comfortable for the rest of their lives in their old hometown. Miko seemed to be the most affected by Asad's departure. She locked herself in her room for a whole day afterwards, playing her violin and practicing everything he taught her. Crying most of the time.

Nearing the California coast and loading the treasure onto the RHIB, Cody looked up and asked, "So what do we do with the *Mogadishu*?"

"You mean the *Friend Ship*," Eugene corrected him.

"Right, well whatever it's called, we can't exactly park it next to the baseball stadium in the bay."

"I guess we have to leave it behind," answered Shayla. "It's not like we can hide it anywhere."

"Can we sink it?" chimed Miko, "Please tell me we can sink it. I think there's enough ammunition aboard!"

"I've actually been thinking about this lately," Danny replied. "And it's a pretty great ship. Too awesome to destroy. But people are probably looking for it and that is bad news for us."

"So what are you thinking?" Shayla was captivated.

Danny turned to Eugene, "I have an idea. Set a course with these coordinates." Danny handed him a map.

Eugene studied the map. Confused, he asked, "But this is-"

"I know," Danny interrupted. "Trust me. It's the best thing."

It was a foggy late-August morning in San Francisco. The clouds hung low with only a modest breeze to push them lazily along the coast. The air was crisp and all around was the familiar bustling feel as San Franciscans began their morning commute to work.

Suddenly, everything was not so normal. A fender bender. Cars stopped. Drivers peered out their windows and caught a glimpse of something wholly unexpected: a great black warship sailing under the Golden Gate bridge.

Uncle Cesar and Uncle Jesus grumbled as they were up far earlier than they had hoped to be. They were still downtrodden due to the fact that their boat went missing months ago. Their boat trip canceled, they had more time for petty shoplifting. They took to posting flyers around the dock with recent photos and a promise of a reward they never intended to fulfill. The brothers were about to steal a street performer's can of change when they saw it.

"Yo, Jesus, check it out!" Cesar got his brother's attention and pointed. The mighty ship navigated the shoreline and headed towards the marina. They stared gape-mouthed at the vessel that was clearly well out of place in a setting of skiffs and yachts. It broke through the sign adorning the entrance with ease, leaving it splintered in the water. The entertainer, painted to look like a statue, grabbed his can of change and bolted inland.

"Run!" Cesar took off as the ship plowed over boats and piers, drawing nearer to where Jesus was still frozen in absolute awe. It turned a perfect 90 degrees, sweeping out dozens and dozens of smaller boats in its wake as it plowed straight into land. The hull broke through the boating supplies shop ashore slowly, but without showing any sign of resistance. Employees fled screaming from the shards of broken glass and collapsing roof. Eventually, it came to a stop just inches from the still staring Uncle Jesus. He could only look on in disbelief.

Meanwhile, at the lighthouse, the Castaway Kids were hoisting their final load of treasure up the stairs. "We should get an actual lock for this place if we're gonna keep stuff here for very long," Cody heaved.

"Don't worry, I got it," Miko flicked him a doubloon. "Think they take gold at the hardware store?"

Eugene watched news footage on his phone of the ship plowing into the coast. "Authorities do not know who attacked the harbor," the news anchor reported. "They are relieved that no one was hurt in the incident. Those whose boats were damaged or destroyed in the harbor will be compensated by their insurance companies."

"I'm going to buy this lighthouse, refurbish it, and call it 'Castaway Pointe,'" Danny said as he wiped dust from the window.

"I think that's an awesome idea, Danny," Cody gave him a playful punch on the shoulder.

"I can't believe we're home," Shayla said. "What do you think we missed?"

"Looks like not much has changed," Miko observed, handing out their cell phones. None of them had any missed calls, with the exception of Cody: forty-two voicemails from Erik.

Danny was undeterred, "Things may not have changed much around here, but I think we certainly have."

"You think so?" Eugene replied hopefully.

"Yeah, I mean, look at us. When we left, if we told anyone that we were going to sail the Pacific, fight pirates, save the world, steal a warship, become filthy rich, would anyone have believed us?"

"And now we can't tell anybody about it," Cody interjected. They looked around the room at each other. He was right. Their parents would kill them, not to mention the legal trouble that would likely result from any one of their actions.

"Agreed," said Danny. "This was a trip just for us. Our greatest summer ever!"

"A vow of secrecy then," Shayla declared.

With that, they said their goodbyes and went their separate ways home. They took care to practice elaborate stories to tell their parents about where they were supposed to be all summer to keep from getting in trouble. But Danny had his own business to sort out first.

Danny's first stop was at the bank. After handling some financial matters there regarding his newfound wealth, he walked down to the trolley line and waited. He let several open trolleys come and go until Chester pulled up and let the riders off. Danny stepped up to the front. "Hey, Chester."

"Danny? Is that you?" Chester hardly recognized the boy in front of him. Were it not for his voice, he wouldn't have guessed he was anyone other than a random tourist. "You're looking fit! But I'm sorry buddy, the car's pretty full. I can't give you a freebie today."

"No freebies, Chester. Today I'm a real customer." Danny pulled out of his pocket an emerald the size of a gumball and put it in his hand.

Astonished, Chester could barely string together a sentence "I…I don't think this will fit through the machine…"

"Oh yeah, don't worry about that, I bought a fast pass," Danny swiped his card. "That little guy's for you. Consider it 'thank you interest' for all the jams you've gotten me out of." He took his seat.

"Where did you get this?"

"I went snorkeling in Australia and found an old treasure chest," Danny lied coolly.

"Wow, thanks, Danny!" Chester wasn't entirely sure had just happened or if he should even believe Danny, but he rang the bell and drove on anyways with a great smile on his face. "I gotta take up snorkeling."

Danny hopped off at the liquor store and headed inside. "Mr. Fong?"

The liquor store owner had been reading a newspaper

when Danny caught his attention, "Yes, little boy? I help you?"

"Mr. Fong, it's me, Danny."

"Danny…"

Danny sighed. "Fat Danny. The chubby kid who steals all the candy."

Grabbing his bat from under the desk, Mr. Fong's mood changed on a dime, "You the thief? You get out of my store! I call police!"

"No, wait!" Danny threw his hands up to defend himself, revealing a wad of hundred dollar bills in his fist. "I want to pay you back! Do you have a tab for what I owe you?"

Suspiciously, Mr. Fong reached for his log book. He'd totaled his losses from each of Danny's escapades and kept them in a book with the regular deadbeats and scumbags. He kept one eye on Danny the entire time. "Two hundred fifty one dollar, eighty five cent."

Danny laid out the money on the counter. "Keep the change." He had overpaid substantially. His head held high, he walked to the door. He turned and asked, "Did I give you enough to grab a little snack?"

Mr. Fong nodded, still not certain what kind of trick this was. Danny grabbed himself a treat and headed out.

Up the street he went, back to his uncles' house. Now that he was in shape, the walk up the hill wasn't half as bad as it used to be. It didn't hurt that no one was chasing him, but even still, he had no desire to wait for the next passing trolley. He missed his hometown and soaked up the sights, sounds, and smells of the city.

Stopping in front of the door, Danny took a deep breath and opened it.

Inside on the couch sat Uncle Cesar and Uncle Jesus. They were in their exact same seats, slumped to their usual levels. For once, though, they were not playing video games but watching a news report about the *Friend Ship* having invaded and destroyed part of the San Francisco harbor. A stench of rotten garbage and fast food twirled up Danny's nostrils.

"I'm home," Danny announced. His uncles stirred from their fixation.

"Woah, look at that! Little piggy's about half the size he was when we sent him off to the farm," Cesar sneered.

"Where we gonna get our bacon now?" Jesus chimed in. They both had a laugh.

"Cute, guys," Danny stepped in front of the TV, turning it off. "Now if I could have your attention for a matter of business."

"Hey! Come on, tortuga gorda," Cesar cut in. "What gives?"

Jesus shook his head, "Don't act all high and mighty, you're just the same little fat boy you were three months ago. I'll still use *la chancla* if I have to." Jesus held up a sandal, ready to throw it.

Danny let these comments roll off his back completely unfazed. "I have something very important to say. You see, I've cleared my parents' debt."

Simultaneously, his uncles sat up. "You what?"

"That's right. All of it. Everything in the name of the family trust is clear, including this house. That makes me the rightful owner. Not the bank."

They jumped up. Jesus patted him on the back. "All right! The kid was good for something! Now that we don't need to keep up those loan payments, let's get a bigger TV!"

"Not so fast." His uncles were still smiling, but halted in their celebration. "I said *I'm* the owner. Not us. Me." Their smiles faded as this reality dawned on them. "And as the owner, I'd like to get my money to start working for me. If you'd like to stay here as my legal guardians, you're going to need to start paying rent."

"Rent?" Jesus asked.

"That's right. A fair market rate too. Just because you're family doesn't mean that my investment should be worth any less."

Cesar chuckled nervously, "Danny, we've barely been making ends meet as it is. We can't afford that."

"Oh," Danny raised his eyebrow. "You want to try and find a place around here that's cheaper? Didn't think so. Then I suppose you'll need to get yourselves a second job. And no more stealing or calling me a fat turtle. Those are my terms." Danny headed upstairs to his room. He ran his finger along the hand railing. Dusty. "And if you'd like me to let you keep the insurance money from the boat, I suggest you keep this place clean!"

Into his room, Danny plopped down in bed. He finally dropped the tough guy act and let the smile he'd been holding back creep across his face. He stared up at the ceiling. *His* ceiling. He finally had a home where he was in charge. He reached into his pocket and grabbed his treat from the liquor store: a granola bar.

It wasn't half bad.

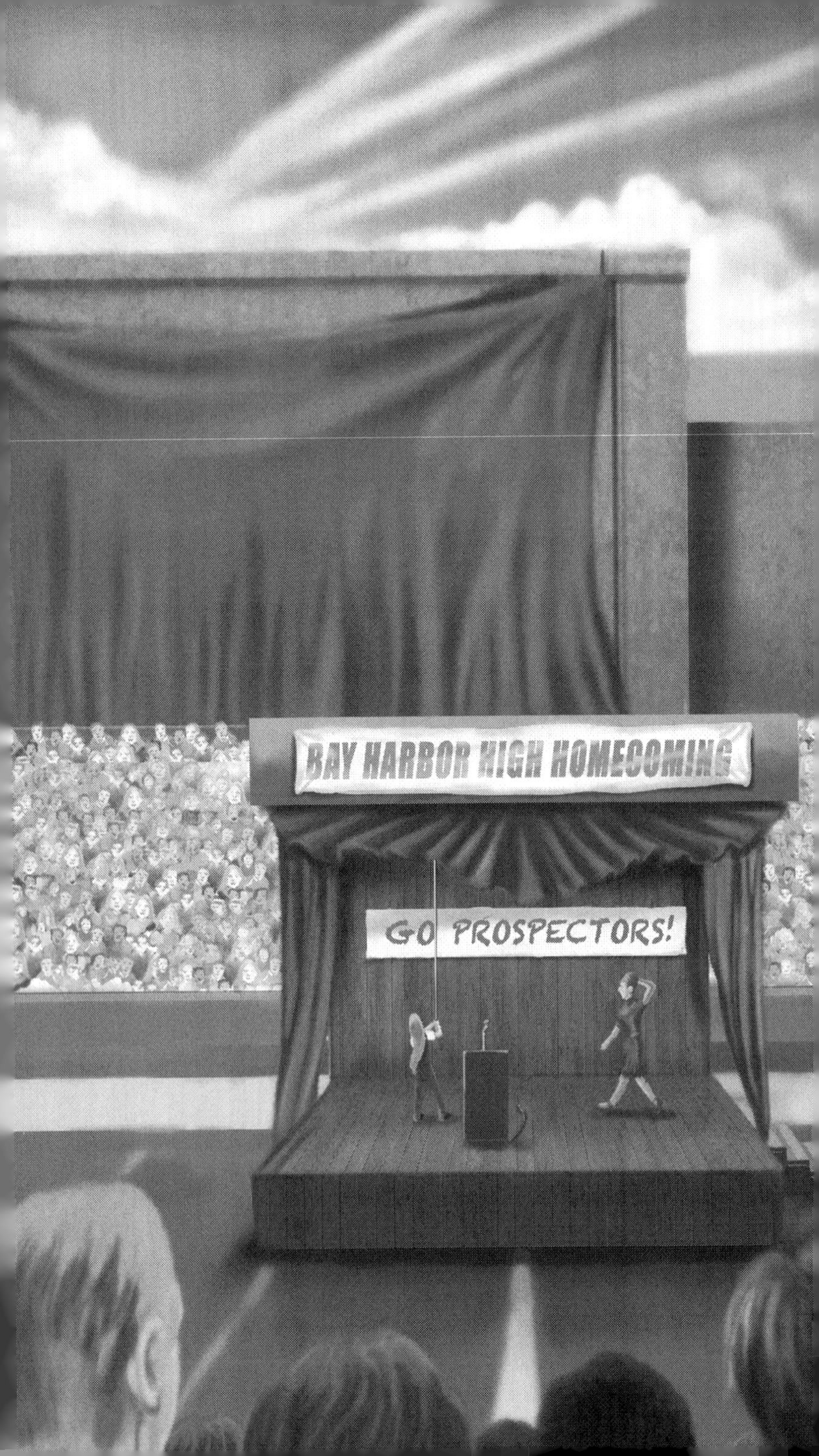
BAY HARBOR HIGH HOMECOMING
GO PROSPECTORS!

EPILOGUE

One Month Later…

It was homecoming night. The Castaway Kids were now freshmen at Bay Harbor High School. They had all kept their promises, and none of them spoke about what happened over the summer. When classmates from junior high asked Danny how he lost all that weight, he looked them in the eye and simply said, "Fat camp." They believed him, and didn't ask questions.

Several kids spoke of their summers non-stop. About the parties, the video game playing, books they read, music they heard, websites they discovered, movies they watched…all of it redundantly over-documented on the internet for the world to see.

One of the comments Miko heard from a classmate of hers was, "You must not have had a very exciting summer, Miko. You didn't post a single picture or say anything about it online. I feel sorry for you."

Eugene's parents thought he learned a lot about bravery and confidence at Wilderness Camp. However, they were a little puzzled about the "prize" he won for being what he said the Camp Counselor's called "Most Improved," which was a smarter-than-average bonobo.

Luckily for Eugene, his parents supported his new friend, and allowed their son to keep him, despite never reading about animal prizes being a part of the camp experience in the brochure. Eugene used a lot of his share of the treasure to buy a giant play-pen for Oliver in their backyard, complete with a greenhouse growing seven banana trees in the middle of it all.

Shayla started the "Wallflower Club," an after-school volunteer program designed to provide an outlet for teenagers interested in the environment to help plant trees and other vegetation around San Francisco.

Cody and Danny trained together, and Cody convinced the coach to allow Danny to try-out again as a walk-on player. He did, and Danny made the football team as a tight-end.

Tonight was their first game together.

A red curtain hung in front of a large brick wall on the side of the school. In front of it, a stage and podium were set up under the bay sky. Not a cloud was in sight. A banner reading "Bay Harbor High Homecoming" was strung up above the stage.

In front of the stage was the 50-yard line of the football field. The crowd cheered as the principal of the school finished her speech to a large crowd of students, faculty, and parents. "And now, to present to you the new mural for Bay Harbor High School, president of the school's environmental volunteer committee, The Wallflower Club, Miss Shayla Nichols!"

The crowd clapped as Shayla took the microphone and addressed the crowd. "Thank you, Mrs. Harris," she said. "And thank you to everyone who helped with this project. Fellow students of Bay Harbor High, I hope that every day you look at this mural, it cheers you up, and reminds you of what a beautiful, green planet we all share and love…" The crowd fell into a hushed "Awww…" Then Shayla continued, "Now let's beat some Tiger butt! Wooo! Go Prospectors!" She pulled the rope attached to the red curtain.

The curtain fell to the ground, revealing an all moss and flower mural of the team's mascot, an 1849 gold-mining prospector holding a pick-ax. It took up the whole side of the brick building and was absolutely gorgeous.

The Bay Harbor High Prospectors took the field. Miko was in the orchestra playing the school's anthem along with the marching band, who performed on the field. Danny and Cody were the first ones to run out of the locker room.

The game was intense, the rivals playing their hearts out. At halftime, the score was 14 -14. Eugene and Oliver wowed the audience with some cool tricks that Oliver had been working on. They both dressed up like prospectors and danced, doing a dance every time their team scored. The crowd loved them both.

The homecoming game was one of the closest ones in years. The score was tied at twenty-one apiece, and there were seven seconds left on the clock. The coach of the Prospectors had not put Danny in the game all night, until one of his receivers got injured when he jumped out of bounds to catch a pass and twisted his ankle on the opposing team's bench.

"Herrera, get in there," grunted the coach.

Danny put his helmet on and joined the offense in a huddle. Cody was quarterback and Erik was his running back. Shayla cheered the loudest when Danny was put in the game.

They finished their huddle and got ready at the line of scrimmage. When Cody yelled, "Hike!" Danny sprinted like a bolt of lightning down the side of the field. Cody threw a Hail Mary pass to him which bounced off of a defender's head. It was caught in mid-air by Danny as he and the football landed together in the end-zone. He had just scored the game-winning touchdown.

The crowd's roar was deafening. The clock had gone all the way down to double-zero. Danny stood up, ripped off his helmet, and hugged his teammates who all jumped on him in a huge pile.

"Nice catch, bro!"

"Woo-hoo! That was awesome!"

"Hell yeah, Herrera! Hell yeah!"

The crowd rushed the field. Fans and students hoisted Danny onto their shoulders chanting "Dan-ny! Dan-ny! Dan-ny!" Shayla made her way through the crowd and the fans put him down in the middle of the stage. He reached his hand out to Shayla through the crowd and helped her up next to him.

She smiled warmly at him, wrapping her arms around his neck. "Well done, Danny." She kissed him. The fans made an embarrassing high-pitched "woooooo" sound, but Danny didn't care. He was elated. He grabbed her hand, grabbed the football with the other, faced the crowd, and held them both high and proud for all to see.

Cody and Erik jumped up on stage too. Cody grabbed Erik's hand, faced the crowd, and held it high and proud. Cody looked over at Danny and winked.

Eugene jumped on stage and had Oliver doing backflips.

Suddenly, from the sky, a black helicopter hovered right above the crowd of people. Danny's eyes grew wide as he whispered to Cody, "You got your suit on, right?"

"Never leave home without it." Cody responded, not taking his eyes off the mysterious chopper. The students and fans parted as the helicopter, which had the U.S. President's seal on the side of it, landed on the 50-yard line, right in the middle of everyone. Secret Service agents appeared to come out of nowhere to greet Marine One as it landed. Bodyguards formed a perimeter around the stadium.

"What's going on?" Shayla asked Danny.

"I don't know," he said, just as confused as everyone else at the game. "But be ready for anything."

Students pulled out their cell phones and started

recording this event. Just then, the President of the United States stepped out of the helicopter.

He walked straight up to the stage, escorted by a few marines in uniform and Secret Service agents. Danny was surprised and baffled that he marched right up to him and Shayla.

The president looked rather serious as he stood in front of the two of them, still holding hands. "Are you Danny Herrera and Shayla Nichols?"

Danny swallowed hard. "Y-yes…yes sir, I am. I'm Danny." He stammered.

"I'm Shayla Nichols, sir," said Shayla, eyes as big as saucers, unable to process what was going on.

"Very good," the president responded. "And is that your cousin, Cody Nichols?"

The President pointed to Cody, for which Shayla replied, "Yes, sir."

"Come on over here, Cody." The president gestured towards the podium. "You too, Eugene. Bring Oliver." He curled his finger towards the stage, beckoning Eugene to go up there. He moved like a zombie to the stage. "And last but not least…Let's see… Where is she…? Where is Miko Tanaka?"

"She's in the school orchestra," Danny pointed her out. "She's right there, Mr. President, sir."

"Ah," he said as he spotted her, waving her up to the stage as well. "I almost didn't recognize her. The footage showed her having straight, black hair. I see she has dyed half of it pink and went for the spiked look. Interesting choice."

Danny was confused. The audience was now clapping for Miko as she made her way to the stage. "Footage, sir?"

"Yes," he explained matter-of-factly. "The self-destruct sequence on Zactrala Island automatically uploaded the recordings from the security cameras to a secured server that is monitored by the FBI. After hundreds of men viewed it all over the last month and a half, they sent me a full report of what you and your friends did there."

"Oh," Danny was trying to comprehend. "We're not in trouble, are we?"

The president chuckled. "Oh, no, no, quite the opposite young man, quite the opposite. You saved America. You young men and women are heroes."

Mrs. Harris adjusted her beehive hairdo as she hustled her way onto the stage next to the podium. She pushed the Homecoming King and Queen aside as she scurried towards the president. "Mr. President! It's an honor to have you visit the school so…unexpectedly! Is there something I can do for you?"

"No, ma'am, that won't be necessary. These are the students I came to see." He nodded at Danny, Cody, Shayla, Eugene, and Miko, who now stood (with Oliver) next to the podium facing the crowd. "Excuse me, Mrs. Harris. I have some business to attend to, it won't take long." He then grabbed the microphone at the podium and addressed the crowd. "How are you San Francisco?" The crowd went nuts. "Sorry for the big entrance. I was in the neighborhood and thought I'd drop in."

He flashed a politician's smile. Danny's hands sweat as he looked out into the crowd, dozens of camera phones pointing in his direction. *Is the president going to tell them what we did?* He thought, *There's no way they would believe him…It would expose everything the military did on that island. People would be outraged.*

The President continued. "I'm kidding of course. I bet you're wondering why I'm here. Well, I'm here to present some awards. Some awards of very high importance, to some of the students here at Bay Harbor High School, who are also very important. This summer, they engaged in acts of heroism that I am not at liberty to discuss the details of. However, rest assured, that their actions single-handedly saved the United States from certain peril.

"Eugene Applebaum and his bonobo, Oliver. Please come up here." Eugene held Oliver's hand and slowly walked up to the president. Eugene waved the president to lean down to his level. He did so and Eugene whispered in his ear. The president nodded, stood back up at the podium, and corrected himself, "I'm sorry, what I meant to say was, Eugene Applebaum and his bonobo *the Amazing Oliver, Best Friends Forever*, please come up here."

Eugene and Oliver took a bow.

"I would like to acknowledge the enormous heart that this young man and his bonobo have shown by defining the meaning of loyalty and friendship in the face of danger." One of the members in his entourage pulled from a beautiful wooden box two star-shaped medallions hanging from blue ribbons. "For this great act, I bestow upon you two The Presidential Medal of Freedom, the highest award a civilian can receive. And now, for the first time ever, an ape named Oliver. Congratulations to the both of you." He shook both Oliver's and Eugene's hands, whispering to them, "Don't let him eat this…Oh and by the way, I really like your capes."

Eugene beamed with excitement. "Thank you, sir! I made them myself!"

The crowd applauded as Oliver and Eugene bowed simultaneously.

The president continued at the podium, "Miko Tanaka, please step forward." She did, nervously spotting her parents in the crowd, who did not look very pleased. "Miko has shown that art and creativity can flourish in even the most remote, desolate, and dangerous of places. Her high spirit, artistic focus, willingness to work with others, and decisive cunning made her an irreplaceable part of the team. Miko's precise violin playing is second only to her tactical shooting skills. Congratulations." He placed another Presidential Medal of Freedom around her neck, shook her hand, and whispered, "I hope you'll come play at the White House someday."

"I'd love to!" Miko smiled. "Can my parents come?"

"Of course."

"Cool!" Miko gave her parents a thumbs up. Her mom fainted, and her dad caught her, smiling.

"Shayla and Cody Nichols, please step forward," the president went on. "Cousins by blood, friends by choice. This young man's athletic ability, naval knowledge, and willingness to lead helped save the lives of his friends, family, and the world. A watchful and caring eye, Cody Nichols has a very bright future ahead of him, and we all need to give him our thanks.

"Shayla Nichols, whose nurturing soul took care of her friends and family by providing them renewable food and much needed medical attention. She's also responsible for saving seeds of hundreds of different types of rare and endangered plant life. The environmental world and America thank you from the bottom of our hearts."

The crowd applauded, cameras flashing everywhere. Shayla and Cody were both given The Presidential Medal of Freedom. The president leaned in to Shayla and asked, "You haven't planted any of those seeds you took, have you?"

"No, Mr. President, I promise," said Shayla. "I've kept them in my refrigerator this whole time. I've been waiting for someone like you to ask for them."

"Good," he said. "You can bring them to the White House and show me and my men what you have. You can take a tour of the Rose Garden while you're there as well."

"Oh my yikes!" Shayla beamed. "That would be awesome!"

The commander-in-chief then shook Cody's hand, whispering only, "Job well done, son. And don't worry, your secret is safe with me." He winked at Erik who was standing towards the back of the stage.

"It's not much of a secret anymore."

"Oh," the president smirked. "Well, congrats."

"Thank you, sir," was all Cody could say.

"And finally," the president concluded. "Danny Herrera, please step forward." Danny wiped his sweaty

304

hands on his dirty football uniform as he took center stage. "Danny has shown an incredible amount of bravery, problem-solving capabilities, patriotism, intelligence, leadership, and the self-discipline to lead these fine young men and women into the conflict of their lives. It was Danny who put them on their adventure, and it was Danny who stopped the evil they faced and made it possible to bring them home safely. He has a rebellious spirit, empathetic heart, and relentlessness to never back down, much like our forefathers and veterans throughout time. Danny also fulfilled a personal quest along the way by reaching the physical goals he set forth for himself. He truly is the face of the ideal American hero. Thank you, Danny."

The crowd exploded with applause. The president placed the Presidential Medal of Freedom around Danny's neck, and whispered to him, "Your parents would be proud of you." Danny couldn't help it. A single tear rolled down his cheek. He had nothing to say. He gripped the president's hand and didn't want to let go. The president gestured towards the podium. Once the lump in his throat disappeared, Danny stepped up to the microphone, trembling.

"Ummm...I don't know what to say really," Danny said. "You all must be really confused, because I can't tell anyone what we did, but what I can say, is that we wouldn't have been able to do it without the final member of our group. His name is Asad Darzi, he's the Muslim son of a pirate doctor from Somalia who saved our lives.

"Asad had every reason to hate us, but he didn't. He did the right thing when no one was looking, and to me, that's the real definition of a hero. I hope that you all look at us as examples of success through diversity. And if Asad were here today, I think he would agree with me."

"Danny!" A voice from the president's helicopter rang out across the crowd. Danny peered past the bright lights at Marine One. Asad waved his arms back and forth, his dad standing next to him, leaning on a cane. They were wearing the finest silk thobes (long garments) and ghutras (headscarves.)

"Asad!" Danny yelled. "Guys look, Asad's here!"

"I thought you might want to see him," the president said. All of the kids ran into the crowd, which parted for them. They met Asad in the middle of the 50-yard line. Danny gave him a huge hug. They all cheered and jumped for joy. Miko was the last to see him, she was beside herself and shaking all over.

"Oh my goodness…I…I can't believe you're here… I never thought…I thought I'd never-" Asad kissed Miko. Cheers rang out across the crowd. Miko's dad fainted.

The Castaway Kids were reunited at last.

"Look at what your president gave me." Asad pulled out a wallet. Inside was a social security card with his name on it. "My father and I are now US citizens!"

The president strolled down to the helicopter. "I have to leave. It was nice meeting all of you. We're busy working on declassifying the incident as we speak. The press is going to have a field day with this little visit. Until then, can I count on your silence?"

"Yes, sir!" They all said in unison.

"Good." He saluted, and all of them popped to attention and saluted him back, including Oliver. "I'll be contacting you shortly regarding a very urgent matter that I need your help with. Until then, enjoy your evening and Godspeed." The president's helicopter flew away into the darkness of night. Mrs. Harris cleared her throat loudly into the microphone.

"Ahem! Attention! Attention everyone!" She said as the crowd turned back to her. "Very exciting things have transpired here tonight. Confusing…but exciting things. But we still have the matter of the homecoming dance beginning in the gym in only thirty minutes. I suggest if we don't want to be late we all scurry off now. Go on, scurry off, scurry off…"

The crowd began dispersing. Some people took pictures with the kids and shook their hands. Others just glared at them jealously. Danny turned to Shayla. "Shayla?"

"Yes, Danny?"

"Will you go with me to the homecoming dance?"

"It's a date." They held hands and kissed.

"Asad?" Miko asked.

"Yes, Miko?"

"Will you…play the violin with me and my band at the homecoming dance?"

"It would be an honor." Asad reached back to his father, who handed him his violin.

Cody turned to Erik. "Erik?"

"Wassup?"

"I'm tired of hiding who I am. I like you. I like you a lot. And I don't care who knows it. Will you be my date for homecoming?"

"You sure you want to do this?"

"Absolutely."

"All right. Under one condition," Erik continued. "Can I wear the power suit? Just once?"

Cody smiled and held his hand. "We'll see." Cody turned to Danny, dancing his eyebrows up and down, before walking off the field together, hand-in-hand.

"Well, Oliver," Eugene sighed. "Looks like it's just you and me. I have some matching tuxedoes in the car we can wear to the dance together. Come on."

Later that night, the Castaway Kids danced, sang, and partied well into the evening to the music of Miko and Asad's punk-rock band. Eugene and Oliver were voted "Best Dressed." Cody and Erik were show-stoppers with their break dancing moves and voted "Cutest Couple." Danny and Shayla shared their first dance together.

While they slow-danced under the disco ball, she looked him in the eyes and said, "Maybe high school won't be so bad."

ABOUT THE AUTHORS

Jon Stremel:

Born and raised in Southern California, Stremel has been writing/directing films, commercials, and plays since junior high school. While living in North Hollywood, CA, he attended The Pasadena Art Center College of Design where he received formal training in filmmaking, screenwriting and children's literature. He joined the Navy in 2010 and wrote a great deal of The Castaway Kids while on deployment in the Middle East. This is his first book. Stremel currently resides in Virginia Beach, VA.

Chris Graue:

A native of Torrance, California, Chris works with the custodial and youth ministries departments at his local church. In his spare time, he plays several instruments for various bands and spends all of his money on film projects. This is also his first book.

ACKNOWLEDGMENTS

Joseph Bagwell – Illustrator:

Joe is a freelance illustrator and graphic designer from Hampton Roads Virginia with a BFA in Illustration from Savannah College of Art. He attends several horror and science fiction conventions were he sells prints of his original art. He fills his spare time with sculpting, writing stories and enjoying as many movies as he can.

The artwork of this book is dedicated to Edwarda Bagwell: a woman who would help out anyone regardless of their appearance without passing judgment.

Patti Foy – Editor:

Mother of four amazing children, she has been a school teacher for over forty years. She is currently writing and conducting research for sacred and secular material, editing manuscripts, and composing poetry from her home in California.

To find out more about it and the book, visit our website at:
www.castawaykidsbook.com

Made in the USA
Columbia, SC
13 May 2024

35242379R00174